MY NAME IS JASMINE

Shashi Warrier was born in 1959, and, after completing a master's degree in economics, tried his hand at many professions that had nothing to do with economics. He progressed in fits and starts through journalism, consulting, computer software, project management and so on, and then settled down to write. He likes yoga, motorcycles, Hindustani music and good thrillers, and has been learning to cook for a decade or more with little success. He teaches college students how to get their thoughts in order, and is a newspaper columnist and book reviewer. His most memorable achievement has been a solo forty-day 11,000-km motorbike ride around India.

He has written fairy tales, thrillers, literary fiction, satires, and a romance. His ambition is to write a really outstanding fairy tale, but for the time being he's working on a travelogue through his own mind.

He lives in Mangalore, close to a beach, with his painter-writer wife Prita, and their dog Squark.

MY NAME IS JASMINE

Shashi Warrier

SIMON & SCHUSTER

London · New York · Sydney · Toronto · New Delhi

Published in India by Simon & Schuster India, 2025

1 3 5 7 9 10 8 6 4 2

Simon & Schuster India
818, Indraprakash Building,
21, Barakhamba Road,
New Delhi 110001.

www.simonandschuster.co.in

Paperback ISBN: 978-81-983564-5-1
eBook ISBN: 978-81-983564-0-6

Typeset in India by SÜRYA, New Delhi
Printed and bound in India by Replika Press Pvt. Ltd.

This one is for Prita,
who stuck by me through the worst of times.

Prologue

Jasmine

The light is poor as I write this late in the night, at a cramped desk, sitting on a heavy steel chair. It's not just dim, it's gloomy, which is what you'd expect a prison cell to be. Until some days ago, the law wanted to keep me in. Now that I have agreed to do what the police have asked me to, they say I have to stay here to stay safe. As evidence of their good intentions, they offer to get me the food I want, and any other little comforts I might need, like an extra pillow or a blanket or mosquito repellent, though they refuse to send in a plumber to fix the toilet flush. They're taken aback when all I ask for by way of extras are a writing pad and a pen, which they give me without demur, though the pen is felt-tipped. They've promised to take me to a safe place tomorrow, probably a flat, and to set me free as soon as the "paperwork", a tedious and mysterious enterprise, is complete. It seems the law, if not society, is willing to forgive me my sins.

I am not. The blood on my hands won't wash off, and

there are the deaths...deaths can't be reversed. There's much in my life that I wish hadn't happened, and much more that I wish I hadn't done. The burden of those memories weighs down every waking moment of my life.

Two deaths in particular I regret. One is my father's: he died at my hands, not because I wished it, but because of circumstances. I regret his death not because I miss him, or because he was a good man, but because I would have liked him to live knowing the consequences of the way he lived his professional life. He deserved punishment, and what he got, a relatively painless death while being treated for his injuries in a hospital, was much less than he deserved.

The other...I regret that much, much more: that's one of the events this story tells. This death I regret because I would have gladly given my own life for it not to happen. But then, life does to you what it will, and you have to deal with it as best you can. Besides, when I think back of the people in whose stead I wish I had died, I find I wouldn't have a life at all, for the first of them is my mother, who died giving me life.

This story really is about being born again, not all at once but in fits and starts, a process that is still incomplete, and one that I think will never be really done. When I was younger, there were times when I wished I could live shorn of my memories, be born afresh. And then it happened. I woke up one day born afresh. Over the weeks and months that followed, I remembered. A few of those memories that returned were pleasant, but by far the greater share belonged to those that make me cringe and weep in horror. For all that horror, though, I found myself welcoming them back, because they were, in a sense, myself. And, in the end, I found the burden of memory far lighter than the burden of being nameless.

Chapter One

Jasmine

In the beginning it was all slow and gentle. Sounds drifted into my awareness, gathering strength and definition: quick, light footsteps separated by the rustle of cloth, clicks and small thumps, and soft voices whispering in the dark. Then, as my vision improved, I began to see blurs in a light tinged with blue. As the darkness lifted, my vision grew sharper, and the white of a ceiling appeared, with a dusty yellow fan spinning directly above. There were smells, too, strong, some unfamiliar, but bringing disease and injury to mind.

And then came a rushing thirst, all-consuming, a force I couldn't resist. When I tried to ask for water, I found I could only moan through a swollen, dry, painful throat. Someone must have heard my distress, for a dark face moved into my field of vision. Whoever it was seemed to understand, for I felt the cool rim of a glass at my lips, and I drank. A few grateful sips was all I could manage before my throat closed up. By then the fire had eased off and already the comfort of darkness was returning and I sank into it with relief.

I awoke quickly the next time, to the same thirst, to the same little clicks and the hum of the fan revolving above, the same unfamiliar smells, the same blurs that sharpened slowly into objects I knew. This awakening was somehow more complete, I knew, perhaps because there wasn't that darkness to fall back into. Again, I moaned, and someone responded and came to my side: a nurse, I thought, from the cap above the face that responded so quickly. I drank more water with relief and became aware, suddenly, that I was in a place I'd never been to before. By now I thought I might be able to speak so I tried asking the nurse. A stranger's voice emerged from my throat, hoarse and slurred, asking where I was.

"You're in Malkangiri district hospital," the nurse replied, smiling pleasantly. "In the post-operative ward." By now I could see that she wore a white uniform, with a laminated identity card hanging around her neck from a blue tape.

Hospitals were for the sick, I knew. The unfamiliar smells suddenly made sense: they belonged with illness and death. But I had no memory of falling ill. I couldn't feel any pain, either.

"Am I unwell?" I asked.

"Yes," she told me softly. "You fell and hurt your head. You've had an operation, and you're getting better." Then, after a pause, "What's your name?"

Until then I'd taken it for granted that I knew who I was. The possibility that I didn't know hadn't even occurred to me. Everyone has a name, I knew. I searched for it in my mind, but couldn't find one. It'll come, I thought, but instead came a wave of terror, black and heavy and bottomless. It weighed so heavily on my chest that I couldn't breathe. What *was* my name? I didn't know, and when I realized that I didn't know I felt I was falling off a cliff into the darkness.

I must have slept after that, for the next thing I remember is waking up again. This time I woke in a soft pale light, with an aching head and back, and a soreness in the groin. The thirst still raged in my throat, but its earlier intensity was gone. I called, but no one came. As I grew used to the semi-darkness, I groped and found what seemed to be a bell on the table by my bed, and rang it. A whole age later, or perhaps a few minutes later, a nurse came, dragging her unwilling feet along the floor. Unsmiling, she gave me the water I needed, and then, like the one who came before, asked my name.

The terror returned, but now it was tempered by experience. That terror stayed with me over the days I spent in that grimy little hospital ward. Its grip loosened sometimes, but it never let go completely.

But this time I wasn't quite as unprepared. By now I had understood that there was a lot I knew, about all kinds of things. I knew, for instance, that everyone has a name, usually one that their parents gave them when they were born, and a home, where they go to. A sadness caught in my throat when I realized that I didn't know my name, or my parents, or anything at all about where I came from and where I could go when I didn't need to stay in the hospital.

Thoughts that seemed familiar drifted in and out of my mind through the confusion. Stand firm, was one. Show no weakness, was another, and shed no tears. Speak as little as possible. Give nothing away. These thoughts were reassuring, like orders, remembered faintly, and I followed them because they offered a refuge of some kind, a hint that lost memories lurked just below some horizon, and would somehow emerge to save me. So I held my tongue, bit back my tears, and ignored the rising panic. I tried to collect my thoughts as best I could, and to learn from what I knew, what I could see, and what I felt.

I knew, without being told, that I was a woman. Was that because the nurses were women? I had no idea how hospitals were segregated, but I did know, though I'd no memory of having been in a hospital bed, that segregation was important. Obviously I knew about hospitals and nurses and the smell of medicine and the pain of an injection. I knew that there were many professions, and many things I was not. I was not a nurse or a doctor, or a soldier or a cook, or a clerk or a journalist. I knew I was not a saleswoman or a clerk, or a housewife or a teacher.

I even understood, from what the nurses told me, that I was in the post-operative ward, that I'd had surgery on my head, and would be released to a general ward in the next few days, but I hadn't been in a hospital bed ever before.

I knew that we weren't in the heat of the summer months. Mornings were faintly chill, and a slow fan was all that was needed for comfort. The summer, with its blinding sun, despite the forests and the reservoir nearby, would be much hotter. But then, at the peak of the gentle winter, it would be slightly cooler, so this was probably February or early March. So, I knew about seasons, and the year, and the calendar.

But I had no idea how I came to be in that hospital with a broken head and no memory of anything about myself. Not even my name, that simplest of pieces of myself, except that I was a woman. That was what brought the terror, and the question that lodged immovably in the back of my mind: *Who am I?*

I shook my head and swallowed. The nurse smiled reassuringly. "Don't worry," she said. "You hurt your head. You've forgotten some things, that's all. It'll all come back."

"What's today's date?" I asked.

"Twentieth," she said. "It's the twentieth of February, 2020." She smiled. "My daughter's birthday. She says it's 20-02-2020. A special number. Only zeroes and twos." The smile widened. "She wrote the month first: 02-20-2020. She says they write it like that in America."

"How old is she?" I asked.

"Eight," came the reply. "She made a birthday card with the date on it."

So that was how I remembered the date on which I was born again, to replace the day I was born before. Like the nurse's daughter's eighth birthday, it had only zeroes and twos.

Chapter Two

Jasmine

They left me alone much of the time. I didn't need food, for a needle in my arm fed me sugar water out of a bottle hanging upside down on a frame. I didn't need to use the toilet, for a tube running out of my groin cleared my bladder. Nurses checked my temperature and blood pressure four or five times a day, occasionally took samples of my blood, didn't answer my questions, and left me to stare at the cracks in the ceiling the rest of the time. I drank water sometimes, but only a few sips at a time. Even that was difficult after the thirst became less urgent, but the nurses insisted. "Drink as much water as you can," they said. "It's good for you." I obeyed and drank until the nausea came. My head ached, and my back, and, as the hours passed, slowly, my whole body became a single large ache. I discovered a bandage on my head, and another on my arm, both where the pains were their sharpest.

There was time enough to look around. There was the mosaic floor, clean in patches, swept and swabbed twice a day by disinterested cleaners who paid more attention to their mobile phones than to their work despite the signs, in English and Odiya, saying that phones were prohibited. They seemed to ignore the dust on the narrow window sills and beneath some of the furniture. I tried to strike up conversations with them, but their responses were never more than monosyllables, so I gave up after a few attempts, and instead wondered where I had picked up those notions of cleanliness.

There were the uniformed canteen workers who brought me my meals. The first time one of them brought me a meal, it was breakfast, I told her I couldn't pay. She just shook her head and said, "No need to pay," and went away, making it clear she didn't want to talk. No smile, no talk. The others, too, kept their distance: I didn't know whether they did this on their own or if they were told do so, and I didn't ask, because there were so many other things happening in my own mind that I didn't understand, like the birdsong early in the morning that brought some comfort through a familiarity I couldn't gauge.

And then there were those thoughts with familiarity and the promise of return of memory, words drifting across my mind, that I thought of as ghosts. Those ghostly voices gave advice, some of which seemed surreal. This pain is nothing, they said. You've been through worse, and it hasn't touched you inside. They seemed to be right on both counts, for after a while the pain ceased to trouble me, though I was aware of its presence, and, dimly, the presence of old pain, but no memory of it, or its cause.

The ghosts continued to haunt me, and, as the days passed, I got to know them better, shapeless grey beings that brought advice and floating unconnected words and discomfort and fear. Best of all, they helped the moments go endlessly past. Some of the advice they gave was good but they also brought along fragments of ideas about justice and fairness and fighting for something worthwhile. These seemed vaguely familiar but I couldn't really remember them in any detail. They filled my mind, leaving little space for other thoughts. I had no hunger or thirst, or any need for sleep, it seemed. Instead, there was an all-consuming need to pay attention to the memories I had lost, memories that lurked at the edges of my mind, but went missing when I looked for them.

On the day after I woke up the third time, on the 21st of February, after the nurses finished changing the dressings on my head, a painful process, one of them came back. She asked me to sit up, which I did, though I felt a little dizzy. She helped me onto a trolley by the bed and a female ward attendant wheeled me out of the post-operative ward, past the door where a policewoman stood, to a corridor with rooms on both sides. Four doors along the corridor came a staircase to the left, and, along the staircase, a ramp for the trolley. The policewoman, in her khaki uniform, followed the trolley to a women's ward a floor below, where another nurse helped me into another bed.

While the transfer was on, I got to look at myself from a different set of angles, and tried to figure out what kind of work I did for a living. From what I could see of myself, I was thin. My hands were rough and fingers thick, my wrists bony and my skin scarred, showing cuts and small burns. I worked with my hands, then, but I couldn't remember what I did. Was I a cook, then, with knives and flames and hot pots leaving their marks on my hands? No, that didn't feel right, because...because I knew that I knew very little about food and about cooking. Food for me was a matter of survival, not pleasure...

Did I work in a workshop? That would be very unusual for a woman, but that, too, didn't feel right, for I had no idea what went on in a workshop, and knew nothing about wood or metal. Besides, I'd found over my days in bed that I could read and write English and Odiya and perhaps Hindi as well...too much, perhaps, for a person from a workshop. And what of the ghost of the memory of pain? I knew I'd been through a lot of it, but had no idea how or why or when. What kind of work brought such pain? I couldn't think of any.

This bed, like the ward around it, was grimy. The toilet stank, and floor was damp. There was dust everywhere, and the fan above was still. As I wondered how I knew that the policewoman was a policewoman, and that I used to call them "khakis", I found that I knew that the metal rings tying me to the frame of the bed were a pair of handcuffs, which were meant to keep suspects from running away...

So I was a suspect.

But what did they suspect me of? "Why are you doing this?" I asked the policewoman. "What have I done? Why am I a prisoner?"

"I'm doing it because it's my job," she replied impassively. No smile, like the nurses, but no frown either, just a blank, unemotional look, as if she were preparing to restrain me if I showed signs of violence. The "khaki" look: a threat behind the quiet. I was sure she'd use her stick on me without hesitation if ever the need arose. "I'm here to make sure you don't escape. Orders from my Inspector. You'll have to ask him about the rest of it."

"What have I done to deserve this?" I asked, rattling the single handcuff on my left wrist.

She looked away. Clearly, she wasn't going to answer. I asked the nurses, and they wouldn't tell me, either: perhaps they didn't know. "Wait," one of them, more sympathetic than the rest, told me. "You've taken an injury to your head. You'll remember, by and by."

The time in confinement passed heavily, every second a crawling burden. When I had nothing else to do, I counted them. I made up minutes and hours and I kept track of the dates using a series of cracks in the ceiling, radiating out of a corner to the left of the head of my bed. I was the only patient in the ward, there was no TV, and when I asked if I could have a newspaper, the nurses told me to ask the policewoman, who didn't even bother to reply.

There was little to do but observe. I noticed the passing of the day not only from the light in the windows and the warmth of the room but also the changes of shift among the nurses and the police guards. At first, they all seemed to be the same because they did the same things to me—giving me medication, or telling me to change my gown—but as the days passed by I began to see differences. Some were gentle, others in a hurry. But, to my surprise, even the police constables on guard began to differ, even though they were trained to be impassive and watchful.

I might not have noticed the differences but for their mobile phones. For the first two days they were brusque when someone called. Afterwards, their manner lightened, and from their expressions when they spoke on those phones they became humans. I speculated, from their manner on their phones, whom they were speaking to: husbands, children, parents, and one perhaps had a lover, to whom she spoke with a shyness I never imagined a khaki would have.

And, for some reason that I couldn't identify, I was uncomfortable with that, and the discomfort added to the burden of not remembering. The burden was not my ignorance, I realized, but the uncertainty it created. I tried to put it aside and to think matters through. In a moment of clarity that broke the pressing urgency to know about myself, I realized the urgency wasn't real. I was safe here for now, with bare necessities provided, so all I had to do was keep calm and try to remember. When I remembered, I'd have to go by whatever I remembered, but until then, all I could do was wait and concentrate on getting better. Some vague thought emerged from the back of my mind. "Free your breath," it said. "Breathe deeply, breathe freely." I did that for a while, and found myself calming down just a little. Then I remembered more. I remembered someone telling me, "Watch your breath, watch how you breathe in and out." I did that, too, and found, as my attention shifted from the movement of air in my nose and throat to the movement of my diaphragm, that the calm grew deeper.

Following the calm came a realization. Besides the things I knew I knew, like about the police and hospitals and the languages, there were fragments of memories floating in my mind. Like the one about breathing, for instance. There were sounds. I could remember someone telling me about the breath, but I had no idea who, or when, or under what circumstances. I also remembered bells...I remembered bells ringing out regularly. What bells were they? Where had I heard them? I had no idea of that either.

More matters became clear through logic and thought rather than memory or insight. If I had a family, they'd have gone to the police by now about my disappearance. Either I had no family, or they'd given up on me. Mine was no simple case where I'd get my memory back and find my way to a welcoming family. It had become very obvious that I was on my own. It was going to be painful remembering who I was, and what I'd done to get where I was. The more I thought about it, the surer I got that there was something ugly in my past, and the thought sat like a black monkey on my shoulder.

It haunted me, though, not having a past. Having an ugly past is better than no past at all, I thought, just as having an ugly face is better than no face at all. So I said nothing, and waited, at the very least, for my body to heal, for the pain in my head to go away, and, perhaps, for my mind to heal as well.

The doctors came twice a day, one in the morning and again in the afternoon, followed by a few nurses, on hand to answer questions or take instructions. They asked brusque questions that the nurses answered, performed quick examinations, issued orders to the nurses, ignored my questions, even my presence, and left without speaking to me directly, though I was the reason for their presence. The nurses fed me tablets and syrups, gave me injections, and changed the bottles of sugar solution that fed me, brought and took away bedpans, and told me nothing. On the third day, they took the needles away, and let me eat and go to the toilet, cooperating to the extent of undoing the handcuffs without questions whenever I needed to go.

One day a new doctor led the rounds. He was older than the rest, plump and perfumed, and his white coat was spotless, his stethoscope untouched in one of its pockets, and he brought a little cloud of followers, younger doctors and nurses and some kind of an assistant with a notepad. He came to my bedside, looked me up and down briefly, glanced at the history on the pad to the frame at the foot of the bed, muttered something to one of the regular doctors, and went his way. For some reason I couldn't understand, his coming and going angered me much more than anything else in the hospital.

After his departure came a brief flash of memory that disturbed me because it came with a flood of rage that I had no reason to feel.

This is the enemy. This is the privileged one. This is the one who feeds off the labour of the poor. The worker's sweat pays for the perfume with which he conceals the stench of his own wickedness.

Society and government are set up to work for people like him. Most common people are simply the means that he uses to support himself and others like him.

The government is therefore the enemy. Anyone who supports the enemy is also an enemy.

Did that mean that the tired, sullen nurse who brought

me water and told me about her daughter's birthday was the enemy? Or the other one, the sympathetic one who brought me my first sip of water? Weren't they the ones who saved my life after my head injury? And what of the khaki speaking tenderly on her phone to someone I thought was her lover? Did it make sense, lumping whole groups of strangers as the enemy, regardless of what they did and how they did it? I remembered vaguely that someone had told me this: there were opposed groups of people, groups that were always in conflict. I tried to remember who told me this, but made no progress. But it made me aware that my feelings didn't make sense, and I decided then to try to reason matters out whenever I felt anything strongly. I had plenty of time for that, after all.

After a few days, more khakis came, two men with hard faces and moustaches. After the needles were removed, they began asking questions about myself that I couldn't answer. They railed at me, and I withdrew into silence, wondering why I feared and hated them, why they repelled me so strongly, why I didn't trust them. Faced with my silence, they brought their chief and, with him, a doctor from outside, younger and smiling and more human, who, for a change, directed his questions at me instead of the nurses, and actually listened to the answers. "Do you remember what you had for breakfast?" he asked.

I told him. It was a common poor man's Odiya breakfast of puris and potatoes. He asked a nurse if that was right, and she nodded. "Do you remember the last few days clearly?" he asked.

"From the time that I woke up thirsty, I remember very well," I replied.

"And before that?" he asked.

"Nothing," I replied. The panic rose as I answered, and I gripped the side of the bed hard. "Nothing at all."

"Right," he said, watching carefully. "Don't panic." He smiled reassuringly. "I've seen this before. Give it another few days." He turned to the chief of the khakis, a plump, balding man in his fifties, with the insignia of a deputy superintendent on his epaulettes. The policeman had his service revolver in a buttoned holster to his left, butt forward for a cross-draw, with a lanyard attached to a ring on the end of the pistol grip to prevent a casual attempt to grab the weapon. Even with the holster button undone, he'd be slow to get to it...

"She should continue here for some more time," the doctor said, while I wondered how I knew so much about khakis and weapons..."A few days. No pressure until then. Call me if she remembers."

"How many days?" asked the khaki.

"A week, at least, maybe ten days," replied the doctor. "I'll have another look at her then. After the end of next week."

I sensed that they didn't trust this doctor, either, these khakis, for they were certain that I was lying, and even the doctor's advice, that a certain amount of memory loss is natural, wouldn't budge them on that day.

The khakis were the enemy, I could see that. But this doctor? Dividing people into friends and enemies, grouping them, I realized, only brings trouble. It was obvious. But why was it such a big thing for me? Had I been taught otherwise? By my parents? I had no idea, but I remembered that there were a lot more enemies than there were friends...so many more that I remembered making hiding myself a habit.

The next day, the last day of February according to my cracks-in-the-ceiling calendar, the older khaki, the deputy superintendent, turned up alone, unarmed, in civilian clothes, smiling, a jolly fat man whose smile never got to his eyes. The nurses and the woman khaki left the room when he nodded at them. "Do you remember anything?" he asked, looming over me at my bedside. "My people and the doctor told me you don't."

"No," I said, shaking my head. "Nothing. It's as if I was born here."

He held out a photograph, postcard size. When I didn't take it, he jabbed it at me. "Go on, take it. Have a look."

In the photo was the face and shoulders of a man in his sixties, grizzled and angry, with short grey hair and a high forehead. His face reminded me of the face I saw in the cracked mirror in the bathroom. I shook my head.

"He looks a little like me, I think," I said, "but I don't remember him."

"You told him you're his daughter," he said. "Then you tried to kill him."

"No," I said, shaking my head, realizing that this was something better forgotten. "I don't remember." Was this what I was trying to forget, that I tried to kill my father?

"That's why you're here," he said. "That's why you're in handcuffs, because you attacked him."

I had no idea. "Am I really his daughter?" I asked.

"Yes," he said. "We sent some samples from you and from him to a lab. They looked at the DNA and said that you're his daughter. No doubt about it."

"I don't know..." I began.

He cut me off. "I came to ask you how you found out he's your father."

A great sadness welled up inside me when I thought of not knowing who my father was, one of the fundamental elements of anyone's past. I pushed it aside, and shook my head. "No," I said, "I don't remember."

"You broke into his house to talk to him," he said. "Why? Who taught you how to pick locks?"

Again I shook my head, and didn't speak, for there was a lump in my throat. It was harder than before not to cry. I knew about fathers and mothers, but not about my own. "What about my mother?" I asked, when I got my voice back, when I was sure I wouldn't cry in the presence of this policeman.

He shook his head. "I only know that she's dead," he said. "He got married in 1981, and they had a son. His wife died soon after, and that couldn't have been your mother. She bore him one son…one son who is on his own, working in Hyderabad." He rose to leave. "Your father has made some provision for you. You'll be taken care of in this hospital until you're well. After that…we'll see." He paused to pick up the photo he'd given me. "The doctor told me it's best to let your memories come back on their own." He paused again. "Maybe he's right." He shook his head, his forehead wrinkling in perplexity. "Is there anything you need?" he asked, finally.

I shook my head. "No," I said, "I just need to remember who I am."

He sat down again. "May I give you some advice?" he asked.

"Please," I replied. "Anything."

"Stop this pretence," he said. "This isn't a story."

"But I'm not pretending," I said. "I really don't know."

"We have ways of finding out," he said.

"Go ahead and use them," I said.

"I'm not allowed to. Not without your permission."

"You have my permission."

"You have to sign a letter for that."

"I'll do it now," I said. "Gladly. A lie detector test, or whatever you call it." Even as I said this, I wondered how I knew about lie detectors.

"You can learn to get around a lie detector," he said, "but there are other ways."

"With drugs?" I asked. "With hypnosis? I'll agree to all those as well. Get me the paper. I'll sign it. Since I don't know even my name, I'll put my thumbprint on it if you wish. In anyone's presence, just in case the judge raises questions about it." How did I know all this, I wondered even as I spoke.

His expression changed as he looked at me closely, leaning forward to get closer. "You really don't know," he said, after a long moment's silence, his voice turned soft by surprise.

"That's what I've been trying to tell you all along," I said. I paused, and then the words were wrung out of me. "I'm as desperate to know as you are."

"The doctor says that you'll remember, by and by," he said, rising, his voice a little doubtful now. "We'll wait for that. We'll wait for you to get better. Meanwhile, I'll see if I can get another doctor to look at you."

"Look," I said, "there is something I need. I need the doctors to tell me what's wrong. They just ignore me. They just talk to the nurses."

"I'll talk to them," he promised, softened slightly by his new-found doubt, and left. I lay wondering about my own new-found doubt, for this man no longer seemed like an enemy. Again I thought of my world of black and white, with many enemies and a few friends...what kind of a world had I lived in all these years? What had I learnt? From whom? Suddenly it was on the edge of my mind but I couldn't get at it...

A new doctor came next morning, an older man, grey-haired and lean. Unlike the others, he came alone, without a retinue, carrying a file folder in his hand. He was dressed simply but neatly, in a bush-shirt and dark trousers and sandals. I didn't even know he was a doctor, at first, because he didn't wear a white coat or carry a stethoscope. He looked around, popped outside for a moment, and returned. "I'm Dr Patnaik," he said. He raised his folder. "This says something about what happened to you just before you were brought here, but nothing at all about you before that." He smiled. "I was hoping you might tell me."

"I can't," I told him bluntly. "I don't know."

He nodded. "It must be terrifying," he said, laying the file on the side table. "Like falling...and you've lost something precious." He behaved very differently from the others. He didn't seem to be in a hurry to go somewhere else, for one, and, for another, he talked to me directly, and he didn't talk as if I were four years old. Instead, he made himself comfortable on a plastic chair beside my bed. "They told me that parts of your memory are gone, so I've come to see if we can do something about it. Your file says it's been about ten days since you hurt yourself," he said.

"I don't remember anything before I woke up in this

hospital eight days ago," I told him. "I remember waking up feeling thirsty and in pain, but nothing before that. Nothing at all."

"You don't have to worry about that," he said. "You've hit your head and injured your brain a little, after which you've had some surgery on the brain to remove a blood clot. It takes some time for the brain to recover from that kind of misuse. Is the pain better now?"

"Yes," I said. "It's almost gone."

"It'll go away completely in a few days or maybe weeks," he said. "We don't know yet how long it's going to last. How do you know how many days it has been since you woke up?"

"I've been counting the cracks in the ceiling," I told him. "I have nothing better to do."

He smiled. "At least you're thinking," he said, "You're trying different things. Your memory should come back. Most of it, anyway."

"How do you know?" I asked.

He smiled. "Try to remember the name of the President of Venezuela on January 1, 2018," he said.

I shook my head. "No," I told him. "I can't remember."

"Then try to remember where you were on January 1, 2018," he said.

Again I shook my head. "No. No."

"Is there a difference between these two things?" he asked. "One of them you know but don't remember, the other you probably didn't know at all."

"You're right," I said. "I don't think I ever knew the name of any President of Venezuela, but I did know where I was on January 1, 2018...that one feels as if there's a door in my mind that I can't open." I remembered my last conversation with the doubtful khaki, of memories floating just beyond my grasp.

"Well, that door might open in its own time," he said. "So will a lot of others, and on their own. Worrying about opening them won't help. There are, of course, a few doors that might not open, and others that open only in part, but there are some other things we can do."

"Like what?" I asked.

"There's what we call short-term memory," he said, "and there's long-term memory. It's your long-term memory we're trying to get at."

The words floated up from a well somewhere in my mind. "Yes," I said. "I remember someone telling me about these things."

"Fine," he said. "There are different kinds of long-term memory, mainly two. There's episodic memory, for instance, that's like a sort of diary in which you keep notes about yourself. There's procedural memory, when you do things automatically, like putting on your clothes, or reading and writing. Can you ride a bicycle?"

The sudden question took me off balance. "Yes," I replied, not knowing where the reply came from. Who taught me to ride, I wondered, but there was nothing, not even a faint echo of something far away. "I don't know how I know."

He smiled. "That's all right." He paused. "Those cuts on your hands and arms? My colleague Nilu tells me you got them defending yourself against someone with a knife. My friend, the police officer, tells me you broke into somebody's house without any trouble, and sat waiting for him."

"I don't know anything about that," I told him.

"All it means is that you have some rather unusual skills," he said. "There's more. Most people in your position would be terrified. I know you're afraid, of course, but you're not panicking, and you're doing your best not to show your fear."

"Why do you think I'm not showing my fear?" I asked.

"You *are* showing it," he replied, looking me straight in the eye. "To me you are. I've been trained to look for these things, so it's no use evading. So you tell me. Why are you trying to hide your fear?"

Because I've been trained to do that, I thought, but I don't know who trained me or why or when or where. I didn't think I could tell this man all that, because then there'd be more questions I couldn't answer and then the khakis would come...

"You don't have to tell me," he said after a moment, "but it might help."

"Help with what?" I asked, annoyed. He knew nothing

of what I was going through. How did he think he could help me?

"Talking about what you do remember might jog your memories," he said. "That happens sometimes. But not if you're forced to talk."

I glared at him.

"You're not alone, you know," he said gently. He smiled. "Other people have lost their memories, though only a few lose as much as you've lost. You're putting a lot of pressure on yourself trying to remember. That won't help you get your memory back. Share the pressure, relax. *That* might help you remember." He waited for me to respond, and, when I didn't, continued. "Tell me what you do know, then."

I turned away from his sympathy at first, then reconsidered. "I can read English and Odiya," I told him.

"How did you find that out?" he asked.

"The labels on medicine bottles and the notes that the staff here make and pieces of newspaper that they use for wrapping...I thought about it. I think I know Hindi, too."

"If you know three languages you've had some schooling," he said. "Do you know where you learnt those languages? Or from whom?"

"No," I said.

"Do you read newspapers?" he asked.

"Not here," I said, "but I used to read them occasionally. Not regularly." My head was beginning to throb. "I'm getting a headache," I said.

"Rest, then," he said. "Try not to worry about who you are."

"Will you come again?" I couldn't help asking, and it came out like a plea. This doctor seemed different from the rest.

"I doubt it," he said gently. "I'm just passing through, and dropped in to see you because your regular doctor wanted a second opinion. But trust me, you *will* get most of your memory back. In time."

The next week passed with more of the usual, the regular doctors and nurses and the handcuffs were removed only when I needed to go to the toilet. The aches and pains eased off slowly, and I got used to the food, which wasn't so bad. That left me wondering: was I so poor that prison hospital food was passable? At least it proved to me that I was no cook.

And then, on the evening of March 6th, some fifteen days after I woke up the second time, everything changed. A whole urgent, insistent crowd of khakis came, led by some khakis in mufti. They explained nothing, but sat me on the back seat of a big car, between two women khakis, handcuffed. They took me to the house of some judge, perhaps the district judge, a bored middle-aged man who looked at me, listened to one of the mufti khakis speak softly in his ear, glanced at a file that the khakis gave him, and signed a piece of paper. Back in the hospital, I had a new guard, another woman khaki, standing by. Unlike the nurses who handled the chore before, she was firm about visits to the toilet and bathroom: no lingering, no time to clean the place afterwards.

The new conditions lasted only that one night. In the morning, after an early breakfast, they put me in the car and drove me nearly three hours to Jeypore, where, after a break for a meal of rice and curry of which I ate less than half, and a few hours' wait at the railway station, they put me in a grimy sleeper coach on the afternoon train to Bhubaneshwar, handcuffed, in the company of three hard-eyed khakis, two women and one man, all armed, as if I were a dangerous, desperate murderess. Conscious of being the centre of attention, I sat still and silent on the blue-grey cushioned berth, unable to look passersby in the eye. I couldn't eat, and even swallowing an occasional sip of water from the plastic bottle the khakis gave me was difficult. Night brought relief, because everyone went to bed, as did I, though the khakis didn't let anyone turn out the lights in the compartment. I stayed awake through the night, wondering what had happened to change their attitude so dramatically. The thought persisted: *what had I done to deserve this?* And then came a worse question: *what if I had done something to deserve this?*

On its heels came another thought, even more persistent: why does the presence of strangers make me feel worse? Why do their opinions matter when they don't know what I don't know? But none of those thoughts brought any consolation, and I closed my eyes and kept my mouth shut and counted the seconds and wondered how I knew so much about trains and railway tracks and fishplates...

In Bhubaneshwar, in the bright sunlight of mid-morning, there were more khakis to meet us at the station platform, led by a senior khaki in mufti, the one who had spoken to the judge: he must have taken a better coach in the same train. They all surrounded me, and led me through the parcel office to a waiting convoy, headed through the city and out towards a large grim prison in a compound full of well-spaced-out trees, surrounded by a dirty white high wall topped with Y-shaped fenceposts strung with several strands of barbed wire.

There, in an ante-room by the big main door with a curved top and a judas gate, with an armed guard present, I was checked in by a woman khaki, my name put in a register, my belongings listed, and, after being led through corridors and up brightly lit but gloomy staircases, past a window where I could see a part of a quadrangle, I was placed all by myself in a small whitewashed cell: solitary confinement.

The cell was small and dark. Though I was alone, there was no privacy, because there were bars instead of a door, facing a blank corridor wall. There was lumpy mattress on the floor, and a small, smelly toilet attached to the cell, with a flush that didn't work. Sitting alone in the cell I found myself wondering why being locked up all by myself for doing something wrong that I didn't understand was so familiar. After a moment's reflection, that familiarity brought relief, for now I began to understand that I did have a past, that there were doors in my mind that might open if only I could be patient enough, just like Dr Patnaik had said. The relief was so great I found myself in tears, so great that I sat not knowing that I was crying, despite all the training, despite all the unspoken orders in my mind, despite the ghosts. That was how the warder who brought lunch found me, and, in a rare show of humanity, advised me to cooperate with my questioners.

Chapter Three

Jasmine

Not knowing that I *was* grateful to be left to myself, my jailers left me alone in my cell to consider and panic overnight. I didn't sleep much, partly because of the mosquitoes, and partly because the light was always on, except for brief periods when I thought the power failed. I didn't know the time, or the weather outside, for there wasn't a window. I was alone, but preferred solitude to the company of other prisoners, who were bound to ask the same questions as the nurses, and...I had no idea how they'd treat me, but I thought that, like the policemen who interrogated me first, they'd think I was pretending to have lost my memory. In any case, I didn't want to spend time with anyone privileged to have a memory and an identity.

They resumed the interrogation next morning. After breakfast, a khaki led me out of my cell along the corridors from which I could see other prisoners, all men, all dressed in white uniforms, to a room where two new khakis waited, along with one in civilian clothes. They didn't take up the questioning where they'd left off: they started afresh, starting with my name and parentage. The two men were as different as could be, one tall and plump, the other medium-height and wiry, but in other ways they were identical. Both showed the same impassive scepticism when I told them I didn't know the answers to the questions they asked, and they battered me with the same questions, often changing subjects without warning as if to catch me off balance. I was on the verge of screaming at them to stop repeating themselves when I saw that they were looking for exactly that reaction. Then I began to understand that they were working as a team, and that they were good at what they did, and I began to relax. I kept my cool until the end of the session, when I told the tall man, "I told you I don't remember, and I'm happy to repeat that to you as many times as you wish, but doing all that is just a waste of time."

After this they began to mix plenty of new questions among the old ones, though, and in no sequence at all, so I found that I had to think before answering each one. Where was I on such and such day in 2007, they asked, and again another day in 1993, and another one in 2005, and so on, the dates seemingly chosen at random. They began to ask questions at a rapid pace, as if I were a liar, and not giving me time to think of my lies to confuse me. When I got used to this, I continued to tell them without hesitation that I had no idea where I'd been before 20-02-2020, they asked if I remembered anything significant about those days, and I told them that no, I didn't. The first time I asked why they were asking about those dates, they said they'd wait for me to remember, and afterwards met all my questions with a blank silence.

During a break in the interrogation, I asked why their treatment of me had changed so much overnight. The short interrogator hesitated before answering, "We've been given your case. We're not the state police, we're from the NIA." It seemed they didn't like to share the least bit of information, not even about why they were doing whatever they were doing to you. And then two more thoughts, memories from before 20-02-2020, floated into my mind. The first was that being kept ignorant and starkly aware of your ignorance is one way to break down your resistance.

The second bit of memory was about the NIA, which I knew—I wondered how—investigated cases of terrorism. That sent a jolt of fear through me, because I knew that they were far more powerful and secretive than the regular police, and used very different methods of interrogation. They were a lot more methodical, and weren't held back by having to deal with different state governments in the course of their investigations. So had they got evidence of some kind that I was a terrorist of some kind, I reckoned, and also that I really was a terrorist of some kind, because I knew so much about them.

As the session progressed, I discovered that the man asking the questions seemed to defer to the chief mufti khaki, the one who led the team that brought me to Bhubaneshwar. The chief himself sat back and watched, while the interrogator kept at me with his questions, which he seemed to have memorized, for he never once looked at a piece of paper or a his computer's screen before asking me something.

Despite all that I understood about their technique, the tension kept building up as I claimed ignorance of everything they wanted to know. They stopped at lunchtime, leaving me alone with a single armed guard while they conferred outside. A few minutes later, a warder led me back along the dark corridors back to my cell, to stew again until next morning. As before, they thought they were softening me up, while the reality was quite the opposite. In fact, I had begun to find the solitude itself familiar, and was further reassured. I lay on the worn sheet trying to explain, without success, the familiarity of the solitude, and of solitary confinement without reason.

After breakfast next morning, they led me through the same corridors to the same interrogation room, where I found a familiar and unexpected face amidst the group: Dr Patnaik the psychiatrist, whose smile reassured me a little more. He turned to the chief of the khakis when I entered. "I'll spend some time alone with her," he said. "I'll make my own notes as we speak."

"Give us a copy of your notes when you leave," the chief khaki said.

Dr Patnaik shook his head. "Not unless she allows it, or you get a court order. Medical ethics."

"She's a criminal," said the khaki.

"To me she's a patient," he replied. He smiled. "Innocent until proven guilty. I'm bound by my profession just as much as you're bound by yours."

The khaki gave him a long, hard look and led his colleagues out of the room, the last of them slamming the door shut as he left. When they were all out, Dr Patnaik turned to me. "How have you been all these days?" he asked, with a smile.

"My body has been healing," I said, "and I remember more, but the questions remain, and there are more of them, besides a few vague memories. Otherwise, everything is the same." I paused. I wanted to ask him if he was glad to see me but couldn't. "You said you were unlikely to see me again," I managed instead.

"I work in this city," he said, "and the police called me to consult. When we met first, back in Malkangiri, I had no idea you'd end up here...You said everything is the same? What do you mean?"

"I'm still a prisoner," I said, "except that yesterday was a little different." I told him about how being locked up alone seemed familiar, that I'd been left alone as a form of punishment before, and that it wasn't really a punishment because I wanted to be alone while I thought things over.

"Very good," he said when I finished. "That's very unusual. You're spending a lot of time thinking about your own mind, and you're putting less pressure on yourself and that's good. Most people can't bear their own company hour after hour after hour. That's why solitary confinement works." He paused, as if to collect his thoughts. "There's a big difference between remembering your familiarity with being alone and the other things you remember. This is a personal memory, an experience that you've been through. It's not a procedural memory, not something that you were trained to do."

"I don't understand," I said.

"There's nothing personal in all those other memories," he said. "Those were things you learnt with practice, like riding a bicycle. You forgot who taught you, or when you learnt, or how. All you remember is the skill itself."

"All right," I said.

"But this punishment by being left alone," he continued, "it's something you experienced. You remembered an experience, not a skill. There's some feeling attached to it, and other details that you can't yet identify. There are no feelings attached to those skills, like riding a cycle."

"Now I understand," I said. Then, on impulse, I decided to tell this man my doubts. "There are other things I know. Like languages, riding bicycles, about which you asked me the first time we met." He nodded, and I went on. "I know about policemen. I can recognize them even when they're not in uniform. There's a certain air about them..."

"Does that worry you, knowing how to identify policemen?" he asked.

I nodded. "Yes," I said faintly. "It's something that thieves learn. Criminals of all kinds."

"There's more like that, isn't there?" he asked gently. "Things that make you wonder whether you were a normal member of society, or perhaps something more dangerous?"

"Yes," I replied, with some difficulty. "But there's nothing concrete. Nothing other than vague fears and feelings."

"The memories will come," he said, "and you can tell me whenever you think the time is right." He made some notes on the pad that he had kept open on the table between us. "Look at the bright side. Your memories are returning. We'll deal with them, don't worry."

"I'll tell you now whatever I can remember," I said. "A lot of it seems to be procedural. I know about firearms. I recognized every gun I saw on the way here. Service revolvers, old bolt action rifles, pistols, assault rifles, every one of them. I know how to clean them and fire them. I know that there are different types of police, and their ranks, and their symbols, their hierarchy. At the other hospital they told me that I know how to defend myself, because I took a knife from an old man. They said I broke into his house, and I think I know more about locks than most people. I must be some kind of a felon. Most probably a dangerous one."

"Can you tell me the police hierarchy?" he asked.

I recited the list from memory, up the ranks, starting with constable and ending with director-general. I even knew about the ranks at which you could enter any of the police or paramilitaries...

"You're very worried you might have spent your life doing something wrong," he said. "You don't like the idea that you might have committed one or more serious crimes. You might have killed someone, or something of that kind."

I couldn't speak because there's a lump in my throat, so I nodded.

"If at all you're a criminal," he said, "you clearly aren't a small time, petty criminal."

"But I must be a criminal of some kind," I said.

"Not necessarily," he said. "You could be a police informer. Working for them undercover. That would explain all your knowledge, and their lack of knowledge of you, because only your contact will know you. Perhaps both a criminal and an informer, which would explain why you don't trust the police."

I hadn't thought of being an informer. "It doesn't seem to fit," I said. "It doesn't seem right." I thought about it, realizing that I didn't just distrust the khakis but thought of them as enemies. Besides, the very idea of breaking someone's trust was terrible. "No," I said. "I wasn't an informer. I don't think I'd like to tell lies and gain someone's trust and inform on them..."

"You could be both," he said. "That's a very dangerous way to live, and you have to divide your mind into watertight sections..."

That couldn't be right, of course. "I can't say," I said. "I can't seem to bear the thought of letting someone down, of revealing a secret."

"Does the idea of your being a criminal fit?" he asked. "Of robbing, of stealing, of killing for money, of threatening people? Kidnapping them, demanding a ransom?"

I shook my head.

"I thought so," he said, "because otherwise you wouldn't have volunteered to undergo narco-analysis. But you're afraid all the same."

I nodded. "I am."

"Do you feel guilty?" he asked.

I nodded again, without speaking.

"Let me tell you something about guilt," he said. "Everyone has it. Simply put, you have some guilt, you've seen something bad that you *might* be responsible for, and you jump to the conclusion that you're guilty of it. That doesn't make sense. You're putting two and two together without knowing whether what you have is really two and two."

When he put it that way it seemed to be right. I nodded in slight relief. "There's the possibility," I said.

"There are other possibilities," he replied. "The possibilities don't matter. You'll remember exact details, some of them, in your own good time, and I'm willing to wait. I suggest you be patient with yourself, and don't let the police get into your mind with drugs or hypnosis or anything else."

"But I want to know who I am!" I said. "As soon as possible!"

"You seem to have the wrong notion about these drugs," he said. "The drug they use is sodium thiopental, which reduces your inhibitions, so you talk about things you might not otherwise discuss, or answer questions you might not otherwise answer. There are several problems with this. First, even if you are well, you might have mixed up memories, and you might incriminate someone innocent. Do you want to have some poor guy arrested by the police and interrogated round the clock just because you got some names mixed up?"

I shook my head.

"I thought so. Well, that's possible with drugs and perhaps hypnosis. Someone else might pay the price for your..." He paused, searching for a word. "For your impatience."

"And then, of course, the drug itself could get your memories twisted, mixed up. That's why I'm not prompting you, or giving you bits of your past. I know that they asked you about some dates, and you didn't remember. Well, I'm not going to tell you why they asked you about those dates. Let your memory return on its own."

I just looked at him, not knowing what to say, or what to do.

"You're confused," he said. "Confusion is good, because it gets you thinking. So think about what I just said about narco-analysis and hypnosis and all that. All right?"

"All right," I said.

"We'll leave it at that for the time being," he said. "Since you're committed to being honest, be honest with the police. Answer their questions honestly, though I don't think you should volunteer any information. About your knowledge of weapons and police ranks, for instance."

"I'll think about it," I said.

"Do that," he said. "You seem intelligent. Use your intelligence."

"I understood that they want me to lose my balance," I said. "They want to get me angry or upset with their questions. Their questions are very pointed, and very purposeful. As if they know something I don't. And they change the way they ask. Sometimes they don't give me time to think of the answer, other times they're relaxed. Sometimes they're angry, and sometimes very pleasant."

"They're taking note of every single thing you say," he said. "They ask you the same question in different ways, followed and preceded by different matters, and the moment you give them an answer that's inconsistent with something else you've said, they pounce on that."

"Yes," I said. "That's what I thought. Then I understood that if I get angry at something, they can then use the anger, by having one friendly questioner and one hostile...and then I wondered how I know so much about interrogations."

He shrugged. "It'll all come back in time," he said. "Just be aware of what you know. Don't push it."

"It seems odd that they seem to know more about me than I do," I said.

"You can be sure they know lots of things that you don't," he said. "That doesn't matter. As a doctor talking to a patient, your well-being is my primary responsibility, and I will only advise you on that basis." He paused. "Do you have a lawyer?"

"No," I said. It struck me as funny. A lawyer would have been the last thing I'd look for now. As far as I knew, lawyers never worry about the truth, only about what could work in a court, and the courts were unfair. And, of course, the truth was what I wanted.

"Well, you should have one," he said. "If you don't mind, I'll try to arrange one for you. A good one."

"I can't pay anyone anything," I said. "As far as I know, I have nothing at all."

"I know," he said, rising, "but I'll try anyway."

Chapter Four

Govind Patnaik

Calls late in the night usually meant bad news, especially in the early days of the coronavirus, so I hesitated before picking up the phone when it rang at eleven that March night. I hoped it was a wrong number. I didn't like cellphones, and avoided using mine after retirement. My landline didn't have caller ID, so I had no idea who the caller was. But this call, it turned out, was neither a wrong number nor a bad thing: it was my nephew, Ashok, for whom I have a soft spot, calling from Bhubaneshwar in Odisha, our hometown. "Did I disturb you, Uncle?" he asked. "I know you don't go to bed before midnight."

"Not at all," I said. Then, in a moment of honesty, I added, "I was failing to write my diary for the fourth time this week."

"I thought you might be doing something of the kind," said Ashok. "And how are you getting along?"

"The same old thing," I said. "That's why there's nothing to write in the diary."

"Or too much to put into words?" he asked. "Could it be that you're not clear about what to write?"

I shied away from discussing that. "No," I said, "we're just thinking of keeping safe from the coronavirus."

He tried again. "Only the virus?"

"For the time being," I replied evasively.

He laughed. "As you wish," he said. "I've got an interesting case. Perhaps worth your attention."

He taught psychiatry—an Associate Professor at the All India Institute of Medical Sciences in Bhubaneshwar, and I was a lawyer who had just quit practice in disgust, so I didn't understand how I could contribute to any of his cases. "I don't know much about minds and medicine."

"You know more than you think." He paused. "Specially about minds. But this one needs some legal input."

"What input?" I asked.

"The patient is a woman, about forty years old," he said, switching automatically into clinical mode, which he did when describing patients and ailments. "She hit her head a little over a fortnight ago, and suffered a subdural haematoma...a blood clot inside her skull. One of the doctors at the government hospital operated on her and removed the clot, but she seems to have lost her personal memory."

"All right," I said when he paused, "but her identity should be on record somewhere."

"It is, Uncle," he said. "The police found her unconscious

in the house of a retired deputy superintendent of police. The ex-policeman had been stabbed in the abdomen, and he died four days later, in a hospital. The knife with which he'd been stabbed was lying nearby, just out of his reach. It belonged to him, and had her fingerprints on it, besides his. There were slashes on her hands and forearms, so it looks like he attacked her, she defended herself, took the knife from him, and stabbed him...she remembers none of this.

"The investigating officer sent her fingerprints to the Fingerprint Bureau in Kolkata, and they found a match. Her prints matched a set of prints they got a quarter of a century ago, in a murder case. An unusual case. A group of Maoists..." He paused, perhaps to get back to clinical mode. "Well, they 'executed' a rich landowner back in 1993, not far from Malkangiri. They hacked him to death, and left the body lying in a pool of blood. One of the people in that group left a complete impression of the right palm and fingers on the wall. In the victim's blood. It seems she dipped her hand in the blood on the floor and put the print of her hand on the wall..."

"I see," I said. In my practice I had handled quite a lot of criminal law, mostly white-collar crime, but this was getting gruesome and interesting...

"They've found those fingerprints several times over the years," he said, "always at the sites of attacks by a group allied with the Peoples' War Group, the PWG. In

Odisha and in Bengal, so it looks like she's been all over the place. It seems she's been fighting the system for a long time. Fighting it violently."

"You need someone younger, someone active in such cases," I said. "I know a lot more about white-collar crime. It's been years since I came across anything physical, you know, and I know very little about the laws on terrorism. I can put you onto a former colleague who'll be much more knowledgeable about terrorism law and the National Investigation Agency, the NIA."

"There's a further twist to the case," he said. "The dead ex-cop, one ex-deputy superintendent called Mohanty, told a serving colleague that she claimed to be his daughter. He told the man to send his and this woman's DNA samples to a lab. It turns out she really is his daughter, born before he got married. His bastard child. Not only that, he asked his serving colleague to make sure her medical expenses were met. He emptied out his savings account for the purpose. That's why they operated on her without any fuss."

"Does she know all this?" I asked.

"She remembers nothing about her father, or meeting him, or what went on during that meeting. Not yet, anyway. The police have been made to turn her case over to the NIA, on the assumption she's linked to some terrorist group or other, which makes it a case for the central agencies."

"Who made them do it?" I asked. No police force likes its cases being passed on to a higher authority.

"The local MLA," he replied. "I think he means well."

"Can he justify that assumption?" I asked. "Legally, that is."

"I don't know," he replied. "That's your area. There's the fingerprint record, and there's her ability to take care of herself in a fight and to pick locks. The local police wants to deal with it themselves, but now, after the MLA kicked up a fuss, the chief minister called in the central agencies."

"Why?" I asked, wanting to be sure there'd be no political interference. "From the local police's point of view, one of their own was murdered, so they'll want to keep the case. Now they'll have someone from Delhi snooping in their backyard, which neither the police nor the chief minister will like."

"Yes," he replied. "The dead man was controversial, with a bad reputation. He's been accused of bribe-taking, of using third-degree on suspects, of sexual harassment, of using too much force to keep things quiet. The CM thinks the state police might cover up some of these matters rather than letting it all out. She is a policeman's daughter, after all, and there might be something unsavoury lurking in her story when she remembers it. The local cops might even finish her off..."

"Has the NIA taken it up?" I asked.

"Yes," he replied. "Their investigator asked for a psychiatric's opinion, which got me into the case formally. They're dealing with her through their branch in Bhubaneshwar, and they've got her locked up in the central jail."

"Formally?" I asked. "Does that mean you've been in the case informally before this?"

"An old professor is dying," Ashok said. "In Malkangiri. I visited him ten days ago, just after Mohanty died, before the case went to the NIA. The neurologist at the district hospital happens to be an old student. He asked me to have a look at her. To see if I could find out if she's faking her amnesia."

"Was she?" I asked.

"I didn't think so," he replied.

"So you've seen this woman in two prisons," I said.

"Yes," he said. "Both one-on-one meetings. I didn't want anyone else around, as a matter of professional privacy, and the police agreed to let me see her alone."

"What's your impression of her?" I asked.

He hesitated before answering. "In lay terms, she seems very strong-willed, a disciplinarian, with an overactive conscience, and desperate to get back her memory. She told the police at Malkangiri that she's willing to go through any kind of testing to find out who she is. Narco-analysis, hypnosis, polygraph, anything. Both the neurologist and I have told the police that they shouldn't do anything of the kind until her memory returns."

"That's straightforward, isn't it?" I asked. "All they have to do is wait."

"It's not so simple," he said. "There's pressure on them for two reasons. One is that all these PWG-type groups tend to execute whoever they see as traitors. If this woman's colleagues find out where she is, and that she's under pressure to share what she knows, they'll try to finish her off. And that's one more reason why the NIA think she's lying about her memory. Just in case there's a leak and they find out...

"Second, the NIA's informers say that there's something big coming up soon in Odisha. In months, maybe weeks. They need her to get her memory back as fast as possible in case she knows something about that. The investigating officer from the NIA wants to get into her mind now." He pauses. "There's her history, too. They think, because of her fingerprint record, that she's a killer, and they have no qualms drugging her. In fact, they're very gung-ho about it, and don't understand why I should want to save her."

"And you, obviously, don't agree with them," I said.

"Absolutely not," he said. "Broadly, for two reasons. First, as my patient, she's unwell, she's vulnerable, and those drugs they use for narco-analysis could well damage her mind. Second, narco-analysis is unreliable. What comes out of even a normal mind could be wishful thinking, or a false memory. So there's no way you can rely on information from an amnesiac under those drugs.

Besides, someone who knows what they're doing could ask leading questions to coax the 'right' answers out of the subject. It's been done before.

"And then there's the risk that if she gives the NIA accurate information, her former colleagues will intensify their efforts to finish her off. They do have sympathizers all over the place, people who will tell them if she begins to expose her ex-colleagues. They can also blackmail people in the government. If she got killed in their custody, the NIA will be in big trouble. And if she dies before they've got the last bit of information out of her, it'll be even worse for them. So they're doing their best to keep their investigation away from the state police."

"I see," I said. "Does she know the risks involved in narco-analysis?"

"I explained some of them to her," he replied. "But I don't think she understands just how serious they are. She's promised to think about it."

"What didn't you explain to her?" I asked.

"Well, I didn't tell her of the possibility of her old friends killing her…that would put even more pressure on her now, and pressure is the last thing an amnesiac needs."

"So what would you like me to do?" I asked.

"Explain some of these realities to her," he said. "Things happen that you can't plan for, or anticipate. Here's an example. One of the friends of the dead policeman got hold of a photograph of this woman before her father died. This friend was upset at the death, and, wanting to help find out more about the woman, advertised in one the local papers, with the photograph of her, asking people who might've seen her to come forward, promising a small cash reward. My ex-student in Malkangiri called me to tell me this. This was all before the NIA got the case. The Malkangiri police might know about the ad—I have no idea—but chances are they won't tell the NIA anything even if they follow up on it. In any case, the danger of her erstwhile fellow-Maoists finding out about her is very real, and growing. So represent her if you can. Persuade the NIA to keep her safe in every way."

"Did you tell the NIA about this person who came forward?" I asked.

He hesitated. "Not directly," he said, finally. "I hesitate to volunteer anything to our law enforcement people. They can complicate your life enormously. If I become a witness in the case it'll probably cost me a lot of time. Umm, that's one of the things on which I need your advice."

"I understand," I told him. "Ask your student to send you a cutting of the advertisement."

"I've done that," he said. "He took a photograph of the cutting and emailed it to me."

"Fine," I said. "So now, what do you want me to do?"

"Keep the investigators off her back until she gets back some of her memory. My responsibility ends when she gets reasonably healthy..." He paused again. "And, of course, you must give me legal advice. I don't mind spending time with the patient, or offering an opinion in a court, but I really don't want to get stuck in other aspects of the case."

"And how long do you think she'll take to recover?" I asked.

"No idea," he replied. "Weeks, months...even years. These things are unpredictable." He paused before continuing. "Umm, there's another thing, Uncle. You won't get much of a fee."

"Why not?" I asked. "You just said that her biological father emptied out his savings for her."

"Not his savings," he replied, "only his savings account at the bank, besides a stash of cash. A lot of that has gone into paying for her treatment and so on. Most of his assets are locked up now that he's dead. His legitimate son, a contractor somewhere in Hyderabad, will get the lot once the paperwork is done."

"All right," I said. "I'll book my tickets tomorrow."

"No," he said. "You have to be here tomorrow."

"Give me a few minutes to talk to Janaki," I told him. I'll call you back soon."

Janaki had already found her way to a nearby sofa. "Ashok, is it?" she asked.

"Yes," I told her. "He has a patient who needs legal advice."

"So why does he need to talk to you about it so late at night?" she asked, ever practical.

"He said he wants me to get there tomorrow morning." I explained the reasons for the urgency, the pressure, and so on.

She cut me off in her usual authoritative fashion. "The boy is alone," she said. "No one to look after him. I'll speak to him myself." She took the phone out of my lap and called him. "Ashok," she said, "Uncle says you want him there tomorrow. What's so urgent?"

All I could hear was the murmur of his voice replying on the phone. Then, "Who is this patient?", followed by another long murmur. Then, "How long do you want him there?", and some more murmur. Then, "You know Uncle. He finds it difficult to manage by himself. I don't know how you will take care of him. Two men alone... you'll drink too much, and won't eat properly. God knows how clean your clothes will be." More murmuring, insistent this time round. Then, "Of course I know what to do." Murmurs, again. Then, with finality, "He'll come tomorrow. But if he has to stay for more than a week, I will join you. Someone has to make sure you two take care of yourselves." Murmur. "Yes, you book the tickets and call. You know Uncle's email." She hung up, shaking her head.

"What was that all about?" I asked.

"I don't know," she said. "He's lonely, and confused.

You should spend some time with him. You know him best. And you're like a father to him."

"What about this patient?" I asked, "The one who wants to consult me."

"Aaah!" she said. "I don't know. Unlike you lawyers, I try to see the person underneath. That I can't do from here, no?" I had no idea how to respond, so I simply shrugged. She continued, "If it's a simple case, and you can come back in a few days, fine. Otherwise, I will see for myself what this patient is."

"I heard you telling Ashok," I said. "We'll talk on the phone after I see her. Sit on your questions until then."

Ashok called fifteen minutes later. "Your flight is at half-past-nine, Air India," he said. "It makes a two-hour layover at Hyderabad and gets here at three in the afternoon. I couldn't get you a seat on anything that gets here earlier. It happens to be an economy-class only flight, so I couldn't get you a good seat. Sorry about that."

"That's all right," I told him. "I'll manage."

"Please be at the airport by eight," he said. "I'm looking forward to having you around. It's been very quiet at home lately." He was at a loose end because, his wife, Rohini, had died a little over a year ago, and his eighteen-year-old son had gone off to a medical school in Pondicherry. He lived alone, with a maid coming in every day to cook and clean for him, and the emptiness showed.

"I need a break, too," I tell him. "Janaki seems to find

all this a little strange, but she's let me off for a week. You seem to know all the right buttons to push. Part of being a shrink, I suppose."

"I wish I could do it to my patients," he said ruefully. "I'll pick you up at the airport here."

"We'll spend some time swapping stories," I said. "Good night."

After I hung up, I gave in to the memories rushing into the troughs of my mind, relieved to spend time with something other than the bitterness that usually occupied them.

Sambit, a colleague of Ashok's, calls to say that Ashok has lost his wife, and if I can come and help. I promise to get to Bhubaneswar as soon as possible, and ask him to stick with Ashok until next evening. I spend the rest of the working day briefing assistants on my pending cases, getting them to apply for adjournments in a few key ones, while my secretary books tickets for Janaki and myself.

Ashok has always been different, a loner making his own way, and I've always considered him rather more than a nephew. His parents, my brother and sister-in-law, didn't like the girl he brought home one evening, and asked me to try to talk him out of it. When Janaki and I met the girl, though, our opinions were divided, for I didn't see a reason to tell him not to marry her. While Janaki took an instant dislike to her that she couldn't explain. "You'll see," she said when I asked her why.

I spent an evening trying to talk my brother out of his dislike for the girl. I like to think that my talk worked, but I couldn't get Janaki to budge.

Rohini's parents were as adamant as Janaki. She was from a wealthy, conservative Telugu family in the port city of Vizag and her family had been dead against her marrying an Odiya, and one from a different caste. They wanted her to marry a boy from a family in a similar but not competing business: they thought more in terms of alliances than marriages. For them, the thought of their daughter marrying a doctor with no ambitions of earning was unforgivably stupid. She remained on speaking terms with her one sibling, a younger sister, and one of her younger uncles, but that was it.

And now, here I am, rushing to help him pick up the pieces after her death. Janaki and I arrive in time for the cremation, which Ashok has held up for their son Rahul, who arrives just after us. The lost look in his eyes takes me by surprise. A few nights later, after Rahul's gone to bed, over a drink, he tries to explain why it's so deep. "She was terrified I'd die before her," he tells me. "You know how her own people cut her off. She feared being alone so much that she took care that I never risked my life, that I did everything I could to stretch my life out. It's ironic..."

She died of a stroke that took her by surprise on a quiet winter's afternoon, alone in their flat in Bhubaneswar. "My colleagues told me later that she was unconscious before she knew it," Ashok continues. "That was another irony, because that was the one thing she spoke about every now and again during her last few years, that she dearly wanted someone around when she died.

"I found her when I returned home from the office, slumped in the easy chair in which she took her afternoon nap. I'd let myself in with my latchkey when she didn't open the door after I rang the bell several times. With me, thankfully, was a colleague, an internist, who took charge the moment he saw her. He checked her out, called an ambulance, and held my hand during the terrible hours that followed.

"They told me at the hospital that she had really had a stroke. She was brain-dead by the time we got her to the hospital, and she slipped away during the night. The hours after that remained a blur in my memory. There were visitors, from nearby and far away. Neighbours, friends, colleagues, relatives, clients, all offering words and handshakes and perhaps support, all of which I accepted as if from a great distance. The first moment I remember clearly, then, your arrival, and then Rahul's.

"Rahul brought me back to the present. Rahul had just gone back to college after spending his three-week Christmas vacation with us. You left us alone. Rahul and I sat together for a long while, joined by grief with a depth that we never had while she was alive. Much to my regret."

"I hope you're doing something about that," I tell him. "You didn't have much of that with your own father, if you'll forgive me for saying so."

He nodded. "Of course. Both he and I need it. There are some things that only she could give him, but...he's going to have to grow up fast." Then, with a smile, "You rescued me later that night. I've always been grateful for that."

"I don't remember doing anything like that," I say.

"You did," he said. "There was this lady from next door, Rohini's closest friend, who sort of took over...Shanta."

I remember Shanta, of course, an officious neighbour who had nonetheless taken over the kitchen and taken care of immediate matters. "One of those take-charge ladies," I say. "I remember her."

"Well," Ashok says, "She's harmless. She just doesn't know when to stop, that's all. She tried to force me to have something to help me sleep. With the best intentions. She wanted me to move on. Whatever that means." He paused. "And I...I wanted to dwell on Rohini, at least for a while. Her space beside me was empty, and my mind was full of the smells of jasmine and sandalwood...things she always liked, always kept around her. I didn't want to let go of all that."

I remember Shanta's face hardening when she realized that her well-intentioned interference was unwanted, even unnecessary, as I drew her away, telling her I'd take care of Ashok. "If you want him to be miserable," she said, her resentment showing. But her sense of tradition, that she shouldn't argue with an old man, a stranger, kept me safe.

I don't react. Shanta has been of tremendous help, after all, and she, too, is tired, and grieving in her own way. I lead her firmly out and bolt the door behind her. "I want to be alone with my memories," Ashok says, finishing his drink. "Some of it is guilt, at some of the things that I've done and others that I haven't, but the heaviest burden is that I didn't encourage her to look after herself while she looked after me..."

I know there's more to it than he's saying, but I don't think this is the right time to push him, so I nod and leave him to his grief.

Lying in bed thinking about our conversation on the phone, I wondered what Janaki meant when she told me what she did, and what she thought Ashok was about. After Rohini's death he felt like a train that had reached the end of its rails. He had no idea where to go. Rohini had been his rails. Was Ashok trying to find himself a new set of rails?

What should have been a quiet and comfortable retirement turned into an unending period of regret when the bedrock of my earlier life turned into sand. Or was it quicksand?

I was seventy-three, with faded senses and memory beginning to acquire a haze, when, with a mixture of anger and self-loathing I saw that I spent more than half a century in a profession that is, at its core, shorn of humanity, and even reason. It came on all of a sudden, and quickly became unbearable, I let my partner buy me out. Then I went home to stew.

My profession is the law. No, I'm not a policeman. I'm a lawyer, and a fairly effective one, going by the record. I set up a law firm, and my colleagues and I have argued cases at the Supreme Court of India, representing all kinds of rich and influential people, companies, and parties, and won enough to be considered among the better legal brains in the capital, meaning the best legal brains in the country. Like most successful fellow-lawyers, I've built a cocoon around myself in which it wasn't necessary to question the fundamentals of the profession.

The work pays well, and I enjoy some of the argumentation, which consists mostly of looking for a plausible precedent, which saves judges the trouble of having to think for themselves rather than boilerplate. In retrospect, though, I must admit to tremors of conscience. The first stirring signal that something is wrong comes in 2013. Rahul Gandhi tears up, in public, a copy of an ordinance issued by the government run by his own party, and his own mother, and her choice as Prime Minister.

The ordinance concerns members of parliament and state legislatures who have been convicted of crimes by lower courts. By law, their positions are forfeit: the ordinance says, among other things, that they can continue unless their appeal against the conviction is turned down. With Gandhi describing it as complete nonsense, it's a dead duck, and the Prime Minister, who is away, accepts that assessment when he returns.

Gandhi has a point. He seems immature for a man in his forties, perhaps spoilt, surrounded by sycophants, but what he says gets me thinking of the quality of judgments handed out in lower courts. My work is mostly in courts of appeal, and it's been years since I appeared in even a High Court, but my files are full of lower court judgments that are irrational, or, worse, warped. Revisiting them, I am deflated by the realization that it takes so little talent to find holes in those judgments. So I take a step further, and look at some of the judgments that have not been appealed.

It's a revelation.

The judgments are poorly written, obvious boilerplate material with grammatical errors carried over and perpetuated because no one wants to question the judge in a courtroom, least of all the lawyers whose arguments are being judged. Case records with the police are questionable, the rationale linking evidence to crimes unsatisfactory, and confessions far too common. It's my opinion that many lower court convictions would have been overturned on appeal, but the convicts can't afford to appeal.

Then I look at acquittals, of which there are many. The prosecutor's cases are shabbily written and presented, verbose and hard to understand. The legal system, I realize, runs on gobbledygook that obscures rather than clarifies matters.

We gave up thinking. Instead, we cut and paste.

Slowly, another possibility emerges. What if arguments are presented shoddily on purpose? Prosecutors, like anyone else, can be on the take, as can judges.

That was the first crack in the cocoon. Perhaps cocoon is the wrong word. More often than not, something beautiful emerges from a cocoon. No such thing happened with me. If anything, it was uglier on the inside, so I should call it armour. But I digress.

I began to think about numbers. What proportion of cases are settled in the unsatisfactory lower courts? The answer was hard enough to get, but I did discover that only one case in a hundred goes on appeal to a higher court, say a state high court. From there on, with my limited internet skills, the data began to dry up. I began to understand how difficult it is find out whether the legal system works or not. Then I saw that the opacity was perhaps intentional. You weren't supposed to know that the legal system didn't work the way it was supposed to.

So I went back to the Constitution, and its preamble. That document speaks of justice—for everyone in the country, I presumed—and I thought I'd test that. I had a position of some privilege, and I really had no idea what the law was like for the average citizen, someone without the privileges and the money. The best place to start finding out, I thought, was with my staff, who I thought wouldn't have the privileges of my position. Their view would certainly broaden mine.

One morning I surprise Santosh, my driver, with a question about his family near Lucknow. "I brought them all here," he tells me. "Almost two years ago."

Now I'm surprised that I know so little about someone I see every day. "Why didn't you tell me?" I ask.

He smiles in the rear-view mirror before answering. "I needed some money for it, saab," he says. "When I asked you for a loan, you gave it to me without asking why I needed it. That's why I didn't tell you. And we had no trouble shifting. My brother brought my parents here. That was it."

"And if you had had any trouble?" I asked.

"I would have asked for your help," he replies, "but now I can manage on my own."

"That's very good," I tell him.

"There's also your blessings," he says.

"What do you mean?" I ask, taken aback, for he isn't in the habit of saying such things.

"Saab, I know one or two of the local police," he replies. "One man has become a sub-inspector…you got his brother a job some years ago, before he got his promotion."

I have no idea who he's talking about, but I nod. "So?" I ask.

"He knows that I work for you, so he does what he can for me…"

"Oh!" I say. I'll have to find someone else, I decide, because Santosh enjoys a sort of reflected version of my privilege. "You meet a lot of other drivers, don't you?" I ask. "When you're waiting. Do they also use their employers' names to get ahead?"

"Only a few," he replies. "Very few…I'm lucky to be working for you. And madam."

I have to find other sources. Much to Janaki's indignation,

I begin to go out on foot at odd hours, to talk to people. I dress in my most battered—and most comfortable, I must admit—clothes and disappear for a few hours. What irritates her most is that she has no idea where I go, because I go on foot.

I go to a basti*—a slum—nearby (you're never far from a slum in Delhi unless you're a senior government official) on foot and stop for tea at a busy shop. I think of Haroun Al Rashid, the Sultan who went out incognito, but I'm no Sultan, and these are busy people. None of them speaks to me. After I do it for three days, the shopkeeper, in an odd free moment, asks me where I live. "You look different," he says. "Not like the others who stop to drink my tea."*

"I live nearby," I tell him, waving a hand vaguely in the direction of home. "I used to be a lawyer, but I'm retired now, so I have time to walk around and meet people who live differently."

"It must be a big change from what you were used to," he says, pouring out a glass of tea for another customer.

The other tea-drinker chips in. "We don't see many lawyers," he says. "For most of us it's better not to go to the court. We settle our matters in other ways."

So, here we are, I tell myself. There are two questions: why don't they see lawyers, and what are the other ways in which they settle matters? "What other ways?" I ask, afraid, perhaps, of what he'll say if I ask the first.

His answer is surprisingly simple. "Through families,

friends, contacts, well-wishers...you must know this better than I do. The law is the last resort, because nobody knows how it works. Let me give you an example. Two of my neighbours back in my village got into a fight. One of them hit the other. The man who had been hit, he's a peaceful man, so he went to the police. The policeman on duty noted down his name and that of the man who had hit him, who is a bit of a goon. So both are considered goons. If anyone complains about the man who got hit, the police give him the treatment. So going to the police, or to the court, it costs money, and you never know what's going to happen. And you can always bribe the police. That's what they're there for, to collect their hafta."

Over the next few days, when I stop for tea, more people gather around. I listen a lot, and try to suspend judgment. It's clear that many of these are intelligent people, but without the benefit of a formal education. Or what people with a formal education call education. I learn that the legal system is at best fragile for most people who enter it. Nine out of ten people in the country have no effective access to the courts. Those that do, unless they're well connected or well off, suffer for years, or decades, as cases drag on. Even criminal cases go on for years...I read the papers more carefully and discover that a woman, a delivery person for a food distributor, has, without trial or legal representation, spent a year in prison for shouting at a policeman. On the other hand, influential people accused of rape and murder and kidnapping have been out on bail for decades, and a female lawyer who got drunk *before trying to drive home and killed most of a family but spent almost no time in jail.*

As for civil cases, well, those I do know very well indeed. I know that it's next to impossible to enforce a contract legally in India, unless you have oceans of time and money. We're worse off than, say, Senegal, or even Pakistan, at this. The most common motions in civil courts are for adjournment, and I've been behind more than my fair share of those…I also know that a former chief justice of the Supreme Court said at some point that justice delayed is justice denied. Well, so there we are.

And so, I go back to the books. Law books are old. The law is slow to change, and the legal system even slower. And then I went back to older books, and there I began to get a different view of due process: that the legal system and due process need to be rooted in the process of life itself to hold a society together. If you exclude large numbers from the legal process, you'll have a catastrophe on your hands. It might take generations, but it will happen, and most of our political leaders think only as far as the next elections, which might be five years away at most. The only ones who think beyond that horizon are those who have children who might become politicians. Our bureaucrats rarely think beyond their next tenure, which is similarly brief. So who looks at fifty years hence?

Thinking back, I thought that Rajiv Gandhi did the most damage, when, after the judgment in the Shah Bano case, he used his majority in Parliament to make that judgment irrelevant. That there was damage became clear when four judges of the Supreme Court held a press conference on what they felt ailed the judiciary. I hoped they'd come up with something meaningful when the conference was announced, but the judges seemed to miss the fundamental reason for the existence of the justice system: justice for the people, not just for judges and lawyers and officials who made a living out of it.

Then I began to read the judgments of our senior judges with an eye to simplicity. All of a sudden, our judges became windbags with delusions of intelligence, semi-literates who struggled to produce a comprehensible sentence, but considered themselves great writers. Their judgments were verbose and clotted with cliches, a nightmare for a layperson even to read. I think Emma Arbuthnot, the British judge who decided that Vijay Mallya was fit for extradition, said it right. And so, lacking the courage to throw away a professional lifetime's baggage, I retired to a sullen old age.

It's not in my nature to brood. I tend instead to prepare, to read up as much as I can to determine what to do. But I made little progress with the question of reforming the judicial system without having to destroy and rebuild it.

The one thing I could think of was a return to simplicity. Simple language, simple—but not crude—thinking, and an awareness of what the system was supposed to do. I had no idea, though, how to persuade anyone—not even Janaki, a qualified lawyer who concentrated on social work—that this would change anything. I was wondering about that for the hundredth time when I drifted off to sleep.

Chapter Five

Govind Patnaik

I woke from a rare night of deep sleep with a sharp sense of purpose I hadn't felt for a long time. When I tried to remember why, I had only a vague recollection of having planned to travel early, and I wasn't sure where I was or where I was going. All part of growing old, I thought, and lay quietly until a clear memory of my chat with Ashok returned. I was due to travel to Bhubaneshwar early today to spend some time with Ashok, giving him legal advice about a patient of his, with a possible criminal background.

Janaki was up already. Her bed was empty and I could hear her as she mumbled her daily prayers in the little niche off the dining room. After I finished my ablutions and had a look at the pad beside the phone, the day began to take shape. I was scheduled to get to the airport at eight to take a flight to Bhubaneshwar. I arranged for a cab to pick me up at seven. Janaki, I thought, had packed enough to take care of me for a week's stay with Ashok:

she planned to join us if I had to be there longer than that, bringing with her anything more I might need later.

The long line at the check-in counter moved quickly, and I overheard someone saying that traffic at the airport had decreased since Jet Airways went out of business. Past security, I settled down near the departure gate, conscious of a growing hunger. I'd skipped breakfast because it was too early, and Janaki, who distrusted restaurant food, hadn't been able to persuade me to eat. I couldn't find anything reasonably safe in the array of well-lit and expensive but dubious breakfasts on display. I tried to get a simple cup of coffee but found instead a bewildering range of options, all in French, all coming out of a machine that hissed and smoked like a dragon.

Sitting by the departure gate, wishing for a simple cup of coffee, I considered what I might get from this case. Ashok had left it vague, saying I was to advise him and perhaps his patient. There was no specific mention that he wanted me to take the woman's case. Perhaps it wouldn't be necessary, I thought, but in the back of my mind was the hope that here was a chance to redeem myself after the half-century spent working the legal system for my own benefit.

Why had I been putting in sixty-hour weeks at the office at the age of seventy-three when I'd earned enough for three lifetimes, besides having seen our children grow up and build their own independent lives? Because Janaki said that there were lots of others we could—and did—help. She looked after the house herself, asking only for a part-time maid to sweep and swab the house, and a driver to take her around because she couldn't drive. That was her work ethic in action, I used to think, just like my sixty-hour weeks.

Then I saw that it wasn't a work ethic. There was something false about it. That it was compulsion was very clear. And so I suggested to Janaki that we both take a longish break and spend some time with our children, with Saraswati in London and Ranjit in Chicago, and then think of the future.

When I returned from Chicago, I saw very clearly that I worked only because I wasn't comfortable with myself. Why, after having lived more than seven decades and seen so much of the world I couldn't do that was a puzzle that took me by the throat. So I told the office they could manage without me for a year, after which I'd consider returning to work.

Meanwhile, I wanted to get some paperwork in order. Going through the deeds of some property I'd inherited, I discovered that the property wasn't mine alone in law; several cousins had a legal share in it. Since I had the time, I thought I'd chase the paperwork myself, and discovered another universe altogether.

It was like jumping into icy water. Before my retirement, the driver and the maid used to complain—

to Janaki more than to me—about their difficulties in getting documentation out of the bureaucracy. Ration cards, driving licenses, income certificates, all required long hours of waiting, besides bribes. I couldn't afford to have my driver or maid having to lose a day at work for paperwork, and I took care of all that with a phone call to the right office.

The worm's-eye view of the bureaucracy that I got when I tried to get my own paperwork in order without pulling any strings was very different. I could, of course, make those same phone calls, along with a token payment, but I was curious about how others lived, and, of course, I had to time to indulge myself. Waiting in line as plain Govind Patnaik, I understood how callous the government could be, and how insufficient its services were.

That was my first look at the Constitution of India from below, and it was humbling. Until I retired, I'd praised it, claimed faith in it, and, to the extent I could in arguing my cases, followed it to the letter. Of course it had little weaknesses, but there was a foundation there sufficient to build a country on.

I saw that I was part of an insignificant percentage of the people of the country—the people for whom the Constitution existed—that swore by it. A small percentage of the people had a vague idea what it was about, but no specifics, but the vast majority of the people it was supposed to serve hadn't the least idea about it.

The reality was that government itself violated the Constitution routinely. The denial of my certificates, when I had all the requisite papers ready, was itself a violation, and it was considered normal. Blocking off access to superior officers for lodging complaints was also a violation, but the average citizen was far too terrified of the government to protest. We had grown moral and ethical calluses that we didn't acknowledge we had.

Going back to Ashok's call, I thought, what hope did a lone woman with no memory, no money, and no contacts have of getting what the Constitution promised her? The only answers I could find were dismal, and, against my lawyerly instincts, I found myself rooting for her, regardless of her history.

The plastic coffee was too much for my ageing digestion. I sat with it until the passengers were called, and got rid of it on the way to the aircraft, hoping they'd serve an edible breakfast on board. I tried unsuccessfully to sleep through the first leg, ate the airline breakfast, and, for lack of anything else to do, ate almost everything the airline served on the next. Seven hours later, at Bhubaneshwar, I wilted after an insufficient night's sleep, two cramped flights, and two airline meals. Ashok, thankfully, was right there to pick me up, and we were soon in Ashok's car, on the way to his house near the AIIMS campus.

"What's been happening with your patient?" I asked.

"The police have something," Ashok said when we

were out of the airport's parking lot. "Somebody actually responded to the advertisement that I told you about, carrying this woman's photograph."

"Who?" I asked.

"Relax, Uncle," he said. "We'll do this at home. There's time."

"I suppose it's too late to go see her today," I said.

"Yes," he replied. "We'll both go see her tomorrow. I'll get you introduced, and leave the rest to you. You decide whether you want to be part of this, and, if you do, then which part."

At his house, after a shower, a cup of tea in my hand—it was too early for a whisky, which I knew he'd give me at sunset—he took up the narrative. "A clerk from a hospice run by a church got in touch," he said. "It seems a woman who looked like our amnesiac, wearing the clothes she was wearing when the police got her, visited the hospice on the morning of the day she was caught. She wanted to see one Sister Katherine, a nun who was dying of cancer. The name she gave the clerk was Jasmine.

"Jasmine spent an hour and a half with Sister Katherine before going away, and Katherine died two days later, a few days before Jasmine's father died."

"How did you get to know all this?" I asked.

"The neurologist," he explained. "DSP Mohanty's friend, the one who advertised, went to the police with this, and my ex-student the neurologist got it from them.

All the police officers in the area know him. He networks very well, and keeps in touch. As he did with me."

"Does the NIA's investigating officer here know all this?" I asked.

"I don't know," he replied, "but he will very soon. In any case, there's more. The Malkangiri police checked with the other sisters at the hospice, who told them Sister Katherine spent quite a lot of time at their orphanage. One of them remembered that she was very close to an orphan girl called Jasmine whom she brought to the orphanage in 1978. Jasmine was newborn then...the orphanage named her when they took her in.

"The strange thing is, she ran away from the orphanage in 1991, when she was just thirteen. This woman could well be *that* Jasmine. The age fits. There's a lot more that the police can put together. They have her fingerprints, which they've placed at several Maoist raid scenes in the nineties and the noughties, and they'll spread the word among their informers for more on her."

"So it looks like they're closing in on her," I said.

"Yes," he replied. "But they do take time to conduct their enquiries. They have to be careful, because of the risk of news getting back to her former colleagues."

"Why are you so involved in this?" I asked. "It seems out of character. Especially now that we know she's probably guilty of everything they think she's done."

"Because the charges the police make don't seem to fit

with the person thay have in custody," he said. "She seems like a good person, and intelligent...with a very strong moral sense, in simple terms."

"Is that all?" I asked.

"No," he said, a little reluctantly. "You see, back in the 1980s, when I was completing my MBBS, I spent a couple of years doing volunteer work in Malkangiri. You were already in Delhi at the time, and doing very well. Well, I spent some time in Kalahandi and Phulbani and Koraput—in those days, Malkangiri was part of Koraput—in the poorer villages, and what I saw wasn't very encouraging. There were people whose lands were taken away, families were destroyed, people were starving. And a few very rich families got richer all the time, with the help of government officials and contractors...I suppose it must have been even worse before, especially during the Emergency.

"So when I looked at this woman's history, at when and where she was born, and at her father's history, and at the country's history..." He ran out of steam.

"What?" I asked.

"Well, she was born in early 1978, which means she was conceived in early or middle 1977," he replied. "DSP Mohanty would have been a sub-inspector or something of the kind, fairly young, with a sense of power because of the Emergency. So I keep wondering: what's the story there? Is there something we've missed?"

"Won't she remember about her own origins?" I asked.

"Certainly not," he replied. "She ended up at the orphanage when she was just days old. That part we've lost unless we go to the orphanage and find out how she got there, and who took her there."

"The orphanage will have records," I said. "If they've been reasonably careful, those registers should be around even now."

"There's much that the records won't say," he said. "We'll see...but I think we must try to get to the bottom of this history."

"Does the history justify all the killing, all the violence she's been up to?" I asked.

"Not at all," he said. "I'm talking about understanding, not justification. There's a difference."

Fresh from my exposure to governmental hamhandedness, I could see where the conversation was going, and, after a long day of sitting in a cramped airline seat, didn't want to go there. "There certainly is," I said. Then it occurred to me that he was a psychiatrist, after all, and had seen all kinds of people. "I've been looking again at my own life these past few weeks. I don't really know what to do..." I give him the analogy from the previous day. "Like a train looking for a set of tracks."

"That's very well put," he said slowly. "I've been like that, too, after Rohini died. It happens when you lose a spouse you've lived with for a long time. You lose not just the person but also what she stood for. More so when the nest is empty."

The doorbell rang, and he rose to check. It was the busybody neighbour, Shanta, with a wilted flower and a bit of sandal paste in a leaf: *prasad,* from a Siva temple down the street. After seeing Shanta off, Ashok placed a small smear of sandal paste in the middle of his own forehead with the tip of his right ring finger, then offered me the leaf. I put a bit of paste on my forehead too, and felt its coolness, smelt its fragrance, and remembered Ashok telling me about Rohini.

I could see he knew what I was thinking. Jasmine and sandal. More than anything else, they were reminders of Rohini's faith, a faith that Ashok shared only in name. The depth of her faith had made Ashok uncomfortable. Sitting in Ashok's bright drawing room, I realized that he perhaps wondered equally at my faith in the Constitution, a document as open to question as any of the scriptures Rohini had read regularly. Well, my faith was going...

Sitting there with all this going through my mind, I was taken aback by a prodigious yawn. "I'm sorry to have kept you," Ashok said. "The journey must have tired you out. Take a nap."

"Not the journey," I told him. "I drank coffee at the airport and ate two airline meals after a disturbed night and now I'm paying for it. Sometimes I forget that my stomach is no longer a teenager's."

"Take a nap, Uncle," Ashok said. "You'll feel better after it."

"What about you?" I asked.

"I'll take one, too," he said. "After I make arrangements for dinner."

I woke up in the dark, and when I looked at my watch it said half-past-nine. I'd slept close to three hours, and wouldn't be able to get back to sleep until the small hours. I got up and went to the bathroom to wash up before rejoining Ashok in the dining room. "That was a rather long nap," Ashok said.

"Yes," I replied. "Too long. I feel quite fresh now, but a little disoriented, and I don't know how I'll get to sleep after dinner."

"A couple of shots of Johnny Walker might help," he said, grinning. "I've got a bottle of Blue Label for you. I'll keep you company because I, too, took a nap."

"Very nice," I said. "Whenever you like."

We ate then, rice and crab and beans and aubergine, just as I'd eaten as a child, a meal that took me back to my school days nearly sixty years ago, and then started seriously on the Blue Label.

"What's on your mind?" I asked after he put the leftovers in the fridge.

"Despair," he replied.

"About what?" I asked.

"All kinds of things," he said. He looked up. "Sometimes

I regret having trained as a psychiatrist. You get to see your own nasty side very clearly, and you can't get away from it. And then there are the patients..." He smiled wryly. "You know how it is with some kinds of legal cases. They drag on for years. It's a bit like that with psychiatric patients. Some of them keep coming back again and again..."

"I understand," I told him, "about the training, at least. After I quit working I've had a different level of exposure to our Constitution and it's been saddening, to say the least. I should have known it but didn't. It's part of the nature of being a professional. You learn to compartmentalize. When the compartments begin to break down, you're in trouble."

He looked at me sharply. "Yes," he said. "Keeping your personal life separate from the work you do. That's a killer. But we're so used to those compartments that you sound crazy if you begin to talk about it."

"But you still haven't told me what's on your mind," I reminded him.

He emptied his glass with a long draught and refilled it before he answered. "Guilt," he said. "I didn't really do justice to Rohini. Or Rahul, for that matter."

"That's not what you want to say," I told him. "And you know it."

"Yes," he said. "It's not what I want to say, but that's all I'm going to say tonight. If you keep your eyes open, you'll see tomorrow, and we'll talk after that. If I can bring myself to..."

"Fine," I said. "We'll continue this bit of the discussion afterwards. Whenever you see fit."

"So observe," he said, "and let me know what you see."

"Right," I said. "I'll do that."

"So you tell me, Uncle," he said. "How've you been dealing with retirement?"

I told him about the foundation of my professional life being shaken, and he smiled. "It's like that with me, too," he said, finally. "We keep talking of mental health but we don't know what that really means, except that it's not the absence of disease."

Although I got to bed before midnight and turned off the light at a quarter past, I didn't get to sleep for a long time. I'd always thought of Ashok as having a good, balanced life, being completely unaware of the cracks in his marriage. But then, looking back at my own life with Janaki, I began to get a sense of the depth of its emptiness, the emptiness that had led me to try to fill it with long working days and golfing Sundays and business trips and so on.

Did Janaki feel that same emptiness, I wondered, and try to fill it with housework and education programmes for poor children?

Is that what we're all doing, came the thought, fleeing emptiness and worthlessness?

Was that what I was still doing, I asked, looking for something worthwhile to defend, without charging a fee, a woman with no memory of a violent past?

And then, taking my breath away, leaving me stunned, came doubt. If I thought my mind was free, why was I looking for a fresh beginning in retirement, at the end of my professional life? Wrestling with that brought no comfort, but it did bring sleep, and I slept again, deeply, only to awaken at seven, over an hour past the time I usually rose.

Ashok was up and about when I got to the living room at a quarter-past-seven, and brought me a cup of tea just the way I like it, strong, with a dash of milk and a little sugar to take the bitter edge off. I knew he liked the quiet of the morning, and retreated into my own thoughts as I sipped the tea, wishing I had the newspaper to read. Any newspaper, English, Hindi, or Odiya.

"I don't get a newspaper," Ashok said, reading my mind. "Rohini used to read one, but I get my news online." He produced a newspaper with a bit of a flourish. "I went out and got you one, though, a copy of the local *Times of India*."

"Thank you," I said with some feeling. I felt lost if I didn't have a newspaper with my tea...

Later, over breakfast, I asked him what he'd planned for the day. "Jail first," he replied. "I have to be at the Institute by noon for my first class, so I'll take you over to the jail and introduce you to some of the officials there. I know the Jail Superintendent, so we should be able to see our forgetful lady today. But if the paperwork takes too long, I'll leave you there, and have you picked up whenever you like."

We left at ten for the prison, through suburban streets that, after Delhi's crowds and grime, seemed green and spacious, along the highway and then off it again to the prison complex, readily identifiable by the height of its walls and the fencing on top, to a large parking lot, and thence through a search and then bare corridors to the Superintendent's office, a quiet white-painted room that looked more like a bureaucrat's office. Quiet and organized.

The Superintendent knew Ashok and waved us to visitors' chairs across his desk. He knew of me, apparently, so I got a firm handshake when Ashok introduced us. "To see the woman prisoner in solitary?" he asked. "No problem." He picked up his intercom and spoke softly into it. A subordinate brought papers to fill in and sign, which I did. And then, led by a sub-inspector in the state's prison service, followed by an armed constable. We went through to an interrogation room in a section of the prison that was wholly more unpleasant, where were visible, as were in prisons all over India, the nastier parts of the criminal legal system.

The policeman led us to a windowless room with a

single scarred wooden table and a few chairs, where a woman in prison whites was seated. The door closed behind us, and I was at last face to face with my prospective client. She ignored me, however, and, with a smile that transformed her dark face, said to Ashok, in Odia, "My name is Jasmine."

Chapter Six

Jasmine

Lying alone on the hard mattress with the worn sheet was really no discomfort. It's never pitch dark in a prison, or totally silent. They always leave lights on at key points, plus there's the noise of several hundred people sleeping. After the night meal, brought to my cell by a warder, I lay down to sleep, wondering where the memories came from. Practically every returning memory was a surprise, and seemed new in some sense. I relaxed, and had almost dropped off to sleep when there came outrage, or the memory of it.

Its intensity took me by surprise. I lost my breath for a moment, and then the training reasserted itself. My breath slowed and the outrage ebbed, leaving behind the question: what brought that outrage? A fragment of memory surfaced then, of a plump cleric in a cassock, smiling, telling me that I needed guidance. A nauseating smell of sweat and perfume and soiled clothing seemed to flood my nostrils, and I remembered more.

"Child," he says, smiling, though there's nothing nice about the smile. "You deserve better. You are so intelligent, too intelligent for this little school."

We are alone in a room, in which he sits at a desk by a curtained window while I stand beside him. Through the curtain I can see the bright sunshine outside, and, between the edges of the curtain and the window frame, slices of the banana trees growing in the ground outside. I don't know what to say and I know that it's better to keep quiet when I'm not sure what to say. It's usually better to keep quiet even when I know what to say but I have difficulty doing that, so I'm often in trouble. Like now.

He reaches out and puts his right hand on my left upper arm. "Trust me," he says. "I can make your life a lot easier." He gives my arm a little squeeze. I feel the sweat on his palm. I don't like his touch, so I step back, away from him. Spots of sweat appear on his forehead, and he takes his hand away to wipe his face with a stained kerchief which he refolds afterwards and places carefully in a pocket in the trousers he wears under his cassock.

No wonder he's sweating, I think, wearing all those clothes in this heat. I wonder when he's going to let me go back to the dormitory, where I can join the others in the brief Sunday afternoon break when we can play simple games that don't need equipment; or listen to songs on the radio.

"Your birthday is next week," he says. "What would you like for a present? A cake? New clothes?" He reaches up

with his hand to pat my cheek, but my nerve breaks and I turn and run from the room. I don't like him. I don't trust him. He smiles a lot but his eyes never change. He watches me like a cat watching a lizard. And he stinks. I don't want anything from him.

As I flee, I bump into Sister Elizabeth. Sister Elizabeth teaches us history and social sciences. She comes from some place in Kerala, and she speaks very strangely. When she told us about the discovery of India, I asked her why she said that the Portuguese discovered India, because there were already people living in India. She never did answer that question properly, and she's hated me ever since. "Where are you going?" she asks. "Why aren't you in the dormitory?"

"Father Richard was talking to me," I tell her.

"Why were you running?" she asks.

"I don't like him," I tell her.

"What!" she says. "Why?"

"I don't trust him," I say. I can't find the words to tell her why.

She is angry. "We'll talk to him," she says, dragging me along, down the corridor to Father Richard's room.

"I found this child running down the corridor," Elizabeth tells him. "She says she doesn't like you."

"It's all right," Richard tells her, the fake smile on his face. "I was just trying to find out why she's so angry all the time. I asked her about her birthday, and she ran away."

Elizabeth smiles back. I think she's trying to please him.

"I brought her back so that you can finish your talk."

Richard looks at his watch and sighs. "No," he says. "Later. I have other work." He looks at his watch again. "After vespers." He smiles at her. "Bring her to me then."

"That's difficult," says Elizabeth. "Visitors aren't allowed after five."

"Bring her here," says Richard.

"They're not allowed out after five," says Elizabeth.

"Then it'll have to wait until the next visit," Richard says. "Tomorrow is Sunday, and we'll have many visitors. We will leave Monday morning, so that leaves only this evening."

"Let me see, Father," says Elizabeth.

"Good," says Richard. "Do that. Bring her yourself."

"I will, Father," says Elizabeth. "Immediately after vespers."

"Thanks," Richard tells her. He turns his smile on me and I take a step back. Elizabeth tightens her grip on my arm, at the same place that Richard squeezed. It hurts, but Richard's grip makes me want to vomit.

Elizabeth takes me to Richard's room in the evening, after dinner, which is at half-past-six. "Bishop Wilson will be pleased if we can persuade her to change her ways," she tells him as she pushes me into the room.

"Thank you," Richard says. "Yes, the bishop will be pleased. I'll do my best." He smiles as she leaves the room. I hate that smile.

I stand facing him, the desk between us. I know this is

wrong but I can't oppose Elizabeth. "Come closer," he says. "I won't do anything to harm you."

I edge along the desk, slowly. Now I'm scared. I stop where I was standing in the afternoon. He brings out his kerchief to wipe his hands. It's the same one he used before, and it's dirty. He smells even worse than before, because he's used some perfume to hide the smell of his sweat. He reaches out and holds me by the arm, like he did before. His mouth is open now, and I can't stand the sight of it because it seems dirty. I close my eyes as he pulls me closer. His hand moves down my arm and on my back, onto my bottom, which he squeezes.

I can't bear him anymore. I open my eyes and see that his face is much closer, and I can smell his breath. I'm afraid but I'm not going to cry, or make a sound. He squeezes harder, and there's something really bad in his eyes. Without thinking, I reach out for something on the desk, grab it, and poke him in the face with it. Then I turn and run, bursting through the door, straight into Elizabeth, who's waiting outside.

She grabs me by the arm, as she did in the afternoon. Her grip is strong enough to make me cry out. She drags me back into Richard's room, where he sits holding his dirty kerchief, now bloody, to a cut on his cheek. "What happened, Father?" asks Elizabeth. "I heard you cry out."

"She attacked me," he says. He points at a paperknife lying on the floor, with blood on it. "I might need a doctor."

"I'll get Sister Rose," says Elizabeth. "She'll know what to do. She's a trained nurse. But first let me put this brat

somewhere safe where she can think of what she's done." She drags me off to an empty room further down the corridor, pushes me in, and bolts the door from the outside.

It's dark in the room. There's a little light coming in through the window, that's all. I'm thirsty, but there's nothing in the room. I feel like crying. I'm afraid of what might be in the dark. I make up my mind. Whatever's in the dark can't be worse than Richard or Elizabeth. I feel my way all over the room, hands out. I find a table and a chair and a bench and then a cupboard, but that's all. There are no monsters hidden here. Now I don't feel like crying, so I sit on the bench and wait. I'm still afraid, but I don't need to cry out.

The thirst grows. I haven't had any water since dinner. I think of feeling my way around the room and the fear going away. I don't need to fear the thirst. I might have to wait for some time but they'll let me out. I wait for what seems to be hours before I hear footsteps, and Elizabeth's voice in the corridor.

The light comes on and the door opens. In the doorway stands the Mother Superior, a tall and stout woman with a crucifix prominently displayed on her bosom. To her side is Elizabeth, and behind Elizabeth another nun the edge of whose habit I can just see. "Well, child," says the Mother Superior gently, "didn't you promise me you wouldn't get into trouble again?"

It's very strange. Her gentleness makes me want to cry. But I'm not going to cry before Elizabeth, so I keep quiet, because I'm afraid that if I try to speak I'll cry.

She seems to read my mind. "You're thirsty," she says. She turns to the nun behind Elizabeth, who I can see is Sister Katherine. "Get the child water from the dining hall and bring her to my office."

Sister Katherine and I walk side by side through the corridors, now lit, to the dining hall, inside the orphanage. She pours water into a tumbler from one of the three jugs that are always kept full. Only when I've emptied the glass does she speak. "Did you stab Richard in the face?" she asks.

Now I have my voice. "Yes," I tell her.

We start walking towards the Mother Superior's office, which is outside the orphanage, in the office complex, on the first floor. She walks slowly, so that we can talk. "Why?" she asks.

"He was patting my back, and then his hand went lower down," I say slowly. "I didn't like what he was doing, and he had a strange look on his face…There was spit coming out of his mouth."

She holds my upper arm a little lower down than Elizabeth did, but she's gentle, and I find it reassuring. "Were you afraid when they left you in that room in the dark?" she asks. She knows I'm afraid of the dark.

"In the beginning," I tell her. "But I thought about it…I thought the dark wouldn't do anything worse than Richard or Elizabeth."

"Father Richard," she says. "Sister Elizabeth. You must respect them."

"Not Richard," I tell her. "Not after what he did."

She pauses. I can't see her face in the dark. Her voice is very soft. "Jasmine," she says. "Dear Jasmine, please be careful."

That was how I remembered my name. The fragment of memory stopped there. I had an identity of my own, a past. All of a sudden I had an anchor, but instead of holding me down, it lifted my heart. It was so precious that for a while I forgot to hate Richard...

I was impatient, because reaching the end of that bit of memory was like having a really interesting book taken away in the middle of an especially interesting chapter, but much more intense. I felt light-hearted and frustrated at the same time, and I didn't know what to do about it. The first thing that came to my mind was that I should tell Dr Patnaik, because he seemed to have known that something like this was going to happen, and I was impatient. I felt that telling somebody about this memory might bring more memories out of the shadows, and the impatience grew. I hardly slept that night, hoping the doctor would come soon.

Luck was with me. Sometime in the middle of the morning, two khakis, a man and a woman, entered my cell and told me to follow them. They led me to the same interrogation room when I'd spoken to Dr Patnaik. A few minutes later, the khakis led Dr Patnaik into the room. There was someone with him, an older man, thin and bespectacled.

I thought later that I should have been more careful, for as soon as the khaki had slammed the door close, I stood up and blurted to Dr Patnaik, "My name is Jasmine."

Chapter Seven

Govind Patnaik

The spark was evident from the moment I saw her face light up when she saw Ashok, and told him her name.

I shrank from that spark, or at least from the knowledge of it. Ashok and I were close: we were, in many ways, father and son rather than uncle and nephew. I could see that he was in a crisis, and had no idea how to deal with it without doing himself enormous damage.

But then, I'd seen worse. You can't practice law for five decades without coming across a lot of unreasonable relationships, without seeing the randomness of attraction. I have trouble finding the right word for it: it's not lust, it's not love, it's just an entirely inexplicable, insistent tug at the heart. Its consequences are almost always damaging. Few come through unscathed, and end up better and wiser for the experience, but the vast majority that I've seen are left bitter and unsatisfied. Most people survive it, but I've never seen a case where the relationships involved returned to what they were before, to the *status quo ante.* I felt a tug of sympathy for Ashok, and for the conflict in his mind, and arrived at a clearer understanding of why he wanted me there.

He smiled back at her. "I told you so," he said. "You're beginning to get your bearings." He paused, turning to me. "There's no need to tell you her name," he said. "This is the patient I told you about. The one who's forgotten who she is. She seems to have remembered her name." He turned back to her. "This is Mr Govind Patnaik, a very experienced Supreme Court lawyer. I've asked him to consider taking your case." He hesitated. "He also happens to be my uncle."

I nodded and smiled. For all my experience and professional objectivity and the knowledge that it wasn't her fault by any means, I couldn't help feeling a tinge of resentment at her. In any case, she seemed to be bursting with something to share with Ashok, so I knew what to do. "Would you like me to wait outside for a while?" I asked Ashok. "Your patient might want to talk to you alone."

She shook her head. "There's nothing to hide," she said. "It's just that I remembered some other parts of my past, not just my name."

"Stay," Ashok told me. "You'll get to know your client as she speaks."

I held up a hand. "May I record this?" I asked, and she nodded.

We both sat down, and she began to speak. "I don't know who my parents are," she said. "I was brought up in an orphanage," she hesitated. "A Christian orphanage, where I was in trouble a lot of the time."

"What kind of trouble?" asked Ashok.

"The nuns who taught us didn't like me because I asked too many questions," she replied. She told us about asking why the book said that Vasco da Gama discovered India when there were already more people living in India than in Vasco's own country. "That's the only specific question I remember that got me into trouble, but I remember being used to being scolded and punished. Being alone."

She spoke simply and honestly, and not to Ashok or to me. She was looking inwards, sometimes hesitant, looking for the best word to describe whatever she had remembered, trying to relive the experience. After a professional lifetime of dealing with lies and liars, I thought I had a fine-tuned sense for the truth, and, as far as I could tell, she was sticking to it. As I watched and listened, my resentment dissolved. Whatever there was between Ashok and her was beyond their control, and in the meanwhile there was no subterfuge about her.

Ashok waited for her to run out of words, which she did when she spoke of Sister Katherine calling her Jasmine. "Do you remember the name of the orphanage?" he asked.

"St Xavier's," she replied. "It was outside Malkangiri." She paused. "The nuns used to take a bus to town."

A few questions about details sometimes shake loose more facts out of witnesses than they realized they knew. "Do you remember seeing anything out of the windows?" I asked.

"Banana trees," she said. "Almost ready to be harvested…we used to eat a lot of bananas." She paused. "Maybe a cow. A black cow. With a calf. I think I helped look after them."

"Close your eyes and try to imagine yourself back there," Ashok said.

She closed her eyes for a few seconds, then opened them and shook her head. "It's not like a movie," she said, trying to explain. "There are gaps. It's in patches. It's like a very old movie, with breaks and black spots all over."

"Do you remember how old you were when this happened?" Ashok asked.

"Yes," she said. "I must have been twelve or thirteen… Richard said something about my birthday being the following week…I must have been nearly thirteen. Or twelve. I'm not sure."

"What about smells?" Ashok asked.

"I remember Richard's stink," she says. "Sweat and really bad perfume. And that kerchief…I kept wondering how he could fold up such a horrible thing and put it so carefully in his pocket. As if it were a treasure."

He asked her a few more questions, but she seemed not to remember anything else. An hour after we started, we were ready to leave. "Have you decided whether you'll take my case?" she asked when Ashok told her it was time to leave.

"Not yet," I said. "I'll discuss it with Ashok tonight, decide after that, and let you know tomorrow."

She looked directly into my eyes and seemed to see more perhaps than I wanted her to, for I caught a flash of understanding in her, but she said nothing about it. "All right," she said. She turned to Ashok. "Will you come tomorrow?" she asked him.

"No," he said. "I have classes and meetings all day."

She accepted that, too, without any reaction. "Shall I tell him if I remember anything?" she asked, pointing at me.

"Yes," he said. He paused to think. "If he agrees to take your case," he continued, "not otherwise."

Both of them seemed to have assumed that I had decided to take her case. I let it lie, because indeed I had. Ashok rapped on the door to get the warder's attention, and we didn't speak while we were led to the Superintendent's office, where we found the NIA investigating officer awaiting us.

Since NIA officers don't usually wear uniforms, I couldn't make out his rank, but he was probably a Superintendent or higher, named Ramesh Arora. He was relatively young, and, as we discovered in the course of the next hour or so, extremely sharp behind an easy-going exterior. "I know of you, Mr Patnaik," he said as the Superintendent introduced us. "We study some of your cases to make sure we prosecute correctly."

"That's undeserved," I told him. "Juniors do most of the work. It's been like that for the past twenty years."

"We won't waste time on that," he said. "Instead, let me state our position. We have reliable fingerprint evidence that your client was present at the scene of several terrorism-related incidents in Odisha and northern Andhra Pradesh over a period of two decades. We know that she is the biological daughter of the late Deputy Superintendent Mohanty of the Odisha Police. We are investigating her history before...before the first of the incidents at which we found her fingerprints.

"The big problem is that she claims that she has forgotten her identity, so we can't verify much."

"She doesn't just claim to have lost her memory," Ashok said. "She really *has* lost it. As you know, she once offered to let you narco-analyse her, but I persuaded her not to do that."

Arora nodded. "I know that she is willing to cooperate. I also know that you think that if we force drugs on her, she might lose her memory permanently, or give us misleading information. That is why we haven't pursued that course."

"Her memory is returning," Ashok said. "She now remembers her name and the orphanage. She was at St Xavier's, which is close by."

Arora nodded. "The local police told us. We tried to find the Mother Superior, who is in charge, but she is away at a meeting with the Bishop. We plan to talk to her when she returns tomorrow. Her name is Elizabeth."

"Jasmine talks of a Sister Elizabeth teaching her history," Ashok said. "This must have been in the early 1990s. She thinks she was about twelve or thirteen then, and therefore must be about forty years old now."

"Very good," said Arora, "but we are in a hurry."

"Why?" I asked.

"Because we have reliable information on two things. One, that the group that we think she belongs to is planning a big attack in the next few months, during the festival season, when people are likely to be taken by surprise. She is likely to know about it. Second, there is a planner coordinating some of these militant groups. She might know his identity. Both these pieces of information would be a great help in saving lives, civilian and police.

"We have to find out about these things as soon as possible. It's vital, because we don't know how many lives will be lost."

"What are you trying to say?" asked Ashok.

"Is there anything we can do to help her get her memory back sooner? We can show her around the orphanage, for example, if you think it will help."

"At present, no," said Ashok. "It's equally likely to confuse her, or to mislead her. The best thing to do is to wait. It could be a matter of days, or weeks..."

"Or months," said Arora. "We don't know how much time we have."

"It could well be months, as you say," Ashok said. "But in my considered opinion, the process should be left alone. Any attempt to tamper with it could have very serious consequences."

"Is that a threat?" asked Arora, his eyebrows lifting.

"Not at all," said Ashok, "but if you expose her to sodium thiopental or any such thing, I'll have to take it up with the Human Rights Commission. Remember the Aarushi murder case? Narco-analysis did nothing to clear up the mystery, even though the subject was fine at the time. I know, of course, that you're not interested in directing the witness anywhere..."

Arora nodded. "We'll wait a little longer," he said after a moment's pause. "It's very frustrating for us. We have a job to do, you know."

"I understand," Ashok said. "Let's hope she remembers fast."

"Yes," Arora said. He seemed a little deflated. "There's another risk now. Her old colleagues might come after her now. If that threat becomes serious, we might have to shift her to Delhi."

"How will you know about the threat?" I asked.

"We have some informers," he said. "But we don't get complete information. We get indicators, and when we get multiple indicators pointing at the same thing, we begin to look."

"You might not know in time," I said.

"I'm not going to discuss the quality of my informants or my information," he told me. "It's all very confidential, because some of the informants run the same risks that your client runs…worse risks, actually, because they happen to be out in the real world, without the protection your client has."

We left the jail deeply unsatisfied. That small amount of progress with Jasmine's name apart, we'd come away with very little. In the car on the way back to Ashok's house, I asked, "Why did you bring up the idea of directing the witness under narcosis?"

"I don't know anything about the quality of that investigation," he replied. "But I want him to know that if he drugs her, I'll hit him with everything I can." He smiled grimly. "One of the advantages of working for the government."

"It's not much," I said.

"No," he said. "It's not. But we must use what we have."

Ashok was getting too involved, and I consoled myself with the thought that at least I was beginning to know what kind of a client I was dealing with. On the heels of that came the disturbing realization that Ashok was depending on me to help him navigate these uncharted waters, and I had no idea how.

Chapter Eight

Govind Patnaik

Ashok got me a cab home at his office. He was already a little late for his noon class, and I didn't want to take any more of his time, so I took the cab and went straight back home. I warmed up leftovers from the fridge, and poured myself a large Blue Label to try to sort things out in my mind.

And then, unbidden, sprang memories of women and wistfulness. For large parts of my life with Janaki I'd thought—wistfully—of what might have been if I'd married someone else. The wistfulness never moved me to act, though it did bring a few sleepless nights. Remembering how Ashok struggled with his emotions, I wondered, more seriously: did Janaki ever sense that, and did it trouble her?

Had she ever thought wistfully about another man?

If she had, did her wistfulness ever drive her to...? I couldn't complete the thought. I couldn't bear to complete it. Instead, I went back to the faces I'd wished for in Janaki's place, and discovered, to my surprise, that I remembered none in any detail...

The chemistry—for lack of another word—between Ashok and Jasmine was unmistakable. Not that anything would come of it: Jasmine was going to stay in prison for the foreseeable future, given her past. What would Ashok do? And Jasmine?

Jasmine was too caught up in the mystery of her own past to pay much attention to the chemistry. It struck me then that I trusted Jasmine more than Ashok, at least in this. Remembering the integrity of her responses to questioning, I didn't think she'd try to win Ashok over. After half a century of making quick judgements of people, I found myself struggling with these two.

The scotch brought sleep, and after lunch I gave in to it, waking up only at half-past-four. I could hear someone talking quietly to Ashok outside in the living room, and I joined them there for tea a few minutes later, and found a visitor whom I knew vaguely from earlier visits, Ashok's colleague, who seemed to want to discuss office politics with him. When he went to the toilet, I told Ashok, "I need some time with you alone. I hope it won't be too late."

He nodded. "He'll go by dinnertime, at the latest. His wife won't let him stay any later than that."

And so, after dinner, after we had cleared up the dinner dishes, Ashok and I sat in his quiet study. I didn't see the point in beating around the bush. "What's going on?" I asked him. "You're getting yourself into a mess, aren't you?"

He looked wryly at me. After a pause, he said, "Don't tell me I'm that obvious."

"I've known you all your life," I told him. "I think I sensed something this morning, at the prison."

"What did you sense?" he asked.

I fell back on the only word I could think of. "Chemistry," I said. "Jasmine and you."

"It was there from the first," he said.

"Was that why you dragged me out here?" I asked.

"Partly, yes," he replied. "I know plenty of lawyers around here, but none as good as you. And none at a loose end, like you."

"What do you expect from me?" I asked.

"An ear," he said, smiling wryly. "An ear that doesn't have a mouth attached. No criticism."

I couldn't help laughing at his use of words. "Don't you want me to ask questions?" I asked.

"Feel free," he said, "but don't expect answers all the time." He paused for a moment. "You know how to keep secrets," he added. "You know how not to criticize. I need a confidant."

"There's a conflict of interest right there," I told him. "Keeping Jasmine out of jail could destroy you professionally. And me, if I take the case."

"Nothing will come of it," he said. "She's going to be in prison for the foreseeable future. I just need some comfort."

"Right," I said. "That I can give you. There's something else, though: Janaki told me that she's coming here if this takes more than a week. I don't think we'll get anywhere in a week."

He looked me straight in the eye. "She's been here before, and she knows she's always welcome."

"Ermmm...her ear does have a mouth attached," I tell him. "And you won't be able to hide much from her."

"I know," he said. "That's good. Sometimes we need to face ugly truths. Sometimes we need to be forced to face them. But let's have this week without that mouth."

Later, in bed, waiting for sleep, I thought that I should have withdrawn then, and avoided some of the unpleasantness that was to arise from those ugly truths. But some unpleasantness would have arisen anyway, and I tried often to convince myself that I was able to reduce it, if not eliminate it. It was a small consolation that, in old age, is often the best that you can look for. But then you can never be sure, because the ifs haunt you for the rest of your life.

Chapter Nine

Jasmine

When they led me back to my room I was happy enough. My memory was returning, at its own pace, as Dr Patnaik had said it would. In no particular order, with no particular signal, and in fragments that began and ended abruptly. Most of all, now I had a name, the first bit of an identity.

But now an almost physical restlessness took hold of me. It was a deep impatience for which I couldn't find words, but, as I tried to control it, another thought ran through my mind, saying, "Impatience is your enemy. Never hurry."

I knew that neither the thought nor the voice was mine. Someone had said that to me, and I had no idea who, or the context in which he—it was a man speaking, I was sure, though I didn't know why—said it. For some reason I couldn't remember that man who said it was significant. The hours passed slowly, until I realized that the voice and the words were themselves a fragment of memory returning, that I should be treating this fragment as one more piece falling into place rather than struggling for more.

The warder brought the evening meal, and, though I had no space for food in that state, I forced myself to eat a little, perhaps a quarter of what was on the plate, just to make sure that my body didn't run short of fuel. It seemed a terrible waste of food, but as I sat thinking about it I realized, with a twinge of an emotion I couldn't name, that eating it would be a greater waste: the food would go to waste anyway, and overeating would destroy my health.

I must have dozed off after eating because I came awake with another unrelated memory coming loose in my mind. This one was about blood, the smell of blood. The stench of a lot of blood. An image came, of a pool of blood on a floor. A mosaic floor, I thought, and spotless whitewashed walls. The smell of wet earth and blood and woodsmoke.

What was that about?

And then the images came tumbling through my mind.

On moonless nights in the forest, amidst the trees where the canopy hides the starlight, the darkness is absolute. Each group has one small flashlight, hooded with insulation tape, so only the faintest light shows. The leader uses it intermittently to avoid exposure. We have all been trained to remember the terrain that shows up in the brief flash, and stumble our way noiselessly without much trouble.

My heart is in my mouth. This is the first time. I have been preparing for many months, learning to cover ground silently on my feet, on my hands and knees, crawling on my stomach, or, when the light is sufficient, at a fast walk. Then there's been the training to shoot, which consisted mostly of carrying the rifle long distances without a sling, and swinging it as a weapon, until now the heavy rifle feels light as a twig in my hands. There have been endless lectures, and endless discussions among youngsters like myself after the lectures.

Leading us is a short, curly-haired, dark-skinned man whose face is unclear and whose age is difficult to tell. He could be twenty, or he could be thirty. Ten years from now, he'll look the same. His name is Ravan. It's not his name, it's the name he's chosen for himself. He told us why when he was introduced to the group yesterday. Ravan was evil, and the people set his effigy afire every year as they celebrate his death. "I want to be feared in this rotten society," he said, "as feared as Ravan was in the time of Ram."

Our target is a man in a big old house surrounded by trees, mostly fruit trees and the occasional tamarind. Many of his servants live in the same compound, some in the big house, sleeping on the floor in the verandah at the rear, others in the verandah in front.

Ravan has told us that our biggest weapon is surprise. We must be quiet as we attack. There is a pattern to the sounds of the night, the croak of frogs and the chirp of insects and the occasional hoot of an owl, sometimes the faraway howl of a jackal, the barking of a dog, and, very occasionally, the swish and crackle of an animal in the bush. The people in the house are used to all those noises, but any sound that doesn't fit into the pattern will wake them up.

So, silence. If at all we communicate, we hoot, like an owl, common in these parts. Tonight, there should be no need for any such. We know what is where in the compound, and have been briefed on it, with a map drawn on earth.

One of the men supposed to be asleep outside is awake. He goes to a side of the clearing around the house, and urinates under a tree, yawning. He will be awake for some time, and while he is awake he will be able to sound a warning.

The mood changes. Here is a life at stake. Sleeping men can be silenced easily, but not one who's awake.

The enormity of what we have set out to do on this night strikes me. The thought slows me down. Against that is the seething sense of the injustice of the world, of the system that places humans against each other. Ravan's words sound deeply in my mind: we find less compassion in our hearts for a million starving people a few miles away than for one hungry child in front of us. If you have qualms, remember the starving million, and why they starve.

One of the men behind Ravan, a veteran of a dozen killings, moves quietly forward with a knife. He is not quiet enough, though, and a man's scream pierces the silence. In moments, the complexion of the raid changes again. Lights come on around the house, and inside it.

After that it's mayhem. The objective today is to enter the house and kill its owner, who also owns many thousands of hectares of farmland, besides exclusive rights to several thousand acres of forest land, from which his employees—slaves, actually—collect medicinal herbs and honey and fruit and even brew liquor. He has friends in the government, both politicians and bureaucrats, besides the entire police force in the district. Anyone who tries to file a case against him is doomed.

He has many guards, all armed with machetes. We do take them by surprise, but soon there are three or four independent melees around us, and much screaming and the guards are chopped down. In the dark, I, too, swing my machete, slicing a man's chest and watching him go down.

It only lasts a few minutes, though it seems to go on for hours. Then we are inside the house, among the women, who flee, or lock themselves up in small rooms. We have been told not to worry about them, but concentrate instead on the head of the family, the big landlord.

Ravan finds him, behind a locked door. He does not cower, but stands tall. There is a moment's hesitation, and Ravan moves in, machete swinging, and the rest of us follow, myself among the group. The man is down in moments, bleeding, and for the first time I notice the smell of human blood.

It's no different from a pig's.

He lies dead on the floor of a large bedroom, his blood pooling around him. I look at my partners. All of us are high on victory and adrenaline. On impulse, I bend, put my palm in the pool of the landlord's blood on the mosaic floor, make sure that my palm is all covered, and then leave my handprint on the wall by the old man's bed. Something for them to remember.

A scream jerked me out of the reverie. The flow of memory stopped, leaving me frustrated, full of questions, and with a growing sense of irreparable loss, like being cut off in the middle of a story never to be retold, or being woken up in the middle of a wonderful dream. The moments passed, slowly, heavily. Keep still when you're out of your depth, a voice said in my head, and I followed instructions. By and by, a measure of confidence returned, but by then the disappointment was turning into bitterness. I consoled myself with thoughts of a few days ago. The doctor had said that the memories would come back, and they were doing just that. This one, too, I said to myself, will return in its own time.

And in the meanwhile, I knew how the khakis discovered who I am. That handprint, in red on the blue-tinted whitewash of the landlord's bedroom wall, stayed in my memory. When I examined it closely I could see the segments of my fingers, and some of the lines on the palm. I looked at my own right hand, and imagined I could match its lines with the ones on the wall.

With this memory I began to see that there were things that I knew of that I didn't know I knew about, such as fingerprints and the national fingerprint database. There must have been other raids, other killings, and other fingerprints. What kind of a life have I led, I wondered, bathed in blood and the joy of killing.

Then I remembered the feeling when I left my handprint on the wall. It was one of supreme relief, almost exaltation, at having survived what could have been a lethal battle. I remembered the high, but not one of the blows that laid the landlord low. I didn't think I actually hacked at him, but my memory was no longer reliable.

Thoughts floated in my mind, remnants of something repeated times beyond counting. Now they were just phrases, and seeing these remnants without context, I thought them as perverse, even insane. Somewhere, too, there was a memory of a time when they didn't seem perverse. Never show compassion to a defined enemy: that is to invite disaster. Compassion is false, mercy overrated. And then I remembered Ravan saying: *Your biggest enemy is in yourself.* It is the sympathy that you feel for your enemy. It is false. If you don't defeat it, it will enable your enemy to defeat you.

And so to killing, all in the name of a better future. What kind of future, I didn't remember. Unlike the nuns at the orphanage, who spoke sometimes of a heaven in which you sang God's praises in His presence, Ravan believed that each of us had only this one life, and the only way to give it meaning was to leave the world a better place for others. By killing those who wouldn't go along?

Perhaps I'd earned the handcuffs and a prison sentence. I could only wait for my returning memories to show me, and I wished they would return soon, even if it meant prison. The uncertainty was worse.

I smiled thinking again about the irony of it. I was being interrogated by a policeman who knew more about my past than I did.

Chapter Ten

Govind Patnaik

Ashok's mornings started early, with yoga and music. He was done with these by seven, when he started on his first cup of tea after handing me mine. "What do we do today?" I asked him over my tea.

"We talk to Jasmine, see if she's remembered anything more," he said. "If she has, we look at that. Otherwise, we talk again to the cops and see what her legal standing is. The trouble is the lack of precedent."

"Not really," I tell him. "If she's lost her memory, what we have on our hands is a person willing to cooperate with the police but unable to. Let me see if something like that has happened before. That's what I'd argue. In any case, if you say they shouldn't interrogate her aggressively, they won't."

"If they get desperate they'll get hold of a psychiatrist who'll support their point of view," he said sourly. "I don't know how difficult that is these days..."

"I thought about this case all night," I told him. "I'm

taking it on. We'll find a way to keep the interrogations low key."

"Thanks, Uncle," he said. "This means a lot to me."

"I saw that," I told him. "That's one of the reasons I agreed. The other is that she seems to be someone more or less forced into rebellion, and therefore deserves better. I'll do my best to keep you—and her—out of a bigger mess than you already are in."

"Right," he said. "You might cause some ill-feeling."

"No problem," I replied, "Nothing new about that. But I'd like to get Janaki here. This is going to take a long time."

"Sure." He seemed relieved. "I'll arrange for someone to help her around the house."

"She'll want to see the client."

"Why?" he asked.

"She has a degree in law, though she's never practiced," I explained. "And she's worked with NGOs that rehabilitate people, so she has expertise in matters the two of us don't. Besides, she's a better judge of character than I am, so I want a second opinion."

He smiled. "Don't forget I'm a shrink," he said.

"I'm not forgetting that," I said. "But then you're in too deep."

"Okay," he said, but I could see that he wasn't so happy about it, but he had no choice. "If you call her now I'll book her tickets for tomorrow. Will she manage on her own?"

"She's got better everyday survival skills than I do," I replied. "I bet you she gets here in better shape than I did.

"So it's going to be a long stay," Janaki said when I told her I'd like her to get to Bhubaneshwar as soon as possible. "I knew it."

"Since you know everything," I said, an edge to my voice, "Why don't you tell me what else is going to happen?"

"Don't go sarcastic on me," she said. "Just accept that I'm better at some things than you."

"I already did," I said crossly. "Why do you think I asked you to come right away, and said you've got to meet the client? And why are you so grumpy today?"

"You sound as if you're ordering me around," she replied. "Did you ask if there was anything else I was doing?"

"I didn't," I said. "I thought you'd be worried enough about Ashok and me to come immediately. You were talking of it before I left."

She seemed to accept that. Not even something close to half-a-century of marriage had taught me whether she was angry or just baiting me. "It doesn't matter," she said. "I'll come. Make sure you're there to pick me up."

"Yes," I told her. "Ashok might be busy, in which case we'll just take a cab."

"Is there anything you want me to bring you?" she asked.

"Not really," I told her. "Just bring yourself."

After we were through I turned to Ashok. "Try to fix up a meeting with Jasmine for the day after tomorrow so Janaki can talk to her."

"I'll fix it up tomorrow morning," he said. "Shouldn't be any trouble."

At the airport next afternoon, I had no trouble finding Janaki emerging from the arrival area, but was surprised to find a porter following her with two large suitcases on a trolley. "What's this?" I asked.

"They said I could take 30 kilos worth of luggage," she replied, "and I thought we're going to be here for a while, so I brought some things along that we'll need."

I'd forgotten how difficult it was to travel with her. I was used to travelling for business, depending on hotels and their services, and carried little other than a few changes of clothes, besides documents that I might need. She, on the other hand, distrusted hotels, restaurants, and laundries, and packed lots of clothes and bottles of spices and God knows what else, the process taking a couple of days during which she dithered over what to take and what not to.

"Did you bring the kitchen sink?" I asked.

"Don't get sarcastic, old man," she replied. "Just wait and see."

Ashok, who was home from work when we arrived, gave her a hug and me a smile: he knew exactly what each of us felt about luggage, and, instead of taking sides, enjoyed the skirmishes Janaki and I had. And so, when Janaki emerged from the guest room after her ritual involving a three-quarter-hour post-journey bath, he had her tea and biscuits ready in anticipation of another little battle.

"Did you have a comfortable flight, Auntie?" he asked as he handed her a cup of tea, with two biscuits in the saucer, the way she liked it.

"No," she said, in her forthright manner, after she thanked him for the tea. "The seat covers weren't cleaned properly, and the tea wasn't hot enough, and their lunch was terrible. They make us pay extra for the food, you know, and then give us food that's either useless or indigestible."

"Didn't you pack your own lunch?" asked Ashok.

She glared at him. "I know what you're trying to do, young man," she told him gruffly. Then she smiled, for she did have a soft spot for him. "And I think you might be successful."

"I only asked because I was wondering how you could be so different from Uncle," he said. "He never carries food, carries only one suitcase..."

"I know," she said, gruff again. "I know all his habits better than you. I've lived with him almost all your life. We got married when you were small." She paused. "I won't be able to stay here for more than a week. I have work to do in Delhi, so I'll have to leave him in your care for as long as he takes over this case. That's why I brought extras, because you are as irresponsible as him, and when you are his age, you will find your stomach unhappy."

"Thanks," I said, "but Ashok can take care of himself. And I can take care of myself."

She turned to him and began to discuss me as if I weren't there, and, besides, talking of me as if I were a slightly slow four-year-old, something that always gets me furious. "See," she told him, "he still hasn't learnt how to take care of his stomach. He is more than seventy, but leave him alone and he eats like a ten-year-old. So when he travels, he travels light, but his load becomes his indigestion. So he can't sleep. And what does he do for that? He has a drink or two...I don't like his drinking, not because I mind his drinking but because it upsets his stomach, and I have to live with his stomach even when he is asleep."

In a sudden epiphany I saw the resemblance between mother and daughter. Our daughter, Saraswati, who did exactly this to our son-in-law. In his presence, she spoke of—and to—him as if he were a slow four-year-old. In his absence, she spoke of him with pride. I had no idea that Janaki did that about me, but I was willing to think she did. What Saraswati was saying, really was this: look, my husband is a great guy, but I'm smarter than him...

If that was what Janaki was doing, that was fine by me.

Then it struck me that her behaviour wasn't something I could change, so I might as well stop rising to the bait. Yes, that was what she's doing, offering me bait. It was only a game, one that she'd been playing for a long time without my being aware of it. So I smiled at her, taking her by surprise.

She changed track immediately. "Enough of all this," she said. "What is the programme for tomorrow?"

"I've arranged for all three of us to meet Jasmine at the prison at 11 am," Ashok replied. "We'll spend some time with her and then decide what to do next."

"What do we know about her background?" she asked.

"The police have given me their files on the case. We know whatever they know about her history," Ashok replied. "We know that she visited a dying sister in the hospice, and we've been able to work backwards a little from there...Jasmine was brought up in the orphanage where Katherine worked."

"But you also said that Sister Katherine died in the hospice soon after Jasmine visited, so that link is gone."

"Yes. But Jasmine remembers being in an orphanage. She remembers the name, and enough detail for it to be credible."

"Katherine must have had a friend at the hospice, a confidante," Janaki said.

"Yes," Ashok said. "I got the impression she was at peace there, and anyone in a hospice who's peaceful is very unlikely to be friendless. She must have had someone, among the staff, or the other inmates. The police couldn't find her. I suppose that's because no one at the hospice would be happy talking to the police…I should have followed this up before."

"What?" Janaki asked.

"Following up with the hospice about Katherine's confidante," he replied. "I didn't because it means going all the way to Malkangiri, and that could take a lot of my time."

"That's all right," Janaki said. "You take care of your work. We can do this for you. Just put us on a train to Jeypore, and Uncle and I will do the follow up."

At the prison next morning we didn't have to wait. One of Arora's juniors met us in the prison superintendent's office and got sarcastic with me about the amount of free legal aid a terrorist could get. Janaki settled his hash with a couple of acid sentences that I was sure he wouldn't forget for a long time. We had to wait in the interview room for only a minute or two before they led Jasmine in. She came in, looked tentatively at Janaki, and stood by the door, unsure of herself. Janaki got up, took her by the hand and led her to a chair, saying, in Odiya, "Come, child, be at ease. Are these police looking after you?"

Jasmine stared at her, bemused, and Janaki patted her hand again. "Don't worry," she said, patting my leg with her free hand. "My husband is a very good lawyer. We'll do what we can for you." And then, to my complete surprise, the normally stoic Jasmine burst into tears.

Chapter Eleven

Jasmine

It was only afterwards that I felt ashamed, that I had somehow let myself down.

It was all because of Janaki Patnaik, the lawyer's wife, Dr Patnaik's aunt. It happened earlier, with the jailer who brought me my first meal in this jail and advised me gently to open up, but that occasion lasted only a moment and I managed to hold back my tears until he had gone. This time, though, Mrs Patnaik sat by me holding my hand and I found I couldn't keep my tears to myself.

Her very first word pierced me. "Child," she said, and she said it gently. The only other person who has ever spoken to me like that is Sister Katherine. I don't really remember what she said after that, but it was all in the same tone, and after a few seconds I could no longer hold back the tears. Dr Patnaik, too, had been gentle, but clinical, and professional. There was a distance between us: he wouldn't go beyond clinical boundaries for me. But this lady was different.

I have no clear recollection of what I told her when I had gotten over the fit of crying, but I couldn't hold back the terrible sense of not belonging. I do recollect telling her that the police had been reasonable when they were convinced—the first bunch after the fat khaki in Malkangiri visited me alone, and the second lot after the arrival of Dr Patnaik—that I wasn't pretending I'd lost my memory. I recollect trying to tell her about the terror in the hospital when I first realized that I didn't know who I was, and that I was shorn of my...my roots, perhaps.

My first clear thought afterwards was that this could not be the enemy. From the valley of forgotten thoughts emerged one very familiar thought, as if it had been drilled into me over the years, long ago: identify the enemy. Show it no mercy. Yes, it. You have to think of the enemy as a thing, not as a living being, to avoid the danger of compassion.

As I sat with this thought, I found that there were dimensions to it that we don't often come across. The biggest enemy is within us. That thought, too, was familiar, for it was common in all religions. But there, too, it was misleading, as most religion was misleading.

Kindness to the enemy is more dangerous than the enemy itself.

The real enemy is pity. It's the pity we feel when we see some facets of the enemy, and it must be crushed. We must not let our feelings get in the way of arriving at the greater good.

As I sat wondering why this thought made me so uncomfortable, why pity was such a big deal, another memory began to emerge. Parts of it were unclear, or missing, but I felt I remembered what mattered, what was niggling away at me.

One of the groups has gone missing. There has been no action for many months now, and we moved into this area only yesterday. We were near a village until the day before yesterday, a village we consider friendly, because we help the villagers with their wells and their sowing, and sometimes their harvests as well. We plan to move on tomorrow, using this day for rest. Everyone is tired, but the villagers helped us with supplies so there's enough food to keep us going.

At first the missing man's mates think he's gone off for a swim in a nearby stream, one of our few pleasures in this warm weather, for his small pack of belongings is still very much in place, next to the mat where he slept. A search of the banks of the stream reveals no trace of him.

Then the tracker comes into play. Trackers are people who can follow trails others can't even see, a crushed leaf, a broken twig, a bit of bark gone from a tree, a small dent in a path of beaten earth, the remaining faint aroma of beedi smoke, They are rare, and we are lucky to have such a good one in the group. As a tracker, he's also good at evading other trackers working for the police, and he's saved our lives several times.

This is our first runaway in seven years, and none of us are prepared for it. The priorities are clear. First, we catch the runaway. We have already labelled him a traitor, so we try him. Then we punish him. There is no doubt he is guilty: by our rules, the act of fleeing the camp is sufficient evidence. In a brief discussion session where everyone assembles, the collective decides to go all out to find him.

Catching the runaway requires only the tracker and a few people to help him hold the runaway when he catches up. The remainder of the group is "free", so we use the time to re-examine ourselves, re-educate ourselves. Re-education has largely become, for most of us, listening to speeches, and, for a few of the articulate ones, making them. We've heard them all before, and have no interest in hearing them all over again, because there are pressing matters to be seen to. Food, for instance, and shelter, and cleaning up, the usual processes of life.

But all that is suspended while the search for the traitor proceeds, for he seems to have become the biggest enemy we have. But no. As the leaders speak, we learn the true nature of the enemy, and its name. The name of the enemy is pity.

I know the runaway, of course, but not much about him. He is about seventeen years old, and has been with us for nearly three years. He was blooded a month ago, when he participated in a raid on a plantation from where we abducted a member of the family that owns it. The family paid the ransom, and the abductee was returned, though not in as good a condition as the family might have wished.

The traitor protested, half-heartedly, at how we treated our prisoner. Yes, the man was a prisoner. He had maltreated workers, gathered wealth from their sweat, and paid to have some of them arrested when they protested. Later, the money was paid, and the hostage returned. We released the hostage early one morning, on the outskirts of a small town where someone would see him in a matter of hours, if not minutes, after our colleagues had confirmed that they got the money. We never get to see any money, though…but that's another story.

The group locates the runaway thanks to an informer, who tells us whose house he is in, and in which village. It's a village that we have contributed to, dug wells in, harvested crops at, as part of building our support network. Now this family in the village has let us down, and they must be punished, besides the traitor. The family will be wiped out, and the village. Well, the village will suffer. No government agency reaches it. Its inhabitants have to depend on themselves for water and food, and water can be very scarce indeed. We used to help them with their water supply and the harvest, and will stop that.

A flicker of regret passes through me. There are people in the village who I like. They're poor people: most of them have even less than we do, but we have a network to help us through bad times, or to hide us from the khakis. The regret has grown stronger with the years, but I have no idea when I have felt it before. It's like a ghost.

Towards ten at night, a group of six is assigned to fetch the traitor from his hideout. They come back with the captive, all tied up and gagged, and report that they whipped the entire family with whom he took refuge.

His gag is removed, and his feet hobbled, his ankles tied with a rope that stretches two hand spans, eighteen inches. He can walk, in short strides that make him look like a puppet, but he can't run. His hands tied behind his back by the group that captured him, are freed and retied in front of him. In the firelight, with the whole unit assembled in the clearing, we await the leader. Soon, word reaches us that the leader will arrive only a few hours after sunrise, so we disperse to our beds in the clearing—there is no need for shelter in this weather—after sentry duties are assigned.

I lie sleepless through the night. Our beds are in the open, a little away from the trees, and as the breeze drives the clouds across the sky, I glimpse Mars almost directly above, reddish and unwinking. We have been taught to use the planets to get a sense of direction, no more, but the idea of a planet millions of miles away seems almost magical on these nights.

Somewhere in a treacherous corner of my mind I hope the runaway gets away to a road, and there gets a lift in a lorry or some other vehicle. That's extremely unlikely, because this whole district is marked off as dangerous, and people avoid travelling at night. What about the family that sheltered him? Are they relatives, thinking that the bloodline matters? We have been told never to place family above the global society of humans, of mankind.

I think about it through the night, and find no evidence

of a common humanity. Everywhere we look there is conflict. Even in our little society, there is conflict, and pretence. There is also a method of dealing with conflict. A bureau deliberates decides what is to be done, and that must be done, regardless. There is little room for dissent: the bureau is a black box, with outsiders unable to enter into the details of the arguments that the bureau listens to.

When the runaway is caught, he will be tried by a peoples' court. He has run away, no doubt, and will be found guilty. The court will issue the sentence, which will be death by firing squad, and he will be executed immediately.

Of late, I, too, have been thinking of treachery…

The group returns before dawn, dragging the hostage. Fires and lamps are lit, and the marks on his face become visible. He has been beaten, and has struggled. His clothes are torn, his face bloody, his hair dishevelled, his skin covered in dust, sweat, and blood. He seems to have wept on the way, but his tears have dried up.

He will be kept captive until daylight, and be tried immediately after sunrise. There is no formal prison enclosure. He sits in the clearing, hands tied, ankles hobbled. They offer him nothing, no water or food. In the face of all this hostility, he maintains his composure. He asks for nothing, and does what he is told to do: shut up and keep still.

I volunteer for guard duty. No one is surprised. I have always volunteered for work of any kind that doesn't involve killing, like cooking or cleaning or sentry duty. Work carries its own compensation, regardless. Then comes the thought that hard work is what has enabled me to sleep at night, safe in the conviction that I was doing good.

In the firelight I occasionally see his eyes gleam in his thin, dark face with the big cheekbones and no extra flesh. He sweats in the still air, partly for the warmth, and partly perhaps from the fear that he has decided not to show. His running away was an act of courage, I begin to think. The group who caught him says that he came without fuss, and took his beatings without complaint, except for a bout of tears before they dragged him away from the village. Perhaps he came quietly to minimize the damage the group will do to the villagers, to the people who sheltered him. In that case, his act of coming without fuss is an act of greater courage…

Never have I felt this so strongly before: if the rest of society used upon us the methods that we use on our own, we would not survive. The thought shakes me, leaves me vaguely nauseous. With this comes a decision: I will no longer be a party to torture, or to killing. I never did like the idea of doing these things, but was persuaded to believe they were necessary. That persuasion is wearing off.

By and by the runaway dozes off. His head sags on his shoulders in sleep or utter weariness, I cannot tell which. My fellow sentry, a girl—she is only ten years younger than me but seems like a child—also nods off, and I do not wake her. These stolen moments of solitude are increasingly important, I don't know why.

By daylight we are ready. Leaders of groups within a certain radius have been told, and there are more than a hundred revolutionaries to observe the trial and the execution that will surely follow. Most observers are dull-eyed, but a few, perhaps one in five, seem to be looking forward to the spectacle. For the first time it appears that it's from the ranks of these few, the ones who are going to enjoy the spectacle, that the leaders will be chosen…

No, that's not so. There are good ones among the leaders, people for whom violence is the last resort, the only. There are also those who are scarred by loss…there are stories from these forests to fill a thousand books, if you search for them. Those stories are our energy. They are stories of loss, of the brutality of power, of the corruption of money…stories of the results of the worst of human nature. The stories drive us forward.

What stories? I don't remember a single one of them! I know there are thousands, yet not one comes to mind. Am I going mad?

It can't be. A face hovers in my memory, from not so long ago.

Whose face is it? I know it well, and its owner, but can recall nothing about it now.

The sentries guarding the camp stir at sunup. Others all over the clearing are beginning to stir, and I get up and fold my bedding away just as the visitors arrive. There are three of them, two who are leaders of other groups like ours, and one from the central politburo, where decisions are made.

Everyone defers to him…I tend to avoid him, because he's never been on a raid, or risked him life for anything, but…I have no idea how he got his position.

There are a few people like this, who are not of the group but above it. Some of them spoke from the heart, but there are new ones who don't. They say one thing with their mouths, and another with their eyes.

How many years have I been here, watching? Nothing is clear except what I see now.

At last, the trial, before we eat. The gathering, with empty stomachs, want to get on with the case. There is an accuser, who recites the boy's crimes against the group: desertion at a time of war, corrupting his company…After a while my mind wanders. The boy stands downcast, defenceless, and, when the harangue stops, accepts his sentence, his fate, which is to be delivered immediately.

He is to be shot by a firing squad. Composing the firing squad are the ones closest to the runaway. Of course, there are others, strangers who have done this before, and will make sure that the victim dies, but among those handling the rifles are the people who the leaders think most likely to show mercy.

Pity, the eternal enemy.

Their participation in the shooting will be the end of what's left of their innocence. One more tie to hold them in place. The squad lead their victim to another clearing, and tie him to a tree. There is to be air of ceremony to the execution, mostly to show anyone watching what happens to traitors.

Afterwards, I volunteer for the burial. We don't cremate, because the smoke that rises so thickly above the cremation site will give our location away. The directive is to bury him wrapped in rags—people who die in battle are buried draped in our red flag—in a "neutral" location, which means somewhere in the woods where neither the khakis nor curious villagers will find his remains for a few weeks.

Handling the spade is no big deal. I've got used to digging, though not for graves…I remember digging trenches all day long, but never a grave. The spade's handle fits just so in my hands, and I find the right balance, the easiest way to use it, without thinking, and lose myself in the rhythm of digging…

I skip breakfast. My appetite has disappeared in recent months. Despite the effort of moving every two or three days and of taking down and setting up our camp each time I find hunger a stranger. My clothes hang loose, and a sense of foreboding has been settling on my mind. Something is about to happen.

My fellow-revolutionaries have been concerned, but I've been avoiding talking to them. I think I've been doing this for some time now, and they have learnt to leave me alone.

The dead boy's face is no longer clear in my mind. I can remember the gleam of his eyes and the sweat on his skin but what colour was his skin? What was the colour of his eyes, the shape of his nose? Was he tall or short? There are no fat people amongst us, specially among the youngsters…

My mind surged with questions after this chunk of

memory surfaced. When I'd remembered parts of my past earlier, the parts themselves were clear, and seemed complete. This was a memory with blurred parts, with faces I knew but couldn't remember, names at the tip of my tongue. Perhaps, I thought, Dr Patnaik would come along soon, and I'd be able to talk to him about this.

But with this partial memory came other realizations. I knew the risks of using drugs or hypnosis to help remember the past. These unclear parts...the police, if they so felt, could use them. Or I might be tempted to drop a few false names, waste some police time, for they were, after all, the enemy.

The large gaps were apparent. Those instructions that I remembered, about not crying, about not letting pain show, even the vaguely remembered instruction to volunteer for work that didn't actually turn my stomach: that wasn't from the group. That was from someone part of the group, part of my life, but different. There are pleasant memories of him, but none that I can recall in any detail.

His name? It's somewhere in my mind, but it refuses to come up. The tricks that memory plays are cruel.

Who? Perhaps I owed him my life. If he was the man the police were looking for, and I remembered his name, would I give him up?

I didn't know, but this question raised a conflict in my mind I hadn't had before. For the first time, I wasn't sure whether I'd be able to share my memories with the police. I was glad then that Dr Patnaik had been so firmly against the police interrogating me with drugs or hypnosis.

And then I knew with certainty that I had a violent past, that I had committed crimes that might well be unforgivable...I might have taken lives, or kidnapped innocents.

Dear God, what had I done?

The horror of it struck me, but with the realization of the worst came a kind of peace. In the solitude of my cell, terrible though it was, I understood that I was paying the price for what I had done. The loss of memory was only incidental. Whenever it came back, as I was increasingly sure it would, I could only accept the responsibility for whatever I had done.

Those villagers who sheltered the nameless runaway: what choice did they have, in all humanity? The inhumanity shown by my erstwhile group to the villagers and to the runaway was no different from the inhumanity of the system against which the revolution is aimed. If my group ever came to rule a population, would their rule be better than the government that now rules here? I can remember feeling that it would, that the comradeship of the group and the work we put into developing the villages in our area would enable us to be gentle; but I never saw that gentleness. And perhaps I saw the same comradeship among the armed khakis who fought us in the forests. They, too, were brave, and took the same risks we took. They, too, bled when we shot them. Where lay the difference?

All of a sudden another fragment of memory pops up. Gandhi, the so-called Mahatma. I remember learning that he was bourgeoisie…I remember belittling him and his values. But later I began to see the value of what he did for independence. He worked without violence, and we've had much less violence than neighbouring countries because of his legacy.

Power is power, and power corrupts.

How did I know that phrase?

There was more. The people who lead the group seemed unable to think for themselves. They parrotted what others said. For instance, I remember many leaders rejecting what seemed to be clear evidence that we needed to hold the population steady, to prevent it from rising beyond the limits of what the land could support. I remember calculating our needs. If everyone in the country lived the way we and our network of villages did, the country would have to be three times as big as it is. But I remember reading that Russia needed more people. Our leaders went by that, not by what they saw for themselves. I remember the increasing contradictions in what the leaders said, and I remembered the story of a book called *Animal Farm*. Had someone given me the book to read, or had someone had told me the story. Who?

I remember reading more books, more pamphlets, newspapers. I remember reading in poor light when everyone else was asleep. How did I get that habit?

And then, of course, I arrived at the fundamental question I'd been avoiding all this while. What had I planned to do to the man who was the father I never knew? Had I any plans? And after?

Was I going to give myself up to the khakis? Why?

How did the khakis know so much about me?

I must have left my fingerprints all over the place. We didn't wear gloves on raids: we never had any. The police knew about at least some of my crimes. That was why I was here, in the custody of these men from the NIA, who were much more focussed than the state police.

How did I know so much about the different police forces?

When I came out of this reverie, I had no idea what time it was. All I knew was that I had to meet Dr Patnaik.

Chapter Twelve

Govind Patnaik

The train to Jeypore left Bhubaneshwar a little before eight in the evening, and arrived at Jeypore at about eleven in the morning, doing seven hundred-odd kilometres in fifteen hours. The plan was for Janaki and me to travel to Jeypore and take a cab from there to Malkangiri, where Ashok's old student would have us picked up and taken to a hotel. But as they say, man proposes, God disposes.

Janaki, for all the care that she took on the journey—home cooked food, bottled water, and so on—had a mild attack of diarrhoea on the way so when we got off the train at Jeypore we found a reasonable hotel there instead of taking the three-hour cab ride to Malkangiri. I resisted the temptation to lecture her as she would have lectured me if I'd got the Delhi Belly, and instead, after checking us into a hotel, followed her instructions, found a shop selling ayurvedic medicines, and bought her a sour-smelling powder that she believed cured all gastric ailments.

By half-past-noon she had settled down, and ordered

lunch—rice and curd, which she believed would do her good—from room service. I shared it with her in silence, and, when she napped afterwards, called Ashok's friend Nilu in Malkangiri to tell him that we would move on only after Janaki got over her illness. He took it in his stride, and offered a list of medicines that would help her symptoms, and sniffed disapprovingly when I told him that she preferred herbal remedies. "What's the matter?" I asked.

"Nothing, Uncle," he said. "It's just that I don't trust traditional medicine very much..."

"Why not?" I asked.

"Some of these traditional medicines are centuries old," he said.

"Yes," I said. "They are. So what?"

"Well, Uncle," he said, "in all those centuries that our traditions formed, we never had an average life expectancy of more than forty." Pause. Then he continued, "If that much." Pause again. Then, "And if you look at what the traditional medicine men call lifestyle diseases, well, we never had lifespans long enough to be able to have those lifestyle diseases. No offence intended, Uncle, but you asked."

"I did," I told him. "And you answered very clearly. Thank you. Umm...I'm sorry we've been so much trouble."

"Please don't worry about that," he said. "I'm a bachelor, and in any case I owe Ashok Sir a lot for what

I've learnt from him. Our disciplines coincide sometimes, you know, and it's from him that I learnt the difference. And he speaks of you often, so sometimes I feel that I know you, too."

"Very good of you," I tell him. "I'll call you in the evening when we know better how Janaki is feeling."

"Please do," he said. "Any time. If the trouble continues and you need to see a doctor, let me know. I have a friend there."

"Sure," I said, relieved. "Thanks very much."

Back in the room I found Janaki sitting up watching the local news on TV. The air-conditioning was on high, the temperature set at 18 degrees, and she was bundled up in a blanket to keep warm. "Do you like it this cold?" I asked when I saw her.

"No," she replied shortly. "I don't know how to warm it up."

I found the remote on the tea table and tried to show her how to increase the temperature setting. She waved me away. "I can't see all these tiny little things without my glasses," she said. "You do it...you should have done it before you left."

Again, I got the feeling she was baiting me, but when I saw the irritation on her face I decided she wasn't. She was about to reply equally crossly when it struck me that there was no need to be cross at her at all. Then, again, it struck me that perhaps this was part of the training of henpecked husbands, and I couldn't help smiling. She flared up. "Why are you laughing?" she asked. "Do you like to see me sick?"

"Not at all," I told her. "Would you like something to drink?"

"No," she said snottily. "Not now. After four o'clock. Tea."

"Right," I said. "Rest."

"What else can I do?" she asked grumpily, turning away with a sigh.

A few moments later she let out a soft snore, and I settled down on my side of the bed. Soon, thinking of the discoveries of the day, I, too, dozed off, waking up only at four in the afternoon. Ashok called soon after, saying that Nilu had told him about Janaki's troubles, and that we were not to hesitate to rely on Nilu for medical advice. "He's very straight, Uncle," Ashok said. "Sometimes that gets him into trouble, but you can be sure of him. And his friends."

"Thanks," I said. "You know your aunt. She'll insist on dosing herself with ayurveda, and, for all you know, she'll be better tomorrow. "

"I'll ask Nilu to send you someone to collect samples from both of you," he said. "Get yourself tested for the virus."

"Right," I said. "What's new with you?"

"I went to the prison this morning," he said. "She's

begun to remember things. She told me that she no longer has any doubts that she was part of a Maoist group…and that she regrets it very much."

"So do you want me to return to Bhubaneshwar?" I asked. "Now that she's sure that she was part of a violent group and so on…"

"Not at all," he replied. I could sense the desperation in his voice, no matter how hard he tried to hide it. "Like I said, she regrets it very much. She doesn't remember telling anyone this…Uncle, will it make a difference to the way the system will treat her if there's some evidence that she was trying to reach out to the police when she was caught?"

"Of course it will," I replied, more to reassure him than anything else. "Proving it, or even getting an indication of it, will be difficult."

"You have to follow this up, Uncle," he said tightly. "Go to the convent. Find someone who might help."

"I will," I promised him. The tension in him was evident. If I'd asked right then whether he was emotionally involved with his patient, he would probably have answered, but I didn't because I thought it would be in some sense an intrusion on his privacy. Let him tell me in his own good time, I thought. Meanwhile, I'd do what I could to ease his burden.

Janaki was awake and sitting up in bed when I finished with the call. It was about five in the evening, and she did look rested. "How are you?" I asked. "Ready for your tea?"

"Of course," she said. "If you weren't so intent on your cellphone you'd have noticed that it's late."

I kept silent and put the kettle on to make her tea and myself coffee. It was all from tea bags and instant coffee, but we didn't have much choice because room service would have taken twenty minutes and going down to the restaurant would have been even more troublesome. I was wondering about what to do about Ashok when her voice jerked me back to the here and now. "Do you think we could get a taxi to Malkangiri now?" she asked.

"I think so," I replied. "It's not yet five, so we should be there in time for a late dinner, at least."

"Let's go, then," she said. "Forget the tea."

"Are you sure?" I asked. "There could be trouble on the way."

"I think there won't be," she said. "We'll deal with whatever comes."

There was a knock on the door, and I found a young man in a mask and lab smock standing outside when I opened it. "Samples," he said. "Dr Nilu sent me. Two minutes."

"When will we get the results?" I asked.

"Tomorrow," he replied.

"Can I get them on the phone?" I asked.

"Of course," he replied.

Twenty minutes later, samples given, we were being

ushered out of the hotel into a cab that the hotel staff assured me knew his way around the area, with the suitcases safe in the boot, with a supply of emergency medicine in Janaki's handbag. The driver, a smiling young man who had hefted the suitcases effortlessly into the boot, was smooth and fast, and we were at the hotel in Malkangiri, after nearly three hours nonstop on a bumpy road, in time for a quick wash before a late and sparing dinner. Nilu had just completed his day's practice when we arrived, and when he offered to visit us, I advised him not to bother with the formalities. "But Ashok said that you know the policemen here, and that they respect you, so I might have to rely on you to apply some pressure at the right time."

"Don't worry, Uncle," he said. "I think I can deal with the local police. The thing is, they don't like the NIA taking away their case from them, especially since the daughter of a former colleague is involved."

"They'll have to live with it," I told him. "That's the law. I just hope they won't try to obstruct me."

"I'll put you onto the Deputy Superintendent who had her fingerprints sent to the Bureau," he said. "He knew the woman's father well, but he wasn't prepared for the consequences of what he did with the fingerprints..."

"Will he help?" I asked baldly.

"If nothing else, it will damage him or the dead man, yes," replied Nilu. "You'll see for yourself tomorrow." He chuckled. "Google is a great thing, you know. I told him to look you up on Google and he did. I don't think you need any help from me."

"Don't take that for granted," I told him. "Local support is always useful."

"Sure, Uncle," he replied. "Call me anytime on my cellphone. If I'm busy, I won't pick up, but call you back as soon as I can."

Nilu called early next morning to tell us that we had both tested negative for the virus. "That's a relief," I said. "We really can't afford to slow down. Thanks!"

Janaki elected to stay in bed, so I went to Deputy Superintendent Das's office on my own. Das turned out to be large and jolly, but I could see that the jolliness could disappear in a second: he was a policeman through and through, and had the latent watchfulness and hardness that all policemen acquire with years of service. He was approaching retiring age, but despite his fat he could move fast enough; his bulk didn't hinder him in any way. "You know better than me, sir," he said when I asked him what he would have liked to do with the case. "You know the law. We had to hand it over."

"Yes," I told him. "You would have handed over all the files. Everything on paper, starting with copies of the General Diary entry and the FIR."

He nodded. "There was quite a lot of information. Including the DNA test that Mohanty paid for. I needn't have given them that, but it was mentioned in the paperwork, so there was no point in hiding it."

"True," I said, "but there are often little points that policemen don't note down on paper. Don't deny it. I've seen enough of it."

He nodded. "Yes," he said. "If you ask me, I was fairly sure she is his daughter, because she looks like him. Same nose, same jawline, same eyes...the DNA confirmed it, that's all."

He was delaying, trying to find out what I was after. And I, too, wanted to know where he was heading with this case. "There's very little doubt that she was part of a Maoist group," I told him. "The NIA have enough fingerprint evidence to convict her as a Maoist, even though they can't at present find evidence that she killed or tortured anyone. But my feeling is that she has genuinely turned over a new leaf...that she regrets what she did,"

He nodded. "I think so. She offered to take a narco-analysis test, or a lie-detector. The doctor advised us against it. He actually told me that he would take legal action if we narco-analysed her, since she wasn't in a fit state for that."

"Dr Nilu?" I asked.

"No," he said. "The other one. From Bhubaneshwar. Dr Patnaik."

"Ah!" I said. "My nephew. He got me into the case."

"Please don't mind my asking you this," he said. "Is he also paying your fees?"

"No." I smiled. "I'm retired. Only here because this is an interesting case, a unique case."

He knew there was more to it but didn't ask because he sensed he'd be crossing a line if he did. He did say, though, "I would like the late Deputy Superintendent Mohanty's name to be kept clear, because he was a good friend of mine. He didn't always follow the rules but if you consider his circumstances and his career he did more good than bad. It would be bad for the Force..." In other words, serving policemen, perhaps including himself, could get into trouble if the NIA probed too deeply into Mohanty's past.

"That might be difficult," I told him. "The prosecutor will almost certainly investigate how he came to have this daughter, and then...whatever he did was many decades ago, but in this present environment, with this #MeToo movement. So you can be sure there will be people digging up the past."

Even as I said this, I saw that I was doing something I'd done all my professional life. I ignored my feelings about what I was doing to work towards a greater objective: in this case, keeping Jasmine out of trouble. After all these years of doing it, I found it came automatically, and as I became aware of it I knew that this was going to be my last case. The end didn't justify the means. There was much to think about.

But meanwhile, there was also this case to be won.

"If they could stop with this woman..." his voice trailed off.

"Let me see," I replied. "I can't promise anything, but I'll do my best. It's no use complicating a simple matter."

"All right," he said, leaning forward. "Some of my people spoke to the attendants at the hospice. They saw this woman with Sister Katherine. They were very close, and the Sister was very happy to see her. It's a pity she died so soon after."

"Possibly," I said.

"It seems that Sister Katherine's only other visitor was one Sister Theresa," he said. "Both about the same age, and friends. Of course, Sister Theresa was senior in position. From what I understand, Sister Katherine was never...well, she was never strong enough to take a higher position."

"And do you know where I might find Sister Theresa?" I asked.

"At the church," he said. "She's still at the orphanage. Erm, you have to be very careful with the Mother Superior."

"In what sense?"

"She is very loyal to the church."

Meaning, let sleeping church dogs lie. "To the extent possible, I'll try to see to it that everything stops with the time this woman ran away from the orphanage. As far as possible."

He nodded. "I understand. Some of these things happened decades ago. Records will be difficult to find."

"Thanks very much," I told him. "I'll call you if I need further help."

"May I visit you after you see the Mother Superior?" he asked, rising.

"Of course," I told him. "Call beforehand, just to make sure I'm at the hotel."

He handed me a slip of paper with something written on it. "This is my personal cellphone number. Please don't hesitate to use it if you need to, but please avoid giving the number to anyone else."

I returned to the hotel to find a tall balding young man at the reception counter, asking for me by name. "I'm Patnaik," I told him from behind.

He turned, taken by surprise. "I'm Nilu," he said, offering his hand. "I should have called but I was passing by and wanted to make sure Auntie is well so I thought I'd take a chance."

"Welcome," I told him. "Let's go up and see how she is, but let's give her some warning on the house phone."

Janaki was well enough but bored and restless when we got to the room. She always got ill-tempered when left alone with nothing to do but watch TV but Nilu's presence fixed that. Janaki was always particular about never asking doctors about medical problems—many of my contemporaries do that, getting embarrassingly clinical about their digestive apparatus when they meet a doctor socially—and replied simply when Nilu asked about her. She managed to draw him out in a way I can rarely do with young people, and soon Nilu was talking about wanting to teach, and about how strange patients could be.

As he was running out of steam, I butted in. "What's your feeling about this lady, Jasmine?' I asked.

"She seems to be controlling herself very tightly," he said. "She seemed to be afraid of something. People with memory loss after a head injury are often scared, but that usually passes in a couple of days, especially if they meet people they remember. She was different. She never let go…I'm no psychiatrist, but I think she's survived a lot of trauma. You should be asking Ashok saab these questions."

"I did," I said. "But I also wanted your opinion. You're an observant young man, and you saw her before Ashok did, so I want to get your first impressions."

"Okay," he said. "She's intelligent, has some education, but I don't know how much, but keeps everything to herself so you don't know what she knows. She is also very observant."

"Ashok told me much the same," I said. "Good. And now I must ask: do you know the Mother Superior at St Joseph's orphanage?"

"Yes," he replied. "Most doctors here know her. We all visit the institution from time to time."

"What do you think of her?" I asked.

"She's very strong," he replied, "and quite open-minded. Nothing about helping only Christians; they help anybody who needs it. But she maintains very good discipline with the children."

"Janaki and I intend to meet her tomorrow," I told him. "Hence the questions."

At the orphanage next morning, the Mother Superior, formerly Sister Elizabeth, turned out to be tall and slim and dignified, with a no-nonsense air about her. Despite the heat, her conventional habit was neat, the crucifix at her throat shining, her pale hands dry. Her grip was surprisingly strong. "I never knew Jasmine very well," she said, "but we all knew she was bright and a little rebellious. She was always a good student, and she used to read a lot. She was the only child here who read everything she could get her hands on. She tried reading the New Testament, but found many words she didn't understand, so she read Bible stories instead. We thought that when she grew out of her rebellion, she'd be a very good girl."

"That incident with Brother Richard…" I began.

She cut me off. "That's best forgotten," she said. "It's too long ago now for us to bother, and Richard is no longer amongst us."

"But her encounter with him seems to be the foundation of Jasmine's…erm, career," I said. "She ran away from here after that, straight into dangerous hands."

"This institution has done a lot of good in the decades it's been here," she said. "I'm not going to allow something from twenty-five years ago to hurt it," she said.

"Even if that something caused a chain of deaths outside?" I asked.

"Will that revive the dead?" she asked. "If so, I'll gladly open every record here for your inspection."

"It might not revive the dead," I said, "but it might prevent more such deaths. Besides, if we understand it, the system might understand Jasmine better, and be kinder to her."

"We'll do our best to make sure something like that doesn't recur," she said. "As for the rest of it, if Jasmine is truly penitent, she will also find it in herself to forgive past sins against her, if not forget them. I respect the system of the law, but there are instances where I think a different system might do better."

I didn't say anything about the continuing cases of child abuse and sexual abuse in the church. I didn't want to antagonize Elizabeth, because that could affect my client...I kept my doubts to myself. "In that case," I said, "it's up to us here to demonstrate that she truly is remorseful—I don't want to use the word penitent because it has a very specific meaning in your church."

"The only way I can see for you to do that is to speak to someone with whom my old friend Katherine might have shared what happened when they met."

"Yes," I said. "That's in your hands...I believe that one of the nuns here visited Katherine a few times at the hospice, a Sister Theresa."

She glared at me. "Where did you hear that?" she asked, an edge to her voice.

"Does it matter?" I asked.

"No," she said. "I asked Sister Theresa to visit Katherine from time to time, to find out how she was getting along, whether she needed support from one of us. Nothing unusual there. Theresa reported to me after each meeting, and each time she said that Katherine was getting along as well as could be expected from someone with her illness."

"May I speak to her as well?" I asked.

"Why?"

"I'd like to hear from her what Katherine told her," I explain. "I can question her in ways that you might not be able to. As a lawyer."

Her eyes flicked from me to Janaki and back. "Let me see what I can do," she said after a moment's consideration. "Could you come back in the afternoon?"

"Sure," I said. "What time?"

"Three?"

When we returned after lunch and a short nap, the Mother Superior's office was warm but she was as neat as she'd been in the morning. Also in the room, in a visitor's chair, was a short, plump nun with a pleasant smile: Sister Theresa. It was immediately evident why the Mother had sent Sister Theresa to Katherine's sickbed, for her bedside manner would have been infinitely comforting.

"Sister Katherine told me all kinds of things," she told me when I asked. "She told me that she had watched Jasmine's mother die in childbirth: she said that she had felt a bond with the child in that moment, and took an interest in her that went beyond her duty as a nun. I could understand the strength of that bond. It's not unusual in an orphanage.

"She was sure Jasmine would visit her. She could never explain why. Maybe that's what kept her alive, her faith in the child...and in the end Jasmine did visit her. That faith...

"The last time I saw her was three days before she died, a few days after Jasmine's visit. They called me from the hospice, saying that Katherine was dying, but by the time I reached her bedside her mind was wandering. She didn't recognize me, but I could see she was at peace.

"All I can say is that she must have had a good meeting with Jasmine. Jasmine somehow lived up to that faith she had. I don't know how that could be when you say that Jasmine seems to have murdered people, but that was the impression I got. Perhaps Jasmine was remorseful, penitent..."

"How do you know that she found relief in Jasmine just visiting her?" I asked.

"I don't," said Theresa. "I can't be sure. But then,

the people at the hospice told me that she was smiling when Jasmine left. They all said Jasmine talked a lot and Katherine said very little. She just lay there holding Jasmine's hand and listening."

She could say no more about what must have gone on between the two of them, or about Katherine's state of mind after the meeting, and when I gave up after ten minutes, Sister Theresa left without fuss. "Sister Theresa must be a comfort to anyone who's ill," I said.

The Mother smiled for the first time during our meetings. "Yes. I'm glad you noticed that. We did care for Katherine, you know." The smile disappears. "You can talk to Shanta now. She's an attendant at the hospice, and the police spoke to her. She's terrified of the police. Let's just say that her husband has a history of sorts with them. Please don't threaten her."

"I won't," I told her. "I won't even speak to her. Janaki will, and Janaki will know how to bring her out…Janaki is also a qualified lawyer, by the way, but spends most of her time with NGOs."

Shanta turned out to be small, dark and quiet, in her thirties. At first, she refused to meet Janaki's eyes or mine, but as the chat proceeded she smiled at Janaki every now and then. Janaki started early, asking her about her roots, and discovered that she, too, was an orphan. After the first few sentences, her story came tumbling out. She was married at eighteen to a man who visited the orphanage to select what he thought would be a good housewife. Shanta was willing to go along with him even though he treated her like an unpaid drudge. She didn't find the work very hard, but one night he got drunk and she discovered that his idea of discipline was a good beating. She took the first one quietly, and next morning told him, before he even got out of bed, "If you beat me again, remember to tie me up. Otherwise, I'll catch you some time when you're drunk or asleep, and I'll break your arms." Then, to prove that this wasn't an empty threat, she hit him on the shoulder with a rolling pin that she'd held behind her, and broke his collar-bone.

"Everyone told me he was a good man," she explained. "Even the mother at the orphanage. I believed them, and married him in good faith. I don't blame them, for when he isn't drunk he's a good man, and besides he would have hidden his faults from them. His mother and sisters were even worse...I was lucky he had a job in the town, and didn't live with his parents and sisters on the farm. And I had a job, too, and I was willing to leave him and live alone.

"But he was too weak when drunk to beat me, and he knew I'd hit back. He started getting drunk and brawling. He'd go out and pick fights...people started complaining about him to the police. Once or twice the policemen came home and they were rude and I...I couldn't stand it so I was rude to them too, and you know how they are. But by then I had friends, and the Mother helped, so the police didn't do anything to me. They weren't too bad with him, too. They put him in the lockup once in a while and gave him a beating, but they never put him before a magistrate or sent him to jail. He knows that he's out of jail because of me, so I manage. But he still drinks..."

"So you have to be very careful when you speak to the police," Janaki said.

"Yes," said Shanta. "I have two daughters. If I say something rude to the police, my daughters might have to pay for it. And I have a short temper," she smiled apologetically.

"I understand," Janaki told her. "I, too, have a very short temper." She pointed at me. "My husband is a lawyer. He wants to ask you something about Sister Katherine. Tell him what you can. Nothing will happen to you. He'll take care of it."

When Shanta looked expectantly at me, I asked, "Did you take care of Sister Katherine during her stay at the hospice?"

"Yes," she said. "It wasn't that I took care of her. I had other things to do, but I thought she was lonely. Most old people are lonely, but for her it seemed worse than usual. So when my work was over I'd stop at her bedside to ask how she was.

"One day I asked her what was troubling her, and she told me about another orphan who had been in the orphanage long ago, a girl who ran away.

"Did she tell you the girl's name?" I asked.

"Jasmine," she said. "Jasmine. She told me she'd known her since the moment of her birth. She told me how she carried her to the orphanage, and how when she reached the orphanage she found it difficult to leave the baby. For thirteen years she did her best for the child, but it wasn't good enough."

"She felt guilty about her?" I asked.

"Yes," Shanta said. "There was something in the back of her mind that she never told me."

"What else?"

"She feared that Jasmine had taken a wrong turn after she ran away," came the reply. "She didn't say what. You know how it is for a young girl. It's hard to survive. Sister said that she was pretty. Maybe she took up with a man… but she kept saying that Jasmine was good at heart, and that she'd come visiting someday…she was waiting for that. She said so every time I spoke to her."

"She must have been thrilled when Jasmine did turn up," I said.

"Yes. I told you, she seemed worse off than the other old people in the hospice, lonelier. Well, all that changed when Jasmine came."

"Changed how?" I asked.

"It was as if she was lighter. She smiled all the time, and I asked what happened. She told me that Jasmine had really taken the wrong path, but now she wanted to make amends. She had one errand to run, and after that she was going straight to the police. She also said that Jasmine left happy. At least, she wasn't as troubled as she was when she came."

"Did she tell you what errand?" I asked.

"She wanted to meet someone from her past, Sister said. She didn't explain, and I didn't ask further. I was afraid her spirits might go down, like before."

"Did she tell you what Jasmine had done that she was going to the police?" I asked.

"No…I asked, but she ignored the question so I didn't ask again. I thought it might be prostitution, but if she was going to stop that there'd be no need to go to the police. I thought perhaps she was a thief of some kind. But she didn't look like a thief. Or a prostitute. She seemed quiet and dignified. There was something about her…"

"Did you get a close look at Jasmine?" I asked.

"Yes. I was passing by taking an IV stand to someone's bedside and I got a good look at her. She looked tired, and thin, but her eyes were full of spirit."

"What else did you notice about her?" I asked.

"The thing is, she sat very still. She didn't move much. Most of the time she was with Sister, she sat in one position, not shifting. That's unusual. When people visit patients here, they are usually restless. Jasmine was different. She sat close to Sister Katherine. It was as if they were joined somehow."

"What else did Sister Katherine tell you about her?" I asked.

"Only that she was happy that Jasmine was changing her life. She said that the one big regret in her life was gone, now that Jasmine was going to tell the police about her life."

"Thanks," I said. "That's all I really wanted to confirm, that Jasmine was planning to go to the police. You might have to make a statement to the police confirming what you just told me."

She hesitated. "Must I?" she asked. "Working with the police is always a tension. You never know what they're going to do."

"Don't worry about it," I told her, "I'll be with you if you have to face the police."

When she left, the Mother Superior turned to me again. "Where do you intend to take this?" she asked me. "I ask because I must know of possible consequences."

I thought for a moment before replying. "I came here to find out if I should represent Jasmine in court, if at all it comes to that. From what Shanta has said, Jasmine wanted to return to society. Her intentions at the time she visited Sister Katherine are clear. So, yes, I will represent Jasmine. And, if it so happens that some unpleasant history surfaces during the trial or the investigations, so be it. I will defend Jasmine as best I can."

She listened carefully and considered in silence. She

closed her eyes and touched the crucifix on her chest. "I understand," she said finally. She smiled suddenly, a hint of mischief in her crinkled eyes. "You know, we, meaning this institution and its people, have some...some blots in our book, but others have much bigger ones. We can take care of ourselves. So, go ahead with my blessings. And, if Jasmine eventually returns to the fold, I will welcome her back. We think we know what drove her to do what she did, and we will do what we can to make amends."

"Thank you," I said, surprised and touched. "There is also a practical matter with which you might be able to help."

"I'll do my best," she said. "What is it?"

"You get information from all kinds of people," I said. "You know all kinds of people."

"Yes, I do," she said.

"I need to speak to Jasmine's father's friends." I said, "At least one of the men who were with her the night she visited him."

"Why?" she asked.

"He spoke to them before he died," I explain. "They carried out his wishes. They made sure that she was treated reasonably well. They followed up on the DNA. One of them even posted an advertisement with her photo on it, trying to trace her. They might know something that might help."

"How can I help?" she asked. "What stops you from seeing them directly?"

"Nothing," I replied. "But I have to find one, and build a rapport with him, and that could take time. I need to get back to Bhubaneshwar as soon as possible. If you can convince them that I'm doing this for Jasmine, they might come forth faster."

"One of those men is another retired police officer," she said. "Recently retired, and junior in rank. I might know someone who might know him. Give me a few minutes to make a call or two."

We waited outside for ten long minutes before she called us back in. She wrote something on a slip of paper. "This is Sub-inspector John Samuel's phone number. He was a Catholic once, and hasn't forgotten. You can talk to him directly and fix up a meeting."

"Thanks," I said.

"It's not necessary," she said. "We happen to be working towards the same thing. Jasmine's benefit. I wish you all the best. Go with God."

"Thanks," I said. "I'll call him right away."

"Please do keep me informed," she said in dismissal.

Samuel, on the phone, sounded vigorous and businesslike. "The Mother Superior told me that you might represent Jasmine if she's tried," he said.

"Yes," I told him. "I came here to confirm that she was going to give herself up, and I have done that. This is a complex case and I want to know as much detail as possible about her encounter with her late father. You and the others with you on the night she met him know more of those details than anyone else. Would you be willing to share some of that?"

"Yes," he said. "I made sure that the DNA test was done, and I got it done as quickly as possible. The thing is that he told us that, well, she was the best of the children he had, if she was really his child, and he wanted to do something for her. Now, that's hard to understand for someone who didn't know him, because she eventually caused his death..."

"Did you talk to the people of the NIA?" I asked.

"I did," he said, sadly. "You know how they are. They took notes and recorded our statements but I don't think they cared very much because they were interested in her past."

He didn't say it explicitly but I could sense his dislike of the central agency. "Perhaps we should meet," I said. "We can talk freely."

"Yes," he said. "Mother Superior told me that you want to leave tomorrow. I can come to your hotel, if that suits you."

"Yes, please," I said. "We're going there now from the convent. We should be there in half an hour, and we won't be going out."

"I'll see you in half an hour, then," he said.

In the taxi back to the hotel, Janaki asked, "So, are you satisfied about Jasmine?"

"More or less," I told her. "Now I have a good reason for taking up her case. I know that Jasmine was going to give herself up. It makes a big difference, now that I'm sure."

"Why?" she asked.

"Now I can defend her without qualms."

"What do you mean?" she asked. "I thought you were going to defend her anyway. For Ashok."

"No longer," I replied. "I'll defend her because she wants to go legal. I decided to do that about the time I got some of her history. It's not just for Ashok."

"That's new for you," she said.

"Well, I just decided I'm going to work only for clients who appeal to my...well, my moral side. Regardless of the fees."

She gave me a strange look. "That's what I do," she said, finally. "You worked for money, and me for my conscience."

"Yes," I said. "I'm getting a much better idea now of how bad the system is. I have no idea how to fix it, but at least I'm not going to do anything that violates my conscience."

"Good," she said. "You know it's a luxury."

"Now that I think about it, yes. I didn't have it for all these years. I knew about it in the back of my mind, but now it's come to the front. I shouldn't have postponed it so long, but work just became a habit."

"You can afford it now," she said.

"Yes. But I don't think it's enough, selecting cases where my conscience is involved. That won't fix the system. We have to do something more, something more fundamental, and I'm not sure that's possible."

"What?" she asked.

"I need to think about it a little more. I'll tell you when it's clearer in my own mind."

Samuel came on time and called from the lobby. Janaki was lying down and I didn't want to disturb her so I arranged to meet him in the restaurant. By the time I went down and called him he had found his way to a corner table for four and was sitting at it with a cup of coffee as if he owned the place, with a waiter hovering around. He rose, waved me over, and waited for me to sit down before sitting down himself. "What will you have?" he asked.

"Some coffee," I told him. "But you're my guest."

"Not in this town," he said. "They won't let you pay."

It seemed to be a sort of point of honour for him and I did need him to open up. "Thank you," I said. "For both the coffee and the help you're going to offer me."

"We don't know about the help yet," he said, smiling. "But what do you want to know?"

"Essentially what DSP Mohanty told you and your friends about Jasmine," I told him. "As far as I know, he made provision for Jasmine, who seems to have indirectly caused his death. Why was he so concerned for her when he never showed that kind of concern for his son?"

"See, you have to understand about DSP Mohanty," he said, looking away. "His standards were different. He was a strong man, and he respected strength. He came from a poor family, lost his father early, and then had a...a bad stepfather. But he got past that and became a successful man. He did many things that you might not like, but that was his way." He looked me squarely in the eye. "I come from the same kind of background, so I know."

"I'm a lawyer," I told him. "I've been dealing with the police for almost as long as you've lived. You don't have to explain."

He smiled. "Just making sure."

I nodded. "I understand," I told him. "What you tell me stays between us unless you permit me to share it."

"As I told you," he said, "he respected strength. By the time we got him to hospital he was very weak from the blood loss but when I went to see him, I could see that he really wanted to know about her. He kept telling me she was the bravest girl he'd ever met and that if she were really his daughter he'd be proud of her because he didn't know anyone else like that. 'She slapped me twice,' he kept saying."

"What else did he say?" I asked, intrigued.

"He said she must have done something wrong. She told him she didn't want his money. He thought she had come to him to ask him to use his influence to help her with a case, and he wanted to do that, too."

"What sort of case?" I asked.

"He didn't know," he said. "He said he'd do what he could. If it was a local matter he could...he could ask the investigating officer to take certain decisions..."

"I understand," I said.

"She dared to break into his house," he said. "Everyone knows what kind of man lives in that house. But she didn't care. She faced him. She managed to hit him. When he took the knife to her, she fought back. She wasn't an informer or a policewoman. So she had to be a criminal. Maybe a Maoist. But he didn't care. He wanted to help her. And so I want to help her."

"What did you do after you took him to the hospital?" I asked.

"I took a photo of her on my iPhone," he replied, "and asked a friend to edit it so that she had her eyes open. He told me he had no idea what her eyes were like, so I gave him a photo of DSP Mohanty and told him to go by that. Then I placed an ad in the papers to find out what she might have been. Then the NIA took the case and you know what happened after that."

There wasn't much more to tell, but I could see two things: first, that DSP Mohanty had a tight group of supporters, all people he'd helped in one way or another, and, second, that he had developed a soft spot for the woman who claimed—and was confirmed to be—his daughter, and was instrumental in killing him painfully.

The nature of that soft spot remained a little mystery until Ashok called later that evening to ask what we'd managed to find out. "Quite a lot," I told him. "Enough to confirm that Jasmine had decided to turn herself in to the police. She had one last job to complete before she did that, and I think that had to with her father, the dead retired Deputy Superintendent. What that was we can't tell for sure, but it could well have been to ask him to do what he could to ease the process of her surrender. What we know for sure now is that Jasmine did indeed want to surrender to the police."

"What difference does that make?" Ashok asked.

"Two things," I told him. "In the first place, it gives us a basis on which to ask that she be treated leniently. How leniently will depend on the severity of her crimes and the quality of the information that she gives the police now. We're not sure about either of these.

"Second, now I'm really committed to her as a client. I'll try my best to see her through with the least damage."

His relief almost seemed to float across the radio waves during the long silence that followed this. I waited for him to collect his wits, unwilling to intrude with words on what must seemed to have been a moment of great relief. With a twinge I realized that I had also finally lost him, and couldn't help wondering what part that played in my decisions. But there were questions I wanted to ask him about why Mohanty wanted to help her, about the nature of the attraction he undoubtedly felt for her. "I spoke to a friend of her father's today, another retired police officer. He told me that Mohanty definitely wanted to help her, that he felt she's a strong person, and that if she really were his daughter he'd have been proud of her."

"I never met the man," he said slowly, choosing his words carefully in an almost legal manner. "So I can't comment on that with any certainty, but here's what might be likely: he didn't think he'd die, and he thought she's strong but he was stronger and would ultimately be able to control her. Like you might want to tame a spirited animal."

"That makes some sense," I told him. "Let me think over it. But I do want to see Jasmine as soon as we get back to Bhubaneshwar."

"That's very good, Uncle," he said, "because she's remembered more. She told me about it this morning, and it's not encouraging."

"What do you mean, not encouraging?" I asked.

"She might have participated in some pretty serious crimes," he said. "Also..."

"Also what?" I asked.

"There are things that she might be willing to share with one of you but not with me."

"Of course," I said. "We're always available to listen to her, now that she's my client. It's better I hear these things directly from her rather than through you."

Chapter Thirteen

Jasmine

"I remember an execution," I told Dr Patnaik when the khakis left.

"Tell me whatever you remember," he said. "Don't worry about the order in which you remembered, or about getting the right word, or getting the right sequence of events. Tell me whatever comes to your mind, and don't worry about gaps. We'll put it in some kind of order later."

So I told him about the runaway eighteen-year-old and his eyes gleaming in his dark face in the firelight, and the sweat on his brow and his air of resignation. Then, with growing anger, I told him about the smugness and the certainty of the court, but I couldn't remember many of the words they used. It was the attitude of the judging committee that was stuck in my mind. The absolute certainty of their decision. There was nothing you could do about that certainty. As I remembered, I thought that they were machines, not people.

But even as I told Dr Patnaik I remembered more.

I, too, am a runaway.

I am thirteen years old, and quick on my feet. I am an athlete. I can run, and I can climb.

I am in a garden for a brief look at the sun. I don't remember what crime I have committed. Sister Katherine alone accompanies me. Then an attendant comes to her with a message from the Mother Superior. The attendant watches over me while Sister Katherine goes to the Mother's office.

The attendant is lazy. She seems tired, for she drags her feet. No, she's not tired. I know her. She always drags her feet. She rests when she can. While I walk around, she sits under a tree by the gate, so I won't be able to go that way. She closes her eyes. In a little while her whole body sags.

I take the chance and run. The wall is much higher than my head, and I just go for it. I misjudge the distance and scrape my knees on the rough plaster but my fingers get a grip and I scramble over. There is broken glass at the top of the wall but I can see gaps where the weather has eroded the plastic, or glass wasn't laid properly. I cut my hands and feet a few times but now I can't go back.

I drop on the far side of the wall. There is no one in sight. I duck behind a tree, reach under my skirt, and rip off the end of my chemise. With that bit of cloth I manage to wipe most of the blood off my hands. It doesn't show on my feet.

My feet are bare and the heat of the earth stings. Walking on the road is harder than walking on the earth at the sides. Stronger than the heat, though, is the fear. What will happen to me if they catch me? I don't wonder about this; I dread it. God will send me straight to hell when I die, and they will prepare me for that hell. And if they don't catch me? That seems no better. I'm so full of pain and fear that I don't feel the hunger yet.

My hands have stopped bleeding. As I walk along the road, I see a tree by its side with a lot of people standing in its shade. It's a bus stop, and they're waiting for a bus. A beggar in rags, dirty unwashed clothes, many layers of them, torn and tied up to keep them from falling off, goes from person to person, asking for money to buy food. Will that be my state if they don't catch me?

That burst of memory ended there, at the bus stop. I found Dr Patnaik staring at me strangely. "You remembered something, didn't you?" he asked.

"Yes," I told him. "I, too, was once a runaway, but they didn't catch me. They didn't have the means, like the other group did."

"What were you running from?" he asked.

"Sister Katherine," I told him.

"I don't think so," he said. "Try to remember."

"Perhaps not," I said. "I don't remember exactly, but Sister Katherine was keeping me company. Maybe to make sure I didn't run away. No, that doesn't seem right. I ran when she wasn't there...I chose a time she wasn't there because I wouldn't run away from her...it's all very confusing."

"I understand," he said. "I can see that. There's no hurry to clear the confusion, is there?"

"I don't know," I said.

"Think about it," he said. "You have all the time in the world, actually. Especially now."

"What about the police?" I asked. "They're in a hurry to find out if there are plans of any attack."

"I think the virus has postponed everything," he said. "Including any, erm, revolutionary plans of attack. So don't give in to the pressure."

"What virus?" I asked.

"The coronavirus," he replied. "We're trying to find out what effect it's going to have. Haven't you read about it in the papers? Seen it on TV?"

"No," I said. "What is it?"

"A more virulent and deadly kind of the old SARS virus," he said. "It seems to have come out of China, and it's spread over several countries. We're all waiting to see how it behaves."

"What does it do?" I asked.

"So far it's been hitting older people with other problems," he said. "Heart disease, diabetes, things like that. It seems to destroy their lungs, in a way. Most of the people who've died of it are old or had these other problems. We're still learning more about it. We're beginning to find out what we don't know about it."

"How does something like this start?" I asked. "Was it just created out of thin air?"

"Well, there are several ways it could have started," he said. "It starts with the virus, which is not really a live creature though it tends to replicate when conditions are right. That virus could have lived in an animal, like a bat or an ant-eater, and jumped to humans under the right conditions, which is what they say happened."

"How could this happen?" I asked, still mystified, glad for a brief diversion to another topic. "And how could the virus have come about?"

"Well, it might have existed before," he said. "In other animals, and jumped across under the right conditions. Otherwise, it could have been created in a lab...we're always looking for ways to kill large numbers of people, to use as a threat."

"Where did all this happen?" I asked.

"In a place called Wuhan, in China," he replied. "The Chinese seem to have tried to cover up, and the WHO probably colluded with them, and now it's spread to many countries."

"I didn't know all this," I said. "They keep me isolated. No papers, no TV."

"Let me talk to Uncle about getting you some newspapers, at least," he said. "I'm sure there's some provision for that."

"Will it interfere with my memory?" I asked. That was, after all, the most important thing right now: getting back my own history.

"I don't think so," he said. "But we can't keep you isolated like this."

"It's not important," I told him. "I'm quite happy by myself."

He looked at me strangely. "You're perhaps the only person I know who'd be able to handle this isolation as easily as you," he said, finally. "Good for you."

"Is everything normal now?" I asked. "Virus and all?"

"Not really," he replied. "We've got used to it. We keep doing our jobs, maybe a little slower than before, but we have no idea what the coming week holds for us, or the coming month." He smiled. "But there was something else I wanted to ask. You were running away from the church, and the church didn't have the means...whoever you worked with afterwards had the means. Who were they? Who is the group you refer to?"

"I don't know," I told him slowly. "I do remember turning away from their...their violence. They carried out executions. They tortured people. I know that some of them liked doing it. Some of the leaders liked to watch...I don't remember who and I don't remember why." A wave of revulsion passed through me as I spoke. They were mostly runaways, like me, running from injustice of some kind. But they'd been persuaded to do some terrible things. Perhaps I'd done my share of those terrible things too, but I didn't remember any.

He didn't ask whether I'd been involved in any of

these killings or "executions". He didn't intrude because he knew when he was intruding. I couldn't help wondering what he did other than dealing with me. "Do you mind if I ask you some questions? About you, about your work."

"Go ahead," he said.

"What is your job?" I asked.

"I teach," he said. "I teach at a medical college nearby, and I see a few patients."

"You're a professor," I said.

"If you insist," he replied. "But the label doesn't matter. Teaching is teaching, whether you teach five-year-olds or twenty-five-year-olds."

"Isn't it completely different?" I asked.

"Not really," he said. "If you care for what you're doing, you'll try to find the best way to do it. Teaching is like that. The main thing is to care for your patients, and your students. The techniques come along on their own as long as you remember that your patients matter more than your ideas."

"Do you see a lot of mad people?" I asked.

He shook his head. "There aren't any 'mad' people. They're mostly unwell. Having a mental disease involves just as much suffering as a physical ailment…" He smiled. "You know that. There's nothing wrong with you. You've lost some of your memory and parts of it are coming back. Even so, you're more worried about your memory than the possibility of spending some years in prison."

I'd never looked at it like that. "Are all mind diseases like this?" I asked. "Suffering, I mean."

"No," he replied. "Most, but not all. There are some in which the patient suffers very little but their caregivers get a lot of trouble. In any case, yours is not a mental disease, it's an episode of amnesia brought on by an injury to the head. To the brain...I just wanted you to understand that suffering in the mind is also suffering. It's not trivial. Can you imagine how badly a person must feel to want to kill herself?"

"Is it a lot of trouble for you, coming here?" I asked.

"Not really," he replied. "I get a fee for my time, and so on. In any case, my salary is enough for me to live on."

"Do you spend a lot of time with all your patients?" I asked.

He grimaced. "No," he said after a pause. "I never get enough time with my patients. You see, psychiatry developed in places where the doctor spends three-quarters of an hour or more in a single session with a patient. Here, my first session with most patients is fifteen minutes to half an hour, and every session after that is three to ten minutes. Doctors have to be quick here, because there are so few doctors for such a large population."

"So you're spending much more time with me than with your other patients," I said.

"Most of my other patients," he said. "I have a few with whom I spend lots of time."

"Who are they, if I may ask?" I asked.

"You may ask," he said, smiling, "but I'm not going to tell you. It's confidential. Just be assured that I won't discuss your case with anyone any more than I'd discuss someone else's with you. Except for my uncle, the lawyer, of course, who will have access to all my notes."

"I don't mind," I told him. "But isn't your uncle very old?"

"He's past seventy," he said, "and he's retired. I think he's lost his purpose, and a good case like this might wake him up a little."

"Where is he?" I asked. "You came with him the last couple of times."

"He's in Malkangiri," he replied. "He's gone to meet the Mother Superior of St Joseph's, where you were brought up."

"Why is he doing this?" I asked. I thought the police would have investigated the church and the orphanage."

"Uncle's very particular about details," he said. "Besides, he took his wife along. You noticed how good she is at getting people to open up."

"Yes," I said, remembering how I'd opened up to her. "When will he get back?"

"The day after tomorrow, or the day after that," he said. "Depending on whether they get reservations on the train."

"Okay," I said. "From what you say, it would be good

to have him defending me, though I don't know what difference it'll make if I've done something really terrible… as terrible as some of the things I've seen others doing."

"There are programmes to rehabilitate people like you," he said. "People who come back to society."

I shook my head. "I don't think of that. I don't think of coming back to society, or anything like what you might call a normal life. That's because I don't know what it is. I really don't know what normal is."

"You can always find out," he said. He smiled. "For all you know, it might simply consist of learning to worry about a lot of different things. Worrying about food and water and shelter and electricity and fuel, or just staying alive. That's what most people do most of the time in India."

"That's how it is in the villages I've seen," I said. "Just surviving takes up all their time. There's a lot of fear. Fear of illness, of the weather, about water and food… and there's no government, to speak of, except to collect taxes. In those conditions, just survival can be difficult. I remember…"

"What do you remember?" he asked.

"Drought," I said. "Floods…not at the same time, of course, but I remember the years when the earth was dry and others when the rivers broke their banks."

"And what did you do in those years?" he asked.

"In the dry years we helped villagers dig wells," I said.

"I remember helping them with harvests. Working in the fields in the rain that came at the wrong time."

"Do you remember any details?" he asked. "When? Where? With whom?"

"No," I replied. "I think these are things I used to do long ago."

"Why do you think so?" he asked.

"Just vague...ideas," I said. "Maybe memories of experiences. Like using a hat to keep the rain off my head and eyes. I teel these things sometimes."

"That's nothing to worry about," he said. "You've made quite some progress, I'd say, given your state two weeks after you hurt your head."

"All right," I said. "But now I need your help. What else can you tell about my background?"

He smiled. "A couple of things are very clear," he said. "You were taught to take care of yourself. Even now, you take pains over keeping yourself neat and clean. Within the limitations of where you are, you're well-groomed. I can see that from your nails and your hair. You've been taught to modulate your voice, not to shout. From what I have learnt from the hospital in Malkangiri, you're not averse to any kind of work. You read easily, and you have some kind of education, though it's not formal. I think you read more from wanting to rather than needing to. So, if I were looking at you as a stranger, I'd say you were well brought up, and are thoughtful.

"You've also been through very difficult times. These are conditions under which most people, men or women, would tend to break down at least once. You haven't. You're very disciplined. That implies rigorous teaching, of the kind you might get in the army or the police. The probability is that you've been through comparable stress before. I don't know what those conditions were, but they were not much less taxing than what you're going through now. In other words, you've probably been through worse, and what that is I won't speculate about because that might lead you the wrong way.

"You're also very bright. You learn fast. You haven't had much schooling but you ask searching questions.

"Your general physical condition is good. Your heart rate is about sixty, and your blood pressure 115/75. You are thin but strong for your weight. Your hands are a little roughened, indicating that you've done some physical labour. The scars say the same.

"Your mother tongue is Odiya, and that's the language in which you're most fluent. But you're okay with English, and can manage in Hindi: I'm no judge of that. The chances are that you've travelled, at least around the state and perhaps in Madhya Pradesh as well...

"That's about all I'll tell you now. You're not aware of some of these things because, like most people, you take yourself for granted. This is a chance for you to stop doing that."

"What do you mean?" I asked.

"Look, you're sitting here worrying about the past. Look at the future instead."

"What future do I have?" I asked. "I don't know much about any other kind of life."

"It's partly up to you. Talk to Uncle about it. He's the one who'll argue for you. He's on your side."

I could feel a lump in my throat. I'd never thought of someone being on my side, but now I knew that there were two: this doctor and his lawyer uncle. I'd never thought hopefully about the future. Could I have a future without a past, I thought. As I sat thinking he looked at his watch. "I have patients and students to take care of," he said, rising. "But I'll be back in a few days, with Uncle. Meanwhile, think about making a future for yourself. We'll find a way."

For some reason, it was all I could do not to cry. I nodded at him without speaking because if I had said anything I'd have started crying.

Even after the khaki led me back to my cell I kept silent, wondering about the people on my side. There was something nagging at me in the back of my mind and as I lay there it came to the front like bubbles rising in water that's beginning to boil...slowly at first and then in a rush that set me trembling.

The day is gone, and I hardly know where. It's evening, and my body aches. The day starts at sunrise. We have to fold up our beds and clean ourselves up. Hygiene is important, because illness is costly, but some of the others are not so careful about cleaning their teeth. We don't use toothpaste, but neem twigs from the forest. After cleaning up we get to work…

The work varies from day to day, season to season, place to place. Everyone shares camp duties, cooking and cleaning and preparing food and taking care of the camp. There are always sentries on the lookout. The leaders try to camp at places where it's easy to see someone approaching but that's difficult because we try to camp near a water source, a pond or a stream. But if there's water there are often other people. We have a dozen sites where we camp, and we move from one to another every few days.

Packing up and moving is difficult, because the only way to travel is to walk. I'm getting used to walking in the forest, and going barefoot, but that means stepping carefully. I had trouble learning that, and hurt my feet and shins quite a few times before I understood how to walk without sound and without hurting myself. The others laughed at me at first, but they also helped, so the laughter didn't hurt. Now they don't laugh at me because I can run barefoot now, faster than anyone else…

But these are good people, people who understand trouble. They know hunger and pain and being alone, as well as I do. There are days when we are short of food, and times when we are short of even water. We have learnt to deal with shortages by being together. If everyone is short, it doesn't hurt so much.

These people are my family. I belong to them. They belong to me. I never felt this before joining the group, this sense of belonging. We are going to change the world. We are going to make the whole world like this group, sharing everything and sharing alike.

And then the question arose that had been lying in the back of my mind ever since I discovered that I didn't know my name. Who am I really, I thought, if I am not my name and my body and my history? They are mine, but they are not me. I am a functional human being without any of these memories. So who am I? I found no answers but thinking about it tired me out very fast, and I fell asleep with the thought on my mind.

Chapter Fourteen

Govind Patnaik

I hardly noticed the journey back to Bhubaneshwar, after we left the Mother Superior we knew what to expect. The train was only half an hour behind schedule at Jeypore, and we got to the station and boarded without trouble. Janaki was quiet most of the time after we came away from the Mother Superior. She didn't even try to befriend a family travelling in the same compartment, which was strange, because she responds to the presence of children. "What's the matter?" I asked when I got the chance.

She gave me an angry look. "You don't see certain things."

"Right, I don't," I told her. "You see some things that I don't, I see things you don't. That's the whole idea of doing this together. So it's no use being angry at me."

She sighed. "I'm not angry at you. I'm just angry at... at life. At what it does to you."

"I gave up being angry about it long ago," I told her.

"Otherwise, I wouldn't have been able to do what I've done."

She shook her head. "That woman in jail, Jasmine," she said. "She's in my mind all the time. What would you say in her defence?"

"Fundamentally that society wronged her..." I said. "Use that and her repentance to mitigate the severity of her crimes, whatever they are. And, for the crimes themselves, demonstrate that they were committed by a group to which she belonged but not necessarily by her."

"That won't save her," she said.

"It won't," I say slowly. "Not given the scenes at which the police found her fingerprints. But she can help by giving the police some way to catch her ex-colleagues. Or prevent more mayhem."

"Will she do that?" she asked.

"I don't know," I replied. "As best I can make out, she doesn't trust society well enough to make a complete return. Not yet, at any rate."

"But what choice did she have?" she asked. "Once she was with the group, once she was...once she had bloodied her hands, the rest was inevitable."

"Yes," I replied. "I've been thinking about that, too. What choice does any of us have?"

"Don't be stupid," she said. "Everyone chooses their course of action."

"I'm not so sure," I reply. "Given your value system

and your compulsions, the choices you make—the choices anyone makes—are more or less inevitable."

"Of course, our freedom is restricted," she says. "But that freedom is there. That's the basis of the law that you and I studied, isn't it?"

"Now that I've had time to think about it, I'm not so sure," I replied. "But that's not really relevant. Given what happened to her, well, it's difficult to blame her for what she did. And once she stepped down that path there was no going back. But then she did try to change. I was wondering about the courage that takes to turn your back on something you've invested in for decades."

"When you get philosophical," she said, "I don't know what to say to you. Unless you're drunk, which I know you're not. But you're going to argue her case, aren't you?"

"Not if I can help it," I said.

"What do you mean?" she asked, sitting up straight, a hint of anger in her eyes.

"I mean I hope I can negotiate something on her behalf which will enable us to avoid a trial completely," I tell her. "But we'll have to wait for her to get at least some of her memory back for that."

"Can you do that?" she asked.

"Perhaps," I told her. "If she has information that can help the government catch some of her ex-colleagues, or prevent more crimes...I don't know."

"There's more," she said. "You're not telling me everything."

"No," I said. "There's something else all right. It's just this: the present government has avoided blaming earlier governments for the Maoist movement. It started long before the BJP was even born, and it's killed far more people than anything other than Islamist-based movements in the country."

"So you're wondering if this can be made to look as if we can blame the dynasty for this as well?" she asked. "The result of the Emergency?"

"Well, this movement started much before the Emergency," I said. "Long before. I'm just wondering how political it could get."

"Sometimes I hate this attitude of yours," she said. "It's very manipulative. As if you don't care about her."

"Of course I do," I said. "I'm willing to use everything I can to get her off. Just thinking. It might not come to that."

Ashok was at the railway station to pick us up, masked and armed with a bottle of sanitizer. "I hope the trip wasn't too tiring," he said, taking Janaki's suitcase and starting off towards the exit.

"Not for me," I said. "But Janaki fell ill."

"I'll speak for myself," Janaki said. "An upset stomach. That's over now."

"Good," he said. "You can get to work tomorrow. I've fixed it up."

"What's the matter?" Janaki asked as we turned towards the parking lot.

"I won't be able to stay for long," he replied. "I'll leave you at the prison and get back to work."

"That's not what's worrying you," she said.

"You'll see," he said. "She's started remembering things. Some of the uglier bits of her past."

"We were prepared for that," I said, "and now we have plenty of evidence and at least two reliable witnesses willing to testify that she did want to turn herself in."

"Two reliable witnesses?" he asked.

"One isn't a witness, precisely," I said, "but someone who heard her father's dying statement said that she was to be given some substantial help. A retired policeman friend. He said all this to the NIA but they weren't interested in DSP Mohanty's death. They were after her for other, more urgent reasons. I can't blame them, really, but her memory loss is what is blocking them."

"She's been regaining her memory," Ashok said. "The last time we met she told me about an execution. Her group executed a runaway. He was a youngster who had been forced to join. They demanded two boys from a village with the threat of reprisals if they didn't get the boys. It seems that's one tactic they've been following when they need people."

"Did she participate in the execution?" I asked.

"No. She remembered clearly that she stood guard over him the night before the execution. She remembers volunteering for guard duty whenever she could. It was boring but she had time to think, which the others didn't."

"Ah, yes," I said. "Thinking can subvert you. It's beginning to subvert me."

He gave me a keen look. "I know," he said. "You've changed."

"In what way?" I asked.

"Well, you wouldn't have done this trip for a client the last time we met," he said slowly. "You always focused on winning cases, but left the preparation to others. I was willing to hire people to help you out but the two of you didn't even bring that up. Auntie might have done this trip, but not you."

"Right," I said. "I found out things after retirement."

"We all learn after every upheaval," he said. "It's natural. What did you find out?"

"How sheltered I've been," I said, "and how difficult it is for the average citizen to live." I paused, thinking of my going walkabout and meeting people at the tea shop. "You're right, I've changed."

Janaki laughed. We'd reached the car and as she got into the rear seat, she told Ashok, "For years I've been telling him, but he never listened. Then he retires, and a few months later he's beginning to learn...to grow up."

There she was, baiting me again. I smiled at her, saying nothing, and, after a moment she looked away.

When we arrived at the prison at ten next morning, I began to understand, for the first time, the effect of prison surroundings on people. I'd seen very little of prisons, and was always glad to leave them when the time came, and never thought about how it might be to live. Now I began to wonder how Jasmine survived in such depressing surroundings.

But her face was clear, and her eyes lit up when she saw Ashok. I saw a ghost of some other expression in her eyes when she looked at him, but I couldn't understand it, so I filed it away in my mind, perhaps to ask Jasmine when I had a chance to talk to her alone, after Ashok left.

"I have to leave," Ashok told her. "I have a few meetings that I can't postpone. Uncle here will talk to you about his trip to Malkangiri."

Her disappointment showed, no matter how much she tried to hide it. "When will you be back?" she asked.

"I don't know," Ashok replied. "Perhaps not for the rest of this week."

When he had left and the three of us were seated around the table, I told Jasmine, "There are a few things I want to tell you. We met the Mother Superior at your orphanage. She was a sister there when you…when you left, and remembers you fairly well because of the circumstances under which you left. Sister Elizabeth."

"What did she tell you?" she asked.

"Father Richard is dead," I replied. "She is willing to reopen old matters if doing so will do you any good. She told me that if you are penitent, she will welcome you back."

"I remember Elizabeth," she said. "She's the one who locked me up. The one who believed Richard and not me. I didn't trust her, and I don't think I can trust her now."

"That's up to you," I told her. "She was different with me. She put me in touch with two people who confirmed that you had come to town with the intention of leaving your group, and perhaps turning yourself in to the police. The last thing you wanted to do before that was meet to Sister Katherine at the hospice, which you did. But when you heard what we had to tell you, you changed your mind."

"I remember that," she said softly. "She told me who my father was, that he abandoned my mother. I decided to confront my father. I didn't really want anything from him...I just wanted to shake him up a little. I certainly didn't want him to die because of me."

"He didn't die because of you," I told her. "I met a friend of his, a former policeman who took both of you to the hospital. Regardless of what happened, I believe you wanted to turn yourself in, and I will represent you legally on that basis. Which means, essentially, that we negotiate a future for you. Ashok told me that you remembered an execution, and he showed me his notes on it. Now I must ask you to share your returning memories with me. We'll look for information that might be useful when we negotiate."

"I can't pay you," she said. "I asked other prisoners

what it costs to have a lawyer like you. It's a lot. I don't even have a small fraction of that."

"I'm retired," I told her. "I'm taking your case because it's worthwhile." I can't help smiling at her. "After a lifetime of squeezing clients, I can afford to do yours free of charge. Besides…"

"Besides what?" she asked.

"Ashok asked me to do this."

"Are you doing it for him?" she asked.

"It started that way," I told her. "But after we visited Malkangiri I changed my mind. From what we saw and heard, I'm reasonably sure you were going to turn yourself in to the police anyway. So now I represent you for your sake."

She looked dubiously at Janaki, who smiled at her. "You have to tell him everything you remember," Janaki told her. "Because you never know what's going to be useful."

"But what if I remember killings? Bad things?" she asked.

"None of that matters," said Janaki. "You wanted to change. That's what matters."

"All right," said Jasmine. "I remember guarding our prisoner, and watching his execution."

Chapter Fifteen

Jasmine

The lawyer didn't react when I told him about the execution.

"The timing is what counts," he said. "If this was one of the events that helped you decide against continuing with violence..."

"It was one of many," I told him slowly, for something had emerged, a full-blown memory, and it was very troublesome. I rested my face in my hands because I didn't want to face anyone while this was coming. "I remember meeting my father. I remember that night."

"Talk about it when you're ready," he said. "Take your time."

I straightened up. "I'm ready now," I said. "There's no point in putting it off."

"Do you mind if I record this?" he asked, pulling out his cellphone.

"No," I said. "Go ahead."

When he had turned the recorder on, I found it hard

to collect my thoughts. "It's all right," he said. "Start wherever you like. We can always make corrections, and I'll try not to interrupt the flow."

"Sister Katherine told me his name and address," I began. "Finding his house was simple. I was used to walking all day with little food or rest, carrying a crude backpack—no padded straps, no adjustments, just a sack with two straps—across country roads and jungle paths. So walking around a city with only a small bag to carry was easy.

"The house was in a quiet area where moderately rich people live. His house stood out because it was large and poorly kept. The garden was bedraggled and the paint on the house was faded and stained. It was as if the owner either couldn't afford to keep it in good shape or didn't care.

"It was close to dark when I found the place and a shopkeeper nearby told me that he'd be out. He usually got back in the small hours, after midnight, and in the company of some of his cronies. They would all be drunk, and in a cab. He had a regular cabbie, a former goon and jailbird. He ran errands for my father, and drove him around.

"His friends were mostly ex-policemen like himself, though he was the seniormost in rank, if not in age. All just scraped through to retirement without getting into trouble over taking bribes and various other crimes. Now their indiscretions are limited to getting drunk every night and returning home noisily.

"I waited in a park until it closed at eight, and then found a small cheap restaurant where I stretched out my light dinner of two chapatis and an egg and some chopped onions. Afterwards I drank a cup of strong, sweet coffee, a rare luxury in my days in the forests, which will help me stay awake. At about ten, I set off for my father's house.

"All day I'd thought about what I'd say to him when I met him. He was a stranger, after all, even if he was my biological father…I didn't know what to say to him except that I was curious about where I came from. I didn't know how to explain why I even wanted to see him. But now that the hour was so close, I thought I'd tell him I'm his daughter, and wanted nothing from him but a little help. He was a policeman, after all, so he would know how I could turn myself in with the minimum of trouble for myself. Maybe he could turn it into some advantage for himself…

"I was outside his house a little before eleven. There were streetlamps but very little traffic in this part of town where the well off live. There were patches of darkness all over and I found my way over the compound wall with no trouble. The shopkeeper told me he used to keep a dog, but it had died of old age. I groped my way to the back door in the dark, and found it locked and bolted, as expected, so I went to the front door and picked the lock, which was surprisingly easy. Then I understood that it would take a very brave thief to try to burgle this man's house...

"He wasn't going to be there for an hour or more, so I familiarized myself with the house. I used the torch on a cheap smartphone that I bought when I broke away. The front door opened into a lobby and then a sitting room furnished with old furniture designed for comfort, with a big TV set on one wall and a small table by every chair or sofa in the room. Knowing the man's habits, I could see it was all set up for a group of men to drink in comfort. There was a dining room beyond that, a small bathroom for visitors, and two bedrooms besides a staircase leading to the upper floor. I had a look at that as well, and found two more bedrooms, which had an unused look to them.

"I thought then that it was big enough to house perhaps more than a dozen people in my group...

"I went back downstairs. In the bigger of the two bedrooms downstairs I found a bunch of keys, one of which seemed to work the lock in the front door. I locked the door from the inside and settled down to wait in a chair facing the door. The clock on the wall said it was a quarter past eleven so there was plenty of time...so I explored some more, trying to understand the kind of man he was. From what I found, it seemed his basic nature—bully, toady, thief, braggart—hadn't changed in any way.

"The only thing a man like that might respect is

strength. My only strength was that I had nothing to lose. If he refused to help me, I'd be no worse off than I would be otherwise. If he did offer help, well…I didn't know. But either way there wasn't much of a future for me.

"At about half past midnight I selected a chair in the dining room facing the door to the lobby but hidden from the front door. He wouldn't see me when he came into the house, but he would be able to when he made his way to the big bedroom. The chair had a straight back and no arms so I sat leaning on the table for a while and thought about the different ways in which he might react to finding an intruder in his house, and when he found out that I claimed to be his daughter.

"Whatever he did, it wouldn't be pleasant. But then, I hadn't gone there expecting pleasantness.

"At about one, a car drew up outside the house. I heard the engine and saw the wash of the headlamps, and then heard the rasp of harsh male voices. There was some laughter, and then a car door slammed and the headlamps moved off. Moments later, someone unlocked the door and stepped in, fumbling for the light switch by the doorway. The lobby light came on, and a man walked unsteadily into the dining room. He fumbled again for a light switch, turned it on, and the way to the staircase lit up.

"At first glance, I didn't think I resembled him much. I sat motionless, staring at him, and a few seconds later he saw me. His first word was an expletive. 'Who are you?' he asked. 'What are you doing here?' His voice was deep and harsh and somehow unyielding.

"I replied without thinking; all my plans went out of the window. 'I'm your daughter,' I told him, getting to my feet. 'I've come to see what kind of a man fathered me.'

"'Now that you've seen me,' he said, 'get out before you get into trouble.'

"'Not so fast, old man,' I told him. 'I want to talk.'

"'I don't,' he said, taking a step towards me. 'My house, I do what I like. So fuck off before I throw you out.'

"'Try me,' I said.

"That stopped him, but only for a moment. He smiled bleakly. 'So you claim you're my daughter.' He took another step towards me.

"'Yes,' I told him. 'In May 1977, when you were in charge of a police station not far from here, you kidnapped and raped a young tribal girl. When her parents tried to complain, you had them beaten up, and they died of those beatings. I was born of that rape, and my mother died very soon after that.'

"'So you're my father. You raped my mother, and beat her parents to death.'

"'I wanted to see what kind of a man is brave enough to do that.'

"He smiled again. 'So now you've seen me, now get out.'

"A surge of anger took me by surprise. 'I'm not done yet,' I told him. 'I'll go when I've said what I came here to say.'

"He took a step forward and sat in a chair. 'Don't waste my time, and let me tell you right now: you're not getting any money out of me.'

"'I don't want your money,' I said. 'Not when I know how you earned it. I need your help with the law.'

"He laughed. 'I thought it would be something like that,' he said, 'but I don't do favours for people like you.'

"'People like me?' I asked.

"'Maybe a dozen people have come to me claiming that I'm their father,' he said. 'Some of their claims might even be true, because I spread my seed far and wide when I was young. But so what? I owe them—and you—nothing. And if I don't help you, what are you going to do?'

"That's when the anger broke loose. I took a step towards him and slapped him across the face as hard as I could. If he'd been sober he might have been able to block the blow. He staggered under its impact, and rage showed in his eyes as he aimed a punch at me. He was old and drunk and slow and I dodged the blow easily and slapped him again. He stepped back into the kitchen and I followed him there. It was dark and I stood in the doorway, unsure of what he was doing. Then he turned around and I saw the knife in his hand. I blocked his first low jabs, getting bruised on the forearms nevertheless. I backed into the dining room and he followed me there.

"In the bright light I grabbed his wrist and tried to twist it away but he had bursts of surprising strength. We swayed as we grappled but I managed to keep my balance. But he turned away to break my grip on his wrist. He staggered and lost his balance and fell forward and I fell with him, on him, his wrist still in my grip. I let go, and got back on my feet but he groaned. As a trail of blood emerged beneath him, he gathered the strength to turn over on his back and ended up leaning his head against the wall next to the kitchen door.

"The knife was in his abdomen. It must have been painful, for he groaned again. I wasn't going to remove the knife because that might cause him to bleed out. He lay back, staring at me. For all the pain, there was a reflective look in his eyes. 'You really are different,' he said.

"'Quiet!' I told him. 'Save your breath.'

"He kept staring, and I saw that the rage was still in him. As he lay helpless, I remembered what this man did to my mother and I couldn't help taunting him. 'Don't like the idea of being beaten by a woman, right?' I asked him, keeping my voice level. 'If I wanted to do to you a tenth of what you did to my mother or her parents I'd twist that knife in your gut instead of trying to stop the bleeding.'

"I took my eyes off his eyes for a moment to see if the bleeding had decreased and as I looked away I felt him move. By the time I looked at him again he had straightened up and he was using the last of his strength to come at me. I began to rise and I was off balance when his blow landed in my solar plexus. It would have been enough to knock me down even if I'd been standing still but now I was off balance, on one leg. It threw me backwards. I felt my head hit something sharp and then came the blackness..."

At the end of the telling I found the old lady sitting by my side, holding my hand. "I taunted him," I said. "I shouldn't have. He was already down and dying."

"There was no need," the lawyer says. "I've never found that anger helps anything. But neither does guilt. Guilt is useless. It destroys you without doing anyone else any good. But the most important thing is what I learnt from practicing the law for half a century: both are indulgences. Most of us can't afford them."

"I can't help it," I said. "I have nothing to do but try to remember what my life was. Much of what I remember is about guilt and anger."

"Yes," he said. He smiled. "You go ahead and indulge yourself. I'm here to see that your indulgence doesn't hurt you legally."

I had no memory of kindness like this except from Sister Katherine at the orphanage. The comradeship of the group was different. There was friendship there, but no hint of this softness. It confused me. When I looked up, the old couple was bright-eyed and warm and for the first time I understood what parents could be to a child. I found myself unable to speak, so I simply nodded.

"Enough for today," the old lady said. "We'll come back tomorrow. You can tell us more then."

But the softness and all the talk of the orphanage and Sister Katherine and my father's death had opened some windows in my mind. Another layer of shadow disappeared, and I remembered an old man. Some words floated up in my mind. Grandfather. Monster. Fairy tale. Greed. Terror. Hunger. Then came a specific word in Odiya that started a whole new revelation, like a key in a lock.

Jejo Bapa. An old ghost takes shape.

On the night of the third day after I run away from the orphanage I meet Jejo Bapa. I have been travelling all day with a group of three, a man, a woman, and a sullen boy younger than myself. We have spent many hours in buses, sitting some of the time, standing the rest, often with little room to breathe, oppressed by the odour of earth from the people standing close by. We haven't eaten much, an early breakfast of puris and nothing after that. From early evening we have walked, following a trail in the dying sunlight, and afterwards in the dark.

I wonder about running away again, but these people are kind, as kind as the best of the nuns at the orphanage. They seem to trust me, and I don't want to let them down.

The dark here is heavier and thicker than I've ever seen

before. The clouds overhead block most of the moonlight, and I wonder how the man leading the group knows where he's going. Soon my feet hurt and my back hurts and the bag I carry—it's got a spare set of clothes for me, and a packet that I haven't opened—gets heavier and heavier on my shoulder. But my faith in these people keeps me going.

Just when I think I'm going to fall down, we stop. Ahead are faint lights, embers in ashes, and small houses with lamplight showing in the windows. We are in a small village. All this is new to me because I've never been outside the orphanage before. The place smells different, and sounds different. A man comes out of his house and leads us to another, larger, house where they give us rice and curry to eat, and cool water from earthen pots. There are mattresses and straw mats, rolled up in a corner. I spread one out and go to sleep.

I wake at dawn, to the familiar sound of a rooster. But everything else is new. There are no taps, no running water, no toilets, no bathrooms, no electricity. The woods serve as a toilet, and baths are in the pond nearby, in green water that smells funny. After that there's a breakfast of rice porridge and a small quantity of beans. The people in the village are very poor but they're doing their best for us. They share everything.

Afterwards one of the villagers takes me to another hut where an old man sits on the floor in the middle of the room, a small mini desk in front of him. There are other children in the room, two boys, both below ten, and another girl a little older than them, all sitting on the floor facing him. The old man smiles at me, and his whole face lights up.

After Sister Katherine, he's the only person who's made me feel that I matter.

"Sit," he says, pointing to a space in front of him. "What's your name?"

"Jasmine," I tell him.

"That's a beautiful name," he says. "You can call me Grandfather if you wish. Jejo Bapa." He asks each of the other children in turn what their names are, so I get to know them. "Have you all had breakfast?" he asks.

"Yes," we chorus.

"Are your bellies full?" he asks.

There's a silence. "No," I tell him. "I'm hungry, but only a little."

"Would you like to hear a story?" he asks.

"Yes," we chorus.

"A story about hungry people?" he asks.

"Yes," we chorus again. We all know about being hungry.

So he tells us a story, a fairy tale. It's from a huge collection of fairy tales, he says, that's called the Mahabharata. But one of the stories is different. He tells us about an evil being called Bakasura, who lives near a village. Bakasura eats all kinds of things that people eat, but his favourite food is people. He's enormous, and the villagers have no chance against him even when they're united. When he first arrived there, he threatened to eat all the people in the village, but struck a deal with the village elders. The deal is this: the people of the village deliver a bullock-cart loaded with food to Bakasura every week. Bakasura eats the contents of the cart, the bullock, and the person driving it, and doesn't trouble the villagers otherwise. And the villagers agree that week after week, each family will take turns sending one of its members out to deliver the cart to Bakasura and be eaten. But filling the cart takes almost all the food that the village produces, leaving very little for the villagers, so they're always hungry.

"Just like you," he says.

We listen enthralled as he describes the horror of the agreement. He changes his voice to tell us how Bakasura and the villagers talk to each other. It sounds so real that we hate Bakasura, and wonder why the villagers don't move away to someplace far away until Jejo Bapa tells us how difficult it is to move. "Villages need water," he explains in his regular voice. "So someone would have to go find a vacant place where there's water, which could be very far away. And the villagers would have to move there, with the babies and the children and the cattle and the livestock, and, at the end of the journey, they'd have to build everything all over again. The villagers were tied to the land."

He resumes the story in his storytelling voice. To this village come visitors, a woman and her five sons. One of the sons, Bhima, is very strong. According to the fairly tale, he's as strong as several thousand elephants. The woman and her sons live with a poor family, who share what little food they have with the visitors. Later, as they try to sleep with half-empty bellies—just like yours, or worse, he says in his normal voice—they overhear their hosts talking in the night, arguing about who will take the cart to Bakasura. Even the small children in the family offer to drive the cart out to the monster.

The woman visitor tells the host and his family, "Don't worry about the cart. My second son, Bhima, is very strong. He'll take care of it."

"No," says the host. "You are a guest. You are like God to us. We can't let you risk your lives for us."

But the woman insists, and the host gives in. Next morning, the cart arrives outside the house, all loaded up with the best food that the village can offer. Bhima climbs on to it and drives it out of the village, out of the villagers' sight, to the forest cave where the monster lives. Outside the cave, Bhima halts the cart. He is a big man, with a big appetite, and he is very hungry. He begins to eat the food meant for the monster, enjoying every bit of it.

The monster, lurking in his cave, is also hungry. He emerges and finds a man eating the food meant for him, and is furious. He attacks Bhima, throwing large rocks and uprooted trees at him. Bhima, still hungry, ignores Bakasura until every last bit of the food is gone. Then he turns to face the monster. The battle is short and violent, and Bhima kills Bakasura.

"Who can tell me why this is a fairy tale?" Jejo Bapa asks.

"Because there are no monsters like Bakasura," I say.

Jejo Bapa shakes his head. "No," he says. "There are monsters like Bakasura. It's just that they don't look like monsters."

"Because there aren't any strong men like Bhima," I say.

Again he shakes his head. "There are strong men, and women, mind you, and children. It's just that they don't look like heroes, that's all." He smiles.

We fall silent, until he asks, "Shall I tell you why?"

"Yes," I say, and the others all nod.

"It's a fairy tale because Bakasura never died," he says. "Bhima never killed Bakasura. It's because he's alive that you children don't have enough to eat this morning. It's because he's alive and well that all of us go hungry all the time."

"How do you know?" I ask, surprised. "Isn't it because we don't grow enough food?"

He smiles. "Good question," he says. "You come from a town."

"Yes," I tell him.

"Have you been through the town?" he asks.

"Only a little," I say, hesitantly, because all I remember is what I saw while running away.

"Did you see rich people? People with big houses, people with cars, people with servants? Well-dressed people?"

"Yes," I tell him. I remember a few of those.

"Well," he says, "that's what Bakasura looks like now. For every one of those who lives well, and wastes food, there are ten of us who don't eat enough breakfast."

"But we don't have enough to eat because we're poor!" I say.

"Yes," he says. "And why are we poor? Are you any worse or better than any other person your age? No. Then why do some of you go hungry while others don't?"

I don't know. "Luck?" I ask.

"It's because part of your breakfast goes to Bakasura," he says.

While we're all thinking about this, another question pops up in my mind. "What about Bhima?"

He smiles. "I thought you would come to that. There's a Bhima in all of us, brave and strong. There's also a Bakasura in all of us, greedy and afraid. The choice is yours. Which do you want to be?"

The fragment of memory ended with Jejo Bapa telling me that it's our choice: to be brave and strong, or greedy and afraid. I remember vaguely that when he said that, I thought I wanted to be brave and strong, but wasn't sure how I could be that way. And then, another related memory floated up to the top of my mind.

The doubts live in my mind all the time.

We have the blood of innocents on our hands. We have brought death to our own people, to hungry people, to people who are neither Bhima not Bakasura. There are all kinds of people, I've learnt, and I no longer find it easy to make out friend from foe.

I hear that Jejo Bapa is dying. He has been unwell for

some time now, and has refused to get himself treated. He has a growth in his chest, and has been spitting blood for weeks. He eats very little, and is very weak. He rarely gets out of bed.

I visit him in the same little hut in which I first met him all those years ago. A small thin man with dark skin and white hair, he lies on a thin mat on the floor, with no pillow, and a towel by his head. He has folded the towel neatly but the bloodstains show. Then I look in his eyes and find them as bright and lively as ever. I force myself to smile. "Jejo Bapa," I say. Then my voice fails me. I hold his hand instead.

He squeezes my hand gently as he smiles back. He can't speak, but he mouths the words, "I knew you would come." He pauses for a few shallow breaths. "You're the best." Another pause, then, "Keep thinking." Even that is too much for him, and his eyes cloud over. I sit holding his hand and after a while I feel his fingers squeeze again, and relax. His eyes are closed and his face peaceful. I know without feeling his pulse that he is gone.

It is as if a part of me has died.

It is part of my old pain.

When I become aware of them, they're sitting staring at me. "What happened?" the lady asked. "Do you have a headache?"

I shook my head. "No," I told her, "I remembered more."

"You look tired," she said. "We can come back for this later."

"No," I said. "I'll tell you when it's fresh in my mind..." I anticipated his question. "Record it if you wish."

And then I told them about Jejo Bapa, about the story and about his death and the hole it left in my life. At the end of the telling, I found myself weeping and rocking in the chair like a child. "Ashok should have been here," the old lady said when I was finished. "He would know when to stop you, and how to make sure you don't suffer as your memory returns. I don't know how to deal with this."

"I'm all right," I told him.

"That's not the point," she said. "If it hurts you to remember these things, then it might get harder for you to remember more. I wish I knew what would help, but I don't. We'll try to see to it that Ashok is around when we talk."

I took some time answering. I knew now that there were things I hesitated to bring up with Dr Ashok. "It's all right," I said. "We'll get by."

"That's not good enough," Mr Patnaik said emphatically. "We need you in the best possible condition, with the clearest memories, to try to avoid a trial completely. So, take care of yourself."

After they left and the warder took me back to my cell, I sat unaware of time passing, remembering Jejo Bapa. He planted some seeds in my mind, and I was harvesting the fruit of those seeds: this life in prison was part of the harvest. He had warned us then that our path would be painful and expensive, that only the strongest would survive, but they would…and a new world would be born from that struggle. He told us about the "enemy". He told us of the divide between the exploiters and the exploited. He told us that we were working for a paradise in which everyone got what they needed.

That seemed worthwhile.

After the Patnaiks left, the khakis left me alone. I sat in my room with paper and pen, wondering what to do. Writing was difficult. The words don't come.

I miss the Patnaiks. Not the old one so much, but the younger one, and the old one's wife, the one who made me cry.

But as I think of them, more old ghosts collide and take shape in my mind. A big one takes hold as it takes shape, and doesn't let go because it brings a grief that leaves me unable to swallow.

I'm going to be a mother.

We don't visit doctors except for emergencies, and the few that come visiting…well, they don't come very often. But in our villages are women with knowledge and memories of many childbirths, and many stillborns and dead mothers and unlikely survivals.

Midwives. They supervise births and deaths that often come together. One of them, the oldest around, in her sixties, stares at me as I watch some others working on a canal for the village. When I move away from the group, she approaches me, smiling tentatively. She stands in my way, blocking my path, smiling that same tentative smile. "What is it?" I ask.

"You're with child," she replies. "I can see it in how you walk, in how you behave, in how you smile. Three months."

Something grips at my insides, a kind of joy mixed with a kind of panic. In a moment, the panic settles. A face surfaces in my mind, a face with a ragged beard and fine eyelashes...

The spell is broken. I come back to the reality of my confinement wondering what happened...WHAT HAPPENED TO MY BABY?!

A moment later, another thought follows: WHO IS THE BABY'S FATHER?

The wedge of memory returns, patchy like a movie with large parts missing.

My baby.

"Don't tell anyone," I tell her urgently. She knows our group well enough not to question that, so she nods and moves on, leaving me holding my guilty secret.

When we break for lunch, rice and vegetables and some lentils, I wonder why there's anything to be guilty about. Discipline, comes the answer. Having to take care of a baby will take my mind off the work I have to do, which might involve taking life.

A few people have got permission to live together and have children but that's not easy. Having a baby means access to medical facilities, special food for the mother, and, when the baby is weaned, for it as well, and all sorts of other things that hamper the hit and run and disappear approach we take in our operations. Babies hamper disappearance. They bring love and joy but also conflict, which weakens the revolution.

The revolution.

Jejo Bapa. I will talk to him.

I have to wait some days for a chance to do that. He doesn't stay long in any village, moving more or less at random among some twenty-odd villages where he is known and welcome, spread out over several hundred square kilometres. I find him one summer evening, just after sunset, in a room with a kerosene lamp hung from a hook on the wall, the wick turned low. It's warm, and Jejo Bapa sits bare-chested on the floor. He recognizes me when I appear in his doorway. "Come, sit," he says, "My friends say you want to talk to me."

"Yes," I say. "I need to talk to you alone."

"Of course," he says. He gestures to his host, the owner of this hut, who stands beside me now. The owner nods and leaves the two of us alone.

I enter the room and sit on the floor facing him. It's only sometimes I see how small he is; when I sit, we are level, which means he's about my size. "Jejo Bapa," I say, "I'm pregnant."

He smiles. "Are you happy about it?" he asks.

"Yes," I say. "But I have reservations."

"I've lived long enough not to ask awkward personal questions," he says. "Besides, you're one of my favourite people. So…so you tell me whatever you want to, and stop whenever you want to." The smile widens. "You're the one

who has to face the conflict. The only thing I've got to say is that I won't judge you."

One thing I've learnt from him is how difficult honesty is. I plod on. "If I tell the High Command, they'll tell me to abort the baby, but I don't want to do that."

"Forget the High Command and what they say," he tells me. "Consider this: what happens to your baby if you get seriously hurt, or go to prison, or get killed? Ask yourself these questions and answer yourself, not me."

"I asked, and got the answers," I tell him. "They're not encouraging."

"But...?"

My breath catches. I think I feel tears in my eyes. I grit my teeth for a moment. "In my heart I want the baby. I want to be a mother."

"Would you like your baby to have a childhood like yours?" he asks. "Or perhaps even worse?" He pauses again, breathless. I can see that despite what he said earlier, he's finding it hard to say what he wants to. "To put it another way: do you want to risk a very bad life for your child just for the satisfaction of your desire to be a mother?"

His face is like stone. Once again I see the strength, the steel, and the depth of thought hidden in that frail body. I understand what he's saying, so, in my mind, I spell out the possibilities as he wants me to. If I want the baby, I'll have to leave the group, and then I'll be a fugitive. If I turn myself in to the khakis, even if they protect me in some ways, they'll demand information, and I'll have to betray people who helped me when I was at my lowest, and I still won't be safe, because they'll come after me. If I stay, and disobey orders, I'll be punished. If I obey orders, I'll have to give up the baby. There's no future for the baby, and, without the baby, for me...I can't speak, so I simply shake my head. Then I remember the story he told us as children the first time we met, and ask him, "Did Bhima have to face these questions when he fought Bakasura?"

"I don't know," he says, "but do you think I can tell you anything you don't already know?"

Again I shake my head.

Then comes the question I dread. "Who is the father?"

That burst of memory ended abruptly. I didn't know the answer to that question. There came shadows at the back of my mind, hints of a gentle voice, of tender eyes with long lashes and feathery caresses and poetry whispered in my ears, and of loss and grief, but nothing specific. I now knew of the poetry in my ears but couldn't remember a single line of it. I knew of the grief but couldn't remember who I grieved for, or what.

I had a great sense of loss but had no idea what happened to my baby. Or my husband, or lover, for that matter...

Why did I dread that question? What was I hiding from myself?

Alone in the small bedroom that makes my prison cell,

I wept. For the first time in my new life, I cried without holding back, not knowing whether to be glad or sad that there was no one to hear me. I had no idea how long the fit of crying lasted, but it left me sadder than before.

Then came a large splinter of memory that wasn't of an event, but of something I'd read and recited—and taught—many times. Rules on how to be safe.

Standing Orders for Armed Squads

1. Follow squad discipline unfailingly. Do not function as you please.

2. Squads must move only in the decided formation to the selected destination.

3. When the squad reaches its den, sentries are to be posted and protective cover taken immediately.

4. Weapons must be cleaned every day and after every use in a proper procedure.

5. Daily roll call and briefing must be conducted without fail.

6. Protective patrols must be appointed every day at the perimeter of the den.

7. Squad members must keep their respective weapons by their side. Weapons must not be given to civilians.

8. Grenades are only for those who can throw them twenty metres or more.

9. Jung *[the military manual] must be read and spread. If squad members have difficulty reading it, it must be read to them without fail.*

In hospital and then in prison, time seemed to take on a quality it never had when I was free to move around. In the hospital the sounds were mostly soft but every now and then there would be the shouts as an emergency patient was wheeled in, and occasionally the chatter of ward boys or nurses. In the jail, there were always noises and smells. There was laughter, and shouted commands, and the clang of metal or the bang of doors shutting hard, and, through most of the day, a muted background chatter. I was never alone but always lonely. Now, I realized what kept me from going mad: my loss of memory. Regardless of the time of the day or my physical isolation, I had something compelling to think about, to worry about: my past. The fragments of memory that I got from time to time keep me going.

I took the pen and paper from the small box in which I kept it, and sat down on the hard bed to write. When I put pen to paper, though, I found that the words wouldn't come. I could not write because Dr Ashok was going to read what I wrote, and, for the first time, it occurred to me that here were things about myself that I might not want him to know...

The desolation increased. I put the pen and paper away and sat on the bed, lost in despair. This time, though, I didn't cry. This time the despair was beyond tears.

Chapter Sixteen

Jasmine

Jejo Bapa's paradise would come into being only if everyone against it was eliminated. At the time, it made sense, but not afterwards…

It stopped making sense because someone talked to me about it.

Even in the worst days of summer, mornings are bearable, even pleasant. The sun rises early in these parts, and I have made it a habit to wake up before first light and lie still in the cooling air, doing nothing. There are mosquitoes, and insects, but I have learnt to live with them.

Yesterday I met a man who seems different.

One thing I've learnt in the years with this group is that they only talk of equality. Men are still considered better. Perhaps, in these circumstances, when physical strength matters, it's appropriate. Men can carry bigger loads, walk longer distances, hide better, and tend to be stronger overall. But I've seen women as good, as strong, whom the group doesn't promote as it should. Even me…I've been left behind, for no reason I can see other than my gender. But then, I have noticed that people are rarely as good at what they do as they think they are, and wonder whether I, too, have too good an opinion of my work, so I keep quiet.

But this one was different. We spent a day helping villagers dig an irrigation canal. By early summer, the earth is hard, but we have to dig now to save the water that the rains bring. This man got down to it without complaint, efficiently and without fuss. Afterwards I noticed that although he wears the same kind of clothes as the rest of us, he takes pains to keep himself clean, and as neat as possible. Despite the hard labour, he is pleasant at the end of the day, and willing to help with cooking the night's meal, which is rice.

Over the next few days, he surprises me even more. "Did you grow up with missionaries?" he asks one quiet evening.

"Yes," I tell him. I wonder how he knows, so I ask.

"Habits," he tells me. "Different types of schools teach people different habits, different ways of living, different ways of speaking. You seem to have studied in a convent school. Very few people here come from convent schools, so it's easy to pick you out."

"How do you know all this?" I ask, surprised.

"I think about what I see," he replied.

"And what else do you know?" I ask.

"That there is no such thing as good or bad," he replies.

"What do you mean," I ask. "That's stupid!"

"It's only that you feel something is good or bad," he says. "That's got no meaning. Like fair and unfair."

I think of Jejo Bapa and the story of Bakasura and almost throw up. What is this man saying, I wonder. I turn away, disappointed. I thought he was intelligent. But his words don't leave me; instead, they come back later, at night, when I try to sleep. Much else that he said makes sense, but this…if this, like the other things he said, is true, then…

Then everything I've done is worthless.

And so, the next evening, I ask him, "Did you mean what you said? About good and bad?"

"Yes," he replies. His pleasant smile is gone, his eyes serious and sad. I notice his eyelashes then, and wonder why I'm noticing such useless details. "You must have figured it out for yourself." He sees the doubt on my face, and smiles. "What you've done is a waste. The consolation is that whatever else you might have done is equally a waste."

"No," I tell him firmly. "It can't be."

"Then why do you go back to that thought?" he asks.

I have no answer. "What do we do, then?" I ask. "How do we choose?"

"Choose what?" he asks.

"Choose the right thing to do!" I say, irritated at his evasion.

"But we just said that there's no right thing," he says seriously.

"Then what do we choose?" I ask.

"Are you sure we choose?" he asks.

"Don't we?" I ask.

"I don't know about you," he says.

"What about you?" I ask.

He smiles. "I don't know that either," he says.

I'm completely lost now. I have no idea what he means, but there's something fundamentally sincere about him that says he's not joking or poking fun at me. "What do you mean?" I ask.

"I don't know who or what I am," he says, "so I don't know whether I choose."

I'm getting irritated. "You're just playing with words," I tell him.

"No," he replies. "I have...I have urges. I don't know where they come from. If they are part of me, then I choose. If they are not, then they choose...not I. So, are those urges part of me or not? I don't know, but I resist them, and therefore I feel that they are not part of me."

"What do you mean, urges?" I ask.

"All kinds of urges," he replies. "Urge to eat, to fight, to flee...to have sex. To talk to you on quiet evenings. To listen to poetry."

I remember wanting to stroke his eyelashes...What was that, I wonder. "I also have urges like that," I tell him. "But they're mostly because of things that happened to me. Things that people did to me."

"When someone hits you, you hit back?" he asks.

"Yes. But only when they hit hard."

"How hard a hit would you take, and from whom?" he asks.

"I don't know," I tell him. "Because I haven't thought about it in much detail."

"I have," he tells me. "The thing is, I don't know, either."

"It would depend on the situation," I say.

"You know about frogs and hot water?" he asks.

"No," I tell him.

"If you put a frog in cool water," he says, "and you heat it up slowly, the frog will get used to the increasing heat of the water and die..."

"I didn't know that," I say.

"Sometimes I think we're like frogs," he says. "We're adapting to worse and worse and eventually we'll die."

"Is that what you think is going to happen?" I ask.

"I hope not," he says. "But I don't know why."

"What do you mean?" I ask. "Don't you value life?"

He looks at me flatly. "What if I say I don't?"

"What do you live for, then?" I ask.

"Good question," he says. "I haven't found an answer to it yet."

Chapter Seventeen

Govind Patnaik

"There's something she's not telling us," I told Janaki in the cab on the way to Ashok's flat. There was some traffic, and progress was slow.

"I know," she replied. "It's to do with Ashok."

"I think there's more to it," I said, "but whatever it is, we need to get it out of the way. For his sake and hers."

"What did you mean when you said you'll try to avoid a trial completely?" she asked, changing tack, which she does when she disagrees with something I've said but doesn't want open warfare.

"Just that," I replied. "If she can come up with some information that helps the police catch one of the leaders of one of those bloody groups, or if she can prevent some attack on a police post or something, well, we can see if we can cut a deal. Otherwise, she's going to spend some time in prison."

"I don't think she'll go back to the violence," she said. "No matter what."

"She won't," I replied. "But I wonder who that Jejo Bapa was. He seems to have hit all the right buttons. He was more dangerous than she ever was, and he caught them all at the right age, when they were young, or they'd just suffered. The thing is, I never thought they'd use a story like that."

"Why?" asked Janaki.

"It's from what might be called a religious scripture," I replied. "Straight out of the Mahabharata. It's a bit of myth that hard-core communists would reject. But this old guy...well, he really picked a good story."

"They use anything they can to persuade," she said. "And maybe he was just passing it on. He might have heard it in a similar context."

"Yes," I said, going off on another track. "But it's people who think like that, and get their thoughts out, who are more dangerous. If they're persuasive, and they get to the right audience."

"The law can't deal with them," she said.

"No, it can't," I said. "You can't use the law to control thoughts even if they're dangerous. Unless they actively incite violence. And even that's a grey area, by any standard."

"But then we can't do anything to people who twist things around like this!" she said, her voice rising. "That's not fair!"

"There's nothing wrong with twisting a story around

like that," I said. "That's what free speech and free thought are about."

"That's not free speech," she said. "That's brainwashing."

"All education is brainwashing," I said. "You learn a point of view, that's all."

"Of course not!" she said. "A real education teaches you to ask questions."

"Within certain limits," I said. "For instance, my legal education helps me argue a case better, but it doesn't teach me to question whether the system is the best way to run things. Despite the gross misuse of the system, the backlogs, the corruption in the system..."

"That's chaos," she said. "No society can afford that."

"We don't know," I said. "That's what we fear will happen."

"You're talking nonsense, old man," she said. "We know that democracy is best."

"All right," I said. I'd been troubled all through the journey and this case, wondering about just such matters. What struck me was that we had very little data on it, which came as a surprise, though it shouldn't have. We really didn't know if any system was better than any other. I didn't know much about methods in history, but I was increasingly aware that it was warped. One way or another, every version of history was warped.

When I really thought about it, I couldn't decide whether anything was better than anything else...

"What's the matter, old man?" she asked as I paid off the cabbie. "You just stopped arguing."

"Nothing," I said. "I really don't know most of the things I thought I did, that's all."

She gave me a strange look. "You've been different after you retired," she said. "You started taking those walks and talking to strangers. Maybe you should get back to work. Just to keep yourself from going senile."

I smiled. "If I am going senile," I said, "we're going to be in big trouble if I get back to work. We can ask Ashok, though."

She did, that evening, when Ashok returned from work. "Do you think Uncle's going senile?" she asked. "He's changed after he retired. He gets these strange moods when he doesn't listen and doesn't argue like he used to."

Ashok smiled at her. "Of course not," he said. "He's sharp as ever. It's just that he's adjusting to something new."

"What?" she asked sharply. "He's too old for change."

"He's just had a change," Ashok replied. "Give him time to get used to it."

"He retired a long time ago," she said. "Besides, he's got a case now, and it's a case that interests him."

"Don't worry about him," Ashok said. "This is a tough one, it's a criminal case, he's working on moral grounds now, not for money, and he's got none of the assistance he used to get. Big changes." He smiled some more. "Besides, I think he's reassessing the value of his profession."

She grunted her dissatisfaction and glared at the two of us. "Leave it," I told her. "Why are you getting so upset about it?"

"Because I have to deal with you at home," she said. "Now that you're retired, you're at home all the time." She stalked off to fetch Ashok a cup of tea, which she thumped on the table in front of him.

"We'll sort it out after this case is done," Ashok said, trying to placate her. She was, after all, his favourite aunt.

"What's troubling you?" he asked when she had closed the guest room door.

"The value of my profession," I said. I couldn't help smiling with more than a touch of bitterness. "And my own contribution to it."

"What started this?" he asked.

"We were talking about freedom of speech," I told him. "Freedom of expression."

"What about it?" he asked.

"People use it to lie, and to hide," I said. "And my profession thrives on that tendency. If fewer people told lies, our profession would die out."

"So would mine," he said. "That's one of things we do: try to understand why people lie, and when."

"So?" I asked.

"So everyone lies," he said. "It's only a matter of degree.

Remember Jesus? 'Let him that is without sin cast the first stone?' This might not be exactly correct, but I think that's what he meant. So we're dealing with a whole range of greys, from almost white to almost black, but there's no pure white and there's no pure black. Laws are just a substitute for thinking things through. They make life easy."

I was stunned. "What do you mean?" I asked. "That the entire legal system is a substitute for thought?"

"In essence, yes," he said. "What should have been guidelines have become rules. Precedents that should show you accumulated wisdom have become examples for the most ridiculous decisions. In the meanwhile, lots of laws that should have been removed stayed. It's like a dictionary. It's always out of date.

"So if you think the legal system is a justice system, you couldn't be more wrong."

"I know," I said. "I've done enough to separate law from justice. But I never thought of it as a substitute for justice. I thought it a framework within which you look at justice."

"It can't be," he said, "because we don't know what justice is. We all have different ideas of it. Different people have different ideas of it, different societies have different ideas of it. But some societies try to force their own values on the others. The ones who can get away with it, mostly."

I looked at him for a moment, revising my opinion of him. He had depths I'd never suspected. "When did you get into all this?" I asked, finally.

"When Rohini died," he replied. "There was time, and I had several good libraries to look up."

"And what did you find?" I asked. "You've obviously got much more to say than that."

"Yes," he said. He paused, poured himself another drink. "I went to the scriptures."

"Nothing wrong with that," I said.

"No, nothing wrong with that," he said. "But these days it seems a dangerous thing to do."

"Well, whatever you say is safe with me," I said.

"Right," he said. "So I went through a lot of material. The first thing I found was that there are a few things that can't be defined in the way we think of defining them. Dharma, for instance. You can't codify it. It's entirely situational. You have to think and feel your way to it. All that stuff they say is rules is really guidelines, no more."

"Nothing new there," I said.

"Right," he said. "So you look at your values. Look at Gandhi and his ahimsa."

"What about it?" I asked.

"Ahimsa became a rule for him," he replied. "That eliminated the need to think of a situation in which violence might be necessary. It wasn't just ahimsa. He said sometime that it's better to let ninety-nine guilty people go free than to punish one innocent. That was thoughtless. I assume he meant that due process is important, and indeed it is. But taking it to this extreme, he freed government from the responsibility of protecting society at large. So I think he made some misjudgements there."

"You know, I tend to agree with you," I said slowly. "To the extent that I sometimes wonder if I've been doing the right thing all these decades that I practiced."

"I sensed that long ago," he said. "While you were too busy to think about why you were doing what you were doing, it was all right. But when your nose came off the grindstone..."

"It was something I couldn't identify," I said.

"That's how a disruption always comes," he said. "As something that troubles you but you can't put your finger on it. Most of the time we just ignore it and keep doing whatever we've been doing or what we've been taught is good for us and so on...

"It's not that the law is useless. In fact, far from it. But somewhere we should keep reminding ourselves that the purpose of the system is more important than the system itself."

"You seem to have got this down pat," I said. "You've been thinking about it."

"Yes," he said. He smiled ruefully. "After Rohini died, I've had nothing much to do in the evenings but sit around and think. And I've been reading. None of what I've told you is new. I went to the scriptures. Many of my patients find relief in religion. I thought I'd explore it, too.

"You've changed more than I thought," I said.

"Perhaps less," he said. "It's just that I have more time these days to think."

Chapter Eighteen

Jasmine

With every returning memory comes a sense of fulfilment but also a deepening feeling of loss, a feeling that another possibility has turned impossible, that another door has closed. I find myself taken aback at the sense of loss; what I've been looking for is more memories. Then I understand: I've been hoping for memories of a certain kind, hoping that my life has gone along certain lines, and when I find memories that go counter to that hope, I feel that loss.

One of the things I hoped for was that my parents were good people. I discovered, however, that my father was just the kind of man that Jejo Bapa called Bakasura. My mother was his victim, and tried to fight back, but lost badly. She lost her parents and her own life to him, and I barely survived.

But there are good people out there. Sister Katherine, whose soft corner for me has been an anchor. And in the very last memory of hers that surfaces, her faith in me shows as strongly as ever.

Sister Katherine's face has changed but I have no trouble recognizing her more than a quarter century after she tried, ineffectively, to defend me.

Her face, thin then, is thinner now. Her cheeks are sunken and her cheekbones are knobs beneath her eyes. Her hair, mostly grey, is sparse enough that her scalp is visible underneath.

Her eyes are different. They were mild, then, and sometimes haunted. As I settle into position by her on her bed, holding her frail hand, I see that her eyes are no longer haunted. A kind of strength shines faintly out of them, through the tears and pain. "Jasmine," she says so softly than I have to bend closer to hear her voice. "My Jasmine. Where were you all these years?"

"Here and there," I tell her, evading the question. "Moving around." At the back of my mind is the thought that if I'd really been hers she should have done more to see that I got fair treatment at the orphanage, but she was always afraid.

"You've had a hard life," she tells me, feeling my hand with her own. "Still so thin. Still so strong." The effort of speaking seems to tire her, and she falls silent.

"I'm well enough," I say. "When I heard that you were ill, I had to see you."

"I knew you'd come," she says. "Thank God, you came in time."

I try to smile. "There's plenty of time," I tell her. "I'll see you out of here."

She smiles back, but, unlike mine, her smile is deep and genuine. The tears and the pain don't matter to her anymore. "Don't lie, Jasmine," she says. "It doesn't suit you. You came because you heard I'm dying." I nod, unable to speak. "They tell me that I'm going to die soon," she continues, "but it's not such a bad thing. I think of it as getting closer to God. But there are a few things I wish I'd done differently." I nod again, helplessly, while she struggles to move just a little, half-sitting up. "I've had a lot of time to think, and I thought a lot about you. There's a lot I want to tell you."

"Don't tire yourself," I tell her. "I'm here."

"I've been tired for a long time, child," she says. "Most of my life. This'll only make me better..." She sinks back on the pillow. She takes a few deep breaths. "I was with you when you were born," she continues, her voice faint but steadying now, "and I held your mother as she died."

"Slowly," I tell her. "Rest."

"Not anymore," she says. "I have to tell you this now. I can see from your face that you're in trouble of some kind, and you might not be able to come back before I die. So I'm going to tell you now, no matter what.

"Your mother told me the story before she died, before you came, and I think she knew she was dying.

"She was beautiful, the way young girls are. When she was seventeen, she was outside, taking a bunch of home-grown bananas to sell to a shopkeeper when a young police officer, a young sub-inspector in charge of the local police station,

caught sight of her. He wanted her, and in the summer of 1977, before the rains, there was nothing to stop a policeman in charge of a police station from taking whatever he wanted.

"At dusk a few days later, when she was on her way home from working on a farm, he stopped her. He was in uniform, and she was terrified. He put her in his jeep and drove her to a small hotel in a town she didn't recognize. When she tried to protest, he hit her and knocked her out.

"When she woke up, she was in a bed in a room she didn't know, and the policeman was sitting in a chair by her side. On a table nearby were bottles and dishes and plates, and he had been eating and drinking. He told her to eat, but she refused. She wanted to go home because her parents, who were then in their thirties, would be worried.

"He told her she would go home when he let her go. Until then, she had better do as he told her to. He'd take care of her parents, he said.

"When she kept refusing, he forced a piece of chicken into her mouth. She fought him, but he was much stronger, and she didn't stand a chance. She began to scream, and he told her that it was of no use. No one would interfere with him.

"He was the law, and, the way things were then, he could kill anyone who interfered with him and no one would ask him any questions."

Despite the urgency gripping her, she pauses from weariness. I hold her hand tightly, for now I want to hear the rest of the story.

My own story, the story no one has ever told me.

She seems to read my mind. For a moment she returns the pressure of my hand, and smiles. "It's been my burden all these years," she says. "You don't know how glad I am to be telling you all this."

But her will is weakening. "I'll tell you briefly," she says after another pause. "He raped your mother several times over the next few days. She lost count of the hours and of the number of times he did it. Then he gave her some cheap new clothes and a hundred-rupee note and told her to go home, which she did.

"When she got home, she found her parents frantic with worry. They'd tried to report her missing at the police station but the police sent them away. Now that she was back, bleeding and wounded, they took her to a local medicine man, and then to the same police station where the man who raped her was in charge.

"When her father persisted with the complaint, the policeman had him arrested as a thief. There was nothing to be done, in those days.

"Her father died in the police station, perhaps because of the beating he got, or from the grief because of what happened to his daughter, your mother. His wife died soon after, and your mother, who was a strong young girl, managed on her own for the next few months. But she was pregnant, and, after some months, she was too ill to work.

"She begged for a living then. She never told me how

exactly she managed to survive those days, and I didn't ask. There wasn't time. I think, perhaps, that sometimes she was a prostitute, but when the child in her belly was too big she couldn't even make a living that way.

"When her pains began, someone sent word to the church. I was there, in the orphanage, and the Mother Superior sent me to take care of your mother. Your mother died, but you lived, and I took you back with me and cared for you as well as I could.

"It wasn't enough. I could never do enough for you.

"I wanted to tell you how you came to be with us at the orphanage, about how brave your mother was, but there were things that I had been taught that said that your mother erred, that she sinned. Ever since, I found my faith weakening. I couldn't understand how a young girl who suffered through what your mother did at your father's hands could be a sinner.

"Now that I have so little time left, I hope I'm going to a God who's kinder than the one they told me about in the church."

She lies back, exhausted. The light in her eyes is already fading. "Two questions," I tell her. "Two names. My mother's, and that policeman's. My father's."

"What will you do to him?" she asks.

"Nothing," I tell her. "I'm curious to see the man who caused me. I want to ask him why he did what he did to my mother."

"Is that all?" she asks.

"No," I tell her. "I'll ask him what will happen if I turn myself in. He used to be a policeman, after all, so he might know how to reduce the trouble."

She gathers the energy to look me in the eye. "You've never lied to me," she says. Then she tells me the names. "He lives nearby. I found out about him a few years ago, and kept track of him."

"How did you do that?" I ask. "And why?"

"One of the boys in the orphanage became a policeman," she says. "He helped me. He got me news. And then I went and watched your father a couple of times. Just two or three times..."

"Why did you do that?" I ask.

"To see if there was anything of you in him," she says. "Or anything of him in you."

"What do you think?" I ask.

"The same spirit," she says, taking me by surprise. "The same strength...I hope you find the good in him when you do meet him. I hope you find it in yourself to forgive him." She pauses. "I always admired your spirit, your strength. You tried to do the right thing always...I failed you."

"No, you didn't," I tell her. "I wouldn't be here if you had." I squeeze her hand. "I'll be back."

"Don't lie, Jasmine," she says. "It doesn't suit you."

"It doesn't," I say. "I'll see you if I can..."

"All right," she says. "You have my love, and my blessing. For what it's worth."

"Thank you very much," I tell her, squeezing her hand. "I won't let you down." She opens her eyes and smiles peacefully at me. "I should move on now," I add.

She squeezes back. "Go," she says. Her voice is fading. "Go with God."

Later, I wait on a concrete bench at a bus stop, wondering what to do next. I'll pay him a visit at night, I decide, and take him by surprise. If it takes him by surprise, will I be able to find the good in him? Or will he show me his worst side? Now I am surprised, for I find that I am afraid I might find only the bad in him. What will I do if that happens?

I emerge from this reverie wondering why I went to see my father really. Was it only curiosity? Yes, comes the answer, but I wasn't curious about him. Instead, I was curious about where I came from. Sister Katherine had the heart to hope that I'd find something good in my father: where did she get that from?

I find myself going back and forth among these returning memories. When I think of them I am confused, because they are little pieces in a gigantic puzzle and I have no way to give them some shape, and myself some perspective. There are good memories and bad ones. So far, the bad ones outnumber the good, but was my life really as bad as the memories indicate?

There were some good times, with Sister Katherine and Jejo Bapa. They occupy places of warmth in my heart. So the memories I have don't actually tell me what my life was like; they're just snapshots of what might be significant moments.

I lie in the dark, trying to get some sort of overview on myself, but it's futile...

Chapter Nineteen

Jasmine

There was regret and a bad taste in the mouth. Why did I taunt my father? It's the kind of thing he'd do, and at the moment, in my anger, I wanted him to experience a dose of what he often gave others. If I hadn't taunted him…but then the ifs were endless. There was no dealing with ifs. I still didn't know about the biggest of the ifs. If I'd had my baby…

What kind of a life would I have been able to give my baby? The God I was told about in the orphanage was unforgiving, as was my group, as was the world itself. Would I want a child to go through what I went through? Here's a surprise! Was losing my baby such a bad thing, then? Perhaps not…

My burden was suddenly different. I was guilty about not being able to bring up a child the way I thought it deserved.

Realizing that seemed to be like removing a key log from a log-jam. Other memories came unexpected, and soon I could piece together what happened after he knocked me out that night. He must have had a mobile phone with him, and called his friends, who came and took the two of us to the hospital.

So why did he help me? I had slapped him, taunted him, driven him to attack me when he should have been lying still...I wondered, would he have survived if he hadn't made that last effort and knocked me down? This was another of those pointless ifs but I found that I couldn't get it out of my mind because it made me somehow responsible for his death and that was a responsibility I did not want.

The thought sprang to mind. I will not cause death. I will not participate in anything that causes it. I would rather not live than kill.

Shadowing this thought came another disquieting question: had I really killed anyone, or just watched as others did? Had I buried the memories of killing because I couldn't bear them?

Did it make a difference whether I killed or only watched?

I didn't know what the legal answer was, but I knew that it seemed to make no difference to the burden of conscience that I was carrying. And then came a memory of what changed me.

The baby. My baby.

Babies are a liability even if both parents are around

to take care of it. We must give up the idea of babies and families because the group is our family and our future. There are child soldiers in some camps, I know, because I was one for a few years. Children of soldiers cannot be treated differently from children brought in through abductions, or inducted in other ways.

"You cannot have a baby. If you are pregnant, get the pregnancy terminated. There are doctors who will do it safely, and you don't have to worry about expenses or rest: we will take care of all that. Our purpose overrides everything else."

I understand that, but there are others who live in comfort in cities, and earn money, and have children who go to expensive colleges abroad.

I remember the seventeen-year-old runaway whom the group tried and executed: he was brought to the group from a village from which the group demanded five youngsters as soldiers. If the village didn't give the group five youngsters, there would be consequences, reprisals…

Somewhere in the back of my mind, Jejo Bapa speaks. "Bakasura demanded a cartload of food and a villager every week, and the villagers delivered because they were afraid."

The irony hits me then, the betrayal. The group is Bakasura. Bhima and Bakasura, they're the same. With that comes a flood of understanding. Bhima and Bakasura, both are only in stories. They're both myths. Here we have the group demanding blood sacrifices in the name of fighting… but fighting what? Blood sacrifices demanded by an unheeding government? What's the difference? The villagers pay both, the taxes that the government demands and the blood and lives that the group demands.

So, who gains from what we do?

Jejo Bapa, what say you?

Why did you tell me that story?

I don't blame him. His youth was over long ago, and he gave it to the struggle. In the early years, maybe there was some truth to the struggle, some integrity. Over the years, when leaders and thinkers like him died and the money became easier to get, the line between Bhima and Bakasura blurred and disappeared.

I'm not sure. I must think it out for myself. I will volunteer for sentry duty whenever I can. Sentry duty, guarding the perimeter, is the most boring activity on the roster, but it gives me time to go wandering through parts of my mind that I don't visit otherwise.

What fills my heart increasingly is loss. Many of the people who joined the group at the time I did are gone. Kesho is gone, taken by a stomach-ache and fever that turned out to be a burst appendix and we couldn't get him to a doctor on time. Tata is gone, taken by a bullet. Muku is gone, taken in the rains by gangrene on a broken leg. Sumi slipped quietly away one night, while we slept, and we never knew why.

Others have done well, grown past the group and joined bigger ones. I'm the only one that remains in this small group. Sometimes I feel left behind. On one of those nights on sentry duty I find in my heart a strange mixture of loss and guilt and resentment and a whole volcano of anger.

The guilt comes from the memory of those who are gone. The question follows: why am I here when they are not? The resentment comes from those who have grown in the organization and now give orders. Am I not good enough to do that? Haven't I done my bit as a soldier? And the anger, that's from the past. That's from Brother Richard and…

Anger that I can't keep my baby. Others have so much, why can't I have just this one little thing after all these years of fighting for the cause?

But my earliest memories are of loss. Why do others have parents but not me? Sister Katherine has told me that my mother fell ill and died when I was born, but nothing about my father.

There is anger at my father, too, the father I never knew. In my mind, he deserted my mother, and, of course, me. Did he desert my mother because of me?

It's all very confusing. I don't know what to do. Under all this, the only clear thought is that I want my baby and they won't let me keep it. It's a her, in my mind, a girl, who'll have a better life than I did. They won't let me keep her.

There is a date. They have an old doctor who removes unwanted babies. They say it has to be done soon, or the mother risks death. They say that motherhood after the age of thirty-five is dangerous. I ask the doctor these things. He tells me that I'm in good physical condition, if slightly underweight, that there is a little risk if a pregnancy is terminated after the first trimester, but there's very little danger to my health from having a baby at this age.

They have lied to me, or, at least, twisted things a little to suit their convenience. The lines are blurring even more. Why do they have to do these things?

I emerged from that memory in tears. I remembered walking through forests to a road and then a bus stop, with another soldier for company. We took a bus to a village where a doctor came at night with a bag of tools. I spoke to the doctor for a little while and then the village midwife stood by while I lay on a raised table with the smell of medicines and disinfectant and the doctor took my baby away.

The worst day of my life, but they said it all went well because I healed well afterwards.

More thoughts came: was I any better than a father who abandoned his daughter?

This was a memory I didn't want, the most oppressive of them all. When I thought about it some more, I realized that at least part of the reason for it being such a burden was that I shrank from the thought of sharing it with Dr Ashok.

But as I went over it, its weight eased, for I remembered that losing my baby was a turning point. I wasn't going to be responsible for another death. Then it struck me that I must have caused death before. But even that brought its own lightness, for now that I knew I had taken life, I was prepared more than ever to lose mine.

If I remembered anything that would save a life, I would tell the khakis. If I remembered anything that would save a life, I would tell the khakis. If that was a betrayal, I was willing to live with the consequences.

With that decision came a kind of peace. I slept. I slept for many hours, and, after more time than I could remember, woke up remembering light rather than dark. In the light came another question to which I had no answer. I knew also that I had decided, earlier, not to take a life myself. No to kill except to save myself. Therefore, I had killed, too. Knowing that brought its own comfort, but also the question: why did I decide not to kill? I didn't know but as I thought about it came another tiny fragment of memory, of just a few moments.

I am walking towards my father's house in the dark, hugging the wall, taking care not to be seen, though there is no one around to see me, increasingly sure that I will ask him for help.

That is all the good I'm looking for in him. I will tell him who I am, and that I want to surrender, that he can take the credit for it. If there is any good in him, he will put me on to someone who will keep me safe until I tell the khakis everything I know.

A wave of remorse came over me then. My father had dismissed me, and I had reacted in anger. Perhaps as he would have. Perhaps there was much of him in me, too...

I wished I remembered the names I was going to give him. I hoped I'd remember them in time.

In time for what, I didn't know.

Thinking about the dark took me back to another time when I was learning to survive.

The dark is your enemy, but it is also your enemy's enemy. You must learn to make it your friend.

Walk in the dark. Eat in the dark. Clean your weapons in the dark.

Attack in the dark.

The weapons drills are most difficult. We have little ammunition for practice. The khakis have better weapons, and ten times the ammunition to practice with. They have automatic rifles, while we mostly have semi-automatics and even a few bolt-loaders. They have night-vision goggles, which we don't have. So we learn to be like ghosts in the dark. We learn to listen, to direct our attention based on sounds, and we learn to move silently.

This is our advantage. Most of our people are tribals, thrown out of society because someone wanted their land or their forests. We know the forests and the dark and the seasons. The khakis are mostly city boys, or farmers. They don't know the ground like we do. Most of them spend a few years, two or three at most, on these difficult tasks. We spend our lives on them. For them, it's a job. For us, it's our lives.

So, where they have plenty, we learn to make do with very little. We have to make up for our lack of power with agility, speed, and surprise. They try to make up for it with local guides, with informers. We have to make up for that by knowing the terrain better.

Once again we learn from old stories. Jejo Bapa tells us about how one of the Pandavas—Bhima's younger brother—learnt to eat in the dark, and went on to become an expert at aiming his arrows by sound alone. And so we learn to do simple things in the dark using blindfolds: eating and drinking and walking. With practice, we learn to depend on our hearing to guide us. Some of us are better in the dark than others, those with sharper hearing and stronger sense of direction, and I find I am among the best.

Being the best is good for a short while. It lifts the spirit briefly, and it takes away the sleep. Then, next morning, when you are told to put on a blindfold and follow a colleague on his way to fetch water from a village well, you realize that you might have been better off not doing so well...

I realize one of the disadvantages of one of the rules that we work on: the best never stop working, while the not-so-good slack off all the time. The leaders, the ones who live soft lives in the cities, are the ones with good tongues and poor bodies...

The regret deepened. We were supposed to be fighting for a fair deal but many fighters never got a fair deal themselves. I'd missed that all along. I'd gone along with Jejo Bapa and his stories. His first story had stayed in my mind; it was still there, the idea of what we were fighting for. Had he known of the dark side of his beliefs?

If he had, he never acknowledged it. He died thinking he was doing good.

Another memory intruded, winding its way through my mind, twisting and turning and tearing me up inside.

"That's a fundamentalist," he says. "Someone who refuses evidence. Someone who refuses to grow up."

"What evidence?" I ask.

I can't see his face in the dark, but I can feel him lying beside me. "Two things. One, that there's always inequality, always unfairness. The evidence is that we created this thing called fairness. Ask a hundred different people about their version of fairness—you have to dig deep—and you'll find a hundred different versions. And confusion.

"The other thing is violence. Violence begets violence."

"I thought you were taking it easy," I say. "So you no longer believe in what we're doing."

"Yes," he says. "But I don't know what else to do. Besides, my only friends are here. And so are you."

"Don't think about me," I tell him. "Think of yourself. Be selfish."

He laughs softly. "We're all selfish," he says. "All of us. All the time."

"Of course not!" I say, sitting up. "Sometimes you talk nonsense."

"I figured it out some time ago," he says as if he hasn't heard me. "You don't respond to the pain of others. You respond to the pain in you from the pain in others."

"Of course I do that," I say. "So that's being selfish?"

"Yes," he says. "That too. Think about it when your anger lets you. Everything you do is selfish."

I don't speak to him for a couple of days after that. What he said seems too stupid to accept. And then, one day, as I bend my back to help a woman carrying a child and a pot of water, and wonder that there are people who won't do this, I see that it is my own discomfort at her discomfort that I am addressing...

So I go back to him at the next opportunity, a few days later. "So why do people feel differently?" I ask. "Why do some people feel the pain of others while others don't?"

"I have no idea," he says. "Maybe they're born that way. Maybe they're taught. Most probably it's because they're born that way. Look at yourself. You're one of thirty or forty girls—or more, now—in that orphanage. You all grew up together, eating similar food, wearing similar clothes, taught and supervised by the same nuns. But you're here, and the others...do you know where any of the others ended up?"

"No," I said. "I haven't ever been back. There were only two or three I cared about...When I ran away I was angry. Later, I missed them, and Sister Katherine. No one else. A total of maybe four or five people from a place where I spent the first dozen years of my life. I really was poor in some ways."

"And what of the others in this group?" he asked. "Do you know anything about them?"

"Yes," I replied. "Many come from close families that broke up after a death. Some from places as barren as mine."

"And are you richer now?" he asks. "More friends?"

"No," I say slowly. "I was, when I joined the group, in 1991. We were a family. But then, over the years, that weakened and disappeared. Some people died, some others went away, and others...well, others changed."

"Remember, we were talking about people having different ideas of what's fair and what's not?" he asks. "It's like that with goodness, too. As you get to know people better, most of the time, the common ground shrinks and even disappears. It's only with a few that it stays, or grows. That's what happened."

"Has your common ground with the group disappeared?" I ask.

"Yes," he replies. "I no longer believe..."

"What don't you believe?" I ask.

"That this is any way to build a better future," he says.

"Are you serious?" I ask.

He smiles. "Yes," he says.

"I was wondering," I tell him. "You've been far less active recently. For a year."

"Yes," he says. "I'm trying to break away."

"Why are you telling me this?" I ask. "How do you know I won't..."

"Inform on me?" he asks. "I don't know for sure, but I don't think you will."

"So what will you do?" I ask.

"I don't know," he says. "I'm not sure."

"What about you and me?" I ask.

"I can't see a way ahead for us," he says. He doesn't have to say the rest. We both know what happens to deserters. We've seen it.

He doesn't know about the baby. His baby, too.

As that fragment of memory ended, I found myself weeping with an unbearable sense of loss. Following that came a sense of how deeply unfair life could be, and following that...I didn't know. Here was something I didn't want to tell the doctor.

I didn't even remember his name, or his face, though I did remember his voice and that he had long eyelashes. I remember that I learnt much from him, that I should have known he was preparing to die, the sense of loss when he was gone, but not his face or his name.

In the quiet of the night, alone in that room, taken unawares by a wave of wanting to be missed, I wondered if it mattered at all whether I remembered or not.

Chapter Twenty

Jasmine

There was no holding back any longer.

I went to the meeting room with the two old Patnaiks determined to tell them about my baby and about other matters that I remembered but hesitated to tell Dr Patnaik. I didn't know how to start, because I didn't know how they would take it. I was afraid that telling them would destroy their sympathy for me, and yet I didn't want them to have the wrong idea about me.

"Good morning, child," Mrs Patnaik said. "We met the Mother Superior at Malkangiri."

"And?" I asked. "What did she say?"

"She put us on to a sort of helper at the hospice where Sister Katherine died," she continued. "One who took care of Katherine during her last few months there. The helper confirmed that you'd visited Sister Katherine on the afternoon before the night you met your father." She smiled. "Katherine died in peace. She told the helper that you were going to give yourself up, but wanted to meet your father before you did so...so my husband would be glad to argue for you."

A relief welled up in me that I couldn't hold back and for the second time in the presence of these old people I burst into tears. I don't know how long that lasted but they waited patiently for me regain some control. "I think I should tell you what else I've remembered," I told them eventually.

"Take your time," Mr Patnaik said. "Take a break if you wish."

"No," I said. "I should have told you this before..."

He smiled. "There's nothing like that," he said. "I decided to take your case only after I went to Malkangiri and confirmed what I could about your past. So you shouldn't really have told us anything before this. And now, please understand, whatever you tell me—or us—is going to remain between the three of us."

And so I told them the most important of the memories that had returned so far, about my baby. I told them without tears, with the old lady holding my hand, that it was the most difficult thing I'd ever done. That I remembered it as what confirmed my decision about leaving the group. "I had been having doubts for a long time," I told her. "But I wasn't sure until they...until they made me get rid of my baby. My mother stayed alive for me, died for me...I was ashamed I wasn't willing to die for my child. I'm still ashamed..."

"There's nothing to be ashamed of," she said. "Where was your baby's father when this happened?"

"He died," I said. "Just weeks before."

"Was he a part of your group?" she asked.

I nod. I find I might break down again if I talk so I nod again. There's a pain in my throat and I can't see properly, but I manage to keep it under control.

"You were vulnerable then," she said. "Don't hold it against yourself."

Mr Patnaik spoke again. "Don't hold it against yourself regardless," he said. "What's gone is gone. Nothing you feel or do will bring your baby or your partner back."

I nodded again. There's a sympathy in his eyes that I didn't notice before and the lump in my throat grows. In the back of my mind I've got the feeling that I'm letting these people down.

He seemed to read my mind then. "You've been through a lot," he said gently. "I don't know what you've done in the past but it's clear that kindness makes you cry, which says something about the kind of life you've had so far." When I looked at him in surprise, he continued, "You know your weaknesses very well, but not the good in yourself. You were brave enough to risk finding a new life. Even before that, you were fighting for something you thought was right." He smiled wryly. "What would you think of me if I told you that I've successfully defended people in the Supreme Court who I knew were...well, big-time thieves? Stealing enough every year to feed a small town? Stealing money set aside to feed poor children? Other lawyers I know have defended murderers, rapists, drunk drivers who killed. Whatever you've done, I've dealt with much worse. So don't be afraid of these things in your past. We'll deal with whatever comes up."

Again I could only nod. We sat in silence until I found my voice a long minute later. "I remember executions," I said. "I remember young men who tried to escape and were caught and brought back and killed..." The night on guard flashed through my mind. "I stood guard over one of them even though I knew what was going to happen to him."

"And did it happen?" he asked.

"Yes..." I remembered his face in the night.

"Would you like to tell me whatever you remember of that event?" he asked.

"I'll try," I said. I managed to tell him about the chase, the capture, the trial, and the execution. It left me exhausted. "That's all I remember," I told him.

"All right," he said. "You're very tired. Perhaps you've had enough for today. We can resume whenever you wish."

"There's one more thing I want to tell you," I said. Jejo Bapa was on my mind, and the story with which he inspired us.

"If you're sure..." he said.

"There was an old man who died," I tell him. "I don't know his name but we used to call him Jejo Bapa. He greeted us when we joined the group. We were all children; I was the oldest, about thirteen then. We were all thin and poor and had come from places where they didn't really care about us."

"Was that after you ran away from the orphanage?" he asked.

"Yes," I replied, "but I don't remember how long after. I don't remember how I got there but I remember sitting in his hut on the floor, with a few other children, and listening to a story. We had just had a small breakfast of rice and lentils and we were still hungry because there wasn't enough. And he told us a story from the Mahabharata, about Bakasura..."

"I know the story," he said. "About Bhima killing Bakasura."

"Yes," I said. "He said the government was like Bakasura, and we had a choice between being Bakasura and accepting it, or being like Bhima and fighting it."

"That's a powerful story," he said.

"Yes," I said. "It kept us going. The hunger helped. In those days we were hungry most of the time because there was a lot of work and we were growing. Most days it was just rice and some vegetable if we could get any. Sometimes we helped villagers with digging wells and they helped us back, but it was still a poor life. But that story kept us going.

"I really thought of him as a grandfather. He was the only older person I knew who cared. When I went to meet him before he died, he told me to keep thinking, and I did."

"And what did you think?" he asked.

"That most people I knew were so busy just trying to stay alive that they were neither Bakasura nor Bhima. I remembered the story in the hospital in Malkangiri, where there was a tired but sympathetic nurse who brought me water the first time I woke up. She has an eight-year-old daughter whose birthday was February 20th. I wondered how she could be with either Bhima or Bakasura. I wondered that about all the nurses there. But some of the doctors were clearly Bakasura, and Dr Ashok seemed to be on Bhima's side."

He smiled. "Didn't you see that before, among the villagers?"

"No," I said. "They seemed to be victims of the government, mostly. There was an explanation that seemed to make our attitude reasonable. Not just reasonable: it seemed the only way to get a kind of freedom."

He nodded. "I understand," he said. "When I was young, I used to think like that myself some of the time."

"What changed your thoughts?" I asked.

"Evidence," he said, "but that came much later."

"What kind of evidence?" I asked.

"The kind of evidence that bloody revolutions leave behind," he said. "History is full of it. Even recent history."

"Please explain," I said.

"If you look at what followed revolutions that installed Marxist governments or dictatorships," he said, "you'll find that the death toll is probably over a hundred million people in the twentieth century. Take the two most prominent dictators of that time: Stalin and Mao. Between them they killed off at least sixty million of their own people. Stalin lost as many people to purges as to the war. And he probably lost half as many to starvation resulting from his tendency to get rid of people who didn't fit into his weird picture of the world."

"What do you mean?" I asked.

"When the Soviet Union was formed," he said, "there were a few rich farmers who happened to know about farming. There were also lots of smallish farms, often run by families who knew about farming. When Stalin took over, he took over the big farms, but he also took over smaller and fruitful farms run by people who knew what they were doing and handed those farms over to cronies of his cronies, who had little idea how to run a farm well. That resulted in a drop in production of crops which killed several million Ukrainians, for instance…Stalin and Mao each killed many more people than Hitler did, but they're revered while Hitler…well, you wouldn't name a child after him, would you?"

"They told us all this was propaganda," I said. "But there was enough there to get me to see things differently."

"Did they also tell you that all these were mistakes, that the principles work but bad people tried to implement them?" he asked.

"Yes," I replied.

"And what did you think of that?" he asked.

"I didn't find it convincing," I said.

"Well," he said, "I found it unbelievably arrogant."

"Why?" I asked.

"Because this guy is saying that some people made mistakes that killed a hundred million people but don't worry, I know better," he replied. "Doesn't a man who claims to be brighter than Stalin and Lenin and Mao and all their millions of followers seem to be arrogant? Especially when he has trouble keeping his room clean or a group of twenty people organized?"

"Yes," I said.

"And it's the same with religion, or the idea of a country," he said.

"What do you mean?" I asked.

"When someone tells you that they know the core of Hinduism or Christianity or Islam better than the people who've gotten people killed, the same thoughts apply. Don't you think so?" he asked.

"Yes," I said, suddenly carried away by a new set of questions.

"Did you discuss this with anyone else in the group?" he asked.

I didn't know what to say, but I had to tell him about my lover, the father of my baby, whose name I'd forgotten. "Yes," I said, but the hesitation was there and he caught it immediately.

"Was he the father of your baby?" he asked, very quietly.

"Yes," I said. I couldn't continue for a moment, and they both waited patiently.

"I don't remember his name," I said, not wanting to tell them his more intimate features, his voice and his words, which were all I remembered. "He was a little older, soft-voiced, a poet, and he died in an attack...I think he took risks on purpose."

"Didn't he think about what would happen to you if he died?" Mrs Patnaik asked.

"We talked about it sometimes," I said. "We thought differently about death in those days. There would always be the community, the group. They would take care of you." The exhaustion deepened. "I've had enough for today. Can we continue later?"

"Of course," he said, rising. "You're tired, and I need time to consider what you've just told me. But we're here to do what we can for you."

"Thanks," I managed, turning away to hide the easy tears. Why did I cry before them, I wondered as my minder led me back to my room.

Chapter Twenty-one

Govind Patnaik

Janaki, uncharacteristically, kept quiet until we were at Ashok's flat and she had a cup of tea, exactly as she liked it, in her hand. Even then, she only asked, "What do you think?"

"About what?" I asked.

"Don't be silly," she said. "About that girl. Jasmine. Do you think she's really done anything bad? Like killing someone?"

"Possible," I said. "The group would have made sure she did something like that."

"What do you mean?" she asked.

"They would have made her a member of a small raiding party that committed one or more murders," I said. "That makes her guilty, like it or not. Whether or not she fired any of the bullets that killed the victims, she's culpable. It's a sort of initiation into the group, to make sure that if you do give up, you're still a criminal."

"So how are you going to argue it?" she asked.

"She wants to change," I said. "Many such people have been given a chance to begin afresh, sometimes after a brief prison sentence. And if she can remember and relay something useful to the police, well, we might be able to avoid that."

"You sound doubtful," she said.

"I am," I replied.

"Why?" she asked.

"I don't know how the system works," I said.

"What do you mean?" she asked. "You've spent half a century with it."

"With a very small part of it," I said. "A very privileged part of it, and a leisurely part."

"Leisurely, yes," she said. "Privileged, yes. But only a small part of it?"

"Yes," I said.

"What do you mean, a very small part?" she asked, needled.

"Very little of the trouble the public suffers ever reaches the courts," I said. "I've been watching the system from outside and I can't understand how people stand it."

"Is that why you've been disappearing once in a while after you quit?" she asked.

"Yes," I replied.

"Where do you go?" she asked.

"To a *basti* nearby," I said. "There's a man there who sells tea, and I've been visiting him. I'm a regular at his shop now, and his customers have begun to talk to me. I've also been spending more time with Santosh...I'm surprised I put my life in his hands but know so little about him. From what he tells me, he thinks there are advantages of working for me because my name carries some weight."

"That's good, isn't it?" she asked.

"Perhaps," I said, "but why should he have an advantage over a driver who works for, say, a small businessman, or a taxi company, with the same commitment? I'm not saying I grudge him what he gets. But what about the hundreds or thousands of others who work as hard as he does who are less privileged? To put it differently, why should I have any of these privileges I have, besides what I earn from lawyering?"

"It's good your conscience troubles you," she said. "It troubles me, too, but I don't think about it. I just do what I can."

"Well, that's not enough," I said. "That's one of the reasons why I've taken up this case."

"One of the reasons?" she asked.

"Yes. There are others."

"What?"

"It got me thinking," I replied, "about this system that I've spent my life with. This legal system. The justice system."

"And what have you found out?" she asked.

A thought struck me. "It runs on hot air," I replied, grinning.

She didn't like the grin. "Nonsense!" she said emphatically.

"I didn't mean to be funny," I said. "It's just that we run on something very different from what we say we do."

"Are we all hypocrites, then?" she asked, an edge to her voice. She valued the time she spent on her work.

"That's for you to decide," I said.

"No," she said. "You can't say that we run on hot air and then tell me that it's for me to decide. You already decided."

"I did," I said. "For myself."

"So you have to tell me why," she said. "Otherwise, it's you that's running on hot air."

"Okay," I said. "In the first place, it's a legal system, not a justice system. That's because there's no such thing as justice. It's just a word that each of us uses for something different. There might be someone who uses it in the sense Hammurabi did, something we call vengeance. Others might want it to mean some kind of restitution, but that's never part of it. And so on."

"Those are old ideas, old man," she said. "You have to find something else."

"Yes, I will," I said. "Here it is. The legal system is supposed to be uniform. Isn't it?"

"That, too, is old," she said. "We know it isn't. Crimes

aren't reported. Complaints aren't made. Law enforcement is corrupt. A bias is imposed on law enforcement by the government. Nothing new."

"What's new is that the judiciary is absurd," I said.

"Yes, that's new," she said. She thought for a bit. "But you have to defend that. I can understand one or two judges out of the lot being stupid, but the entire judiciary? That's...that's ridiculous."

"Hear me out," I said. "Let me give you an example. Do you know how they decide whether to give someone the death penalty?"

"Yes," she replied. "The rarest of the rare, whatever that means."

"Exactly," I said. "They avoid detail work."

"What do you mean?" she asked.

"Well, they could lay down some guidelines," I said. "Cruelty? Numbers? Premeditation? Coldness? Indifference to the usual human feelings? Cruelty to children? Inhumanity? Lack of remorse at killing? They ignore all this and leave it to the discretion of other judges."

"That's just one thing," she said. "Besides, every time they give a death penalty, the case is reviewed by the Supreme Court, so...you can't make it a matter as simple as ticking a few boxes."

"Of course not," I said. "I'm not trying to, either. But then, they could have said, eliminate the death penalty if it doesn't tick at least two of these boxes. They could set up conditions for leniency or parole..."

"You're making too much of it," she said.

"That's what I used to think," I said, "but I changed my mind when I thought about the backlog of cases. You need to speed up trials and considerations and so on, and one way is to simplify matters so we don't waste time thinking about matters that are already clear."

"I don't know how much difference that's going to make," she said.

"Neither do I," I said, "but if we want reform we've got to start somewhere."

"Okay," she said, "but that's still not enough."

"Yes," I said. "It's not. So here's the clincher. It struck me when I started reading about religion."

"What do you mean?" she asked. "People are free to practice their religion."

"Really?" I asked. "That's the worst thing you've said so far."

"What nonsense!" she exploded. "You're just arguing for the sake of arguing!"

"What if your religion makes you tell others what to do?" I asked. "And if the others can't resist?"

"For example?" she asked.

"The caste system is an outstanding example," I said. "But there are plenty of others. A couple of things in the limelight these days: men telling women what to do, for instance, how to dress, where to go, and so on, and decreeing what's okay to eat and what's not."

"So?" she asked. "We've got to take these things one by one."

"No," I said. "That's just evasion."

"What do you mean?"

"What we need to do is define the rights of every citizen," I said. "And possibly a charter of responsibilities as well. Once you have that, you don't have to consider every religious practice piecemeal: if your designation of rights is strong, you'll be able to shed religious practices that don't belong. And if you keep working on it, you'll have a long-term platform for some kind of public participation in the government."

"But that's difficult," she said. "There's bound to be conflict..."

"Of course people will fight," I said. "We can talk it out, rather than take up arms over the destruction of temples and mosques and churches. We can hope for heated arguments rather than mobs fighting on the street to make progress."

"I don't see it happening," she said.

"That tells you how well we've been educating our people in independent India," I replied. "We're doing just the opposite."

"What do you mean?" she asked.

"The courts say that we have the right to free speech

but within limits," I said, "and one of the limits is that it shouldn't offend peoples' sensitivities. The idea being to maintain public order."

"What's wrong with that?" she asked. "You can't have people inciting others to violence, can you?"

"Let's look at this a little differently," I said. "Do you know that the Iranian Ayatollah who issued the *fatwa* announcing the reward on Salman Rushdie's head didn't read *The Satanic Verses*, which caused all the trouble?"

"So what?" she asked.

"Since the book is banned, we can't discuss it," I said. "Which means we have no idea what's in it, whether the ban is deserved or not, and so on. In any case, it's difficult to talk of freedom of speech in a country where you can't discuss a story rationally."

"But some people find it offensive," she said.

"Right," I said. "Back in the day the Church and most people found talk of the earth not being the centre of the universe offensive. That was the time of the Renaissance in Europe. Is that what we want? A world where we can't have new ideas just because they oppose other ideas that date back a millennium or more? Is that how backward we are?"

"Are you demanding the right to offend?" she asked. "Or to incite hate speech?"

"Offence is a part of progress," I said. "If we had the standards we have now we might not have got rid of the caste system and *sati*. There are still plenty of people who believe in castes, and that women are inferior, and they might well be offended if you say they're wrong. Are you saying that we have the right to offend some people but not others?

"And all this stuff about hate speech. What is hate speech? Could you define it for me? Do you know how much there is in all scriptures that could be called hate speech by our present understanding? Are we going to ban all scriptures? Don't we have to be consistent?"

"You've obviously been thinking about this for some time," she said. "I'll need some time to argue my position."

"Take all the time you need," I said. "But don't go into it with the idea that I'm wrong, that's all."

She snorted and turned away.

The discontent grew.

It didn't let me sleep. That conversation with Janaki—my ideas on how the system works—kept me awake, until I remembered Ashok going back to the scriptures during the worst of times. What did he mean by that?

My father was immensely religious, and also studious. He was never sure of himself on moral or ethical matter. Nor did he ever favour a political ideology. Whenever I asked him why, he just shook his head and smiled. Eventually, under pressure, he once said, "Look, I don't know where I'm going! How do you expect me to tell you which path to take?"

"What do you mean?" I asked. "Have you been drifting all your life?"

"Of course!" he said. "I didn't know it for some years, that's all."

"Do you think I'm drifting?" I asked.

"I don't know," he said. "It's for you to find out."

"What do you mean?" I asked, a little suspicious of his ignorance.

"If I have to explain it to you," he said, "you won't get it."

We were never very close and after I moved to Delhi we drifted apart, maintaining contact often but only for mundane and family matters. I was with him for over a week when he died some two decades ago, but though he'd been conscious the whole while, and in no great discomfort, I hadn't taken the trouble to understand what was in his heart. Now I wished I'd taken the trouble to get closer to him. Maybe he knew something I'd missed.

Bits and pieces of conversations with him drifted through my mind, and then I remembered perhaps the only longish conversation we'd ever had on his faith. It had come up after my mother died, when I was trying to persuade him to shift to Delhi where I would be able to keep an eye on him. "You can't continue here alone," I said. "The house is too big, and you won't be able to maintain it."

"We'll see," he said. "Whatever will be will be."

It was a line he used sometimes to close an argument,

and I hated it because it seemed fake wisdom. It seemed evasive and irresponsible, to say the least. But then, I'd never seen him evade personal responsibility for anything, or to use the least falsehood for his own convenience, so I was careful not to lose my cool. "Back to fate, are we?" I asked. I couldn't keep the sarcasm out of my voice.

He smiled. "I know you don't like it," he said. "But I won't lie to you. Not about my beliefs."

"All these gods and demons that you read about in books written thousands of years ago?" I asked. "How could you believe in them?"

"Some of those demons at least are real for me," he said. "They influence all of us. Or they're influences within us."

"What do you mean?" I asked.

"Let me tell you a story," he said. "A short one."

"All right," I said. I was in no hurry.

"This is the story of our female goddess, Durga," he said. "She goes under many names, but there's a set of seven hundred *sloka*s called the *Durga Saptashati*, which tells her story. A set of stories, actually. The first of those is about a king called Suratha and a merchant called Samadhi who have done their best but get neither the results nor the appreciation for what they've done. They visit a rishi called Medha, and Medha tells them the story of Durga and two demons, Kaitabha and Madhu, who attacked Brahma, who was in a lotus in the navel of Vishnu, who was asleep.

"What struck me were the meanings of the names, Madhu and Kaithaba: honey and insect. I thought then of a honeybee, of a worker bee that spends its life following a compulsion it probably doesn't understand, that's not even aware of...compulsions.

"We all follow compulsions. We're all driven. We have very little freedom, and even looking for what we think of as freedom could well be a compulsion. So the gods and demons, the *devas* and the *asuras*, I think stand for our compulsions. And from what I've seen, all of us have the same compulsions to a different degree. We all have them. That's what we have in common. So the gods and demons are metaphors for the things that drive us. When we get rid of them, we're free."

"Gods and demons both?" I asked. "Compulsions?"

"Yes," he said. "Reality is beyond good or bad. Our scriptures say it. And it seems real to me because we know so little."

"And that freedom from those compulsions—that's what life is about?" I asked.

"I can't tell you," he replied. "I'm not there yet."

"How will you know?" I asked.

"I don't know that either," he replied. "It's something I believe, that's all."

I looked at him in disbelief. "You don't know where you're going, you don't know how, and you don't know when you get there...is that what you're saying?" I asked.

"Yes," he said. "Essentially, yes."

"Can you tell me roughly where you're going?" I asked. "Give me a sense of it."

"*Moksha,*" he replied. "Freedom from compulsion."

"On what basis do you believe that there is such a thing?" I asked. "Or such a state?"

"It's what I was taught in childhood," he said. "It's what we should try to achieve."

"So you believe in all those fairy tales?" I asked.

He sighed. "If you treat them as fairy tales," he said, after a moment's thought, "they become fairy tales."

"How can they be real?" I asked.

"Let me try again," he said. "They're symbols."

"Symbols of what?" I asked.

"I told you. Symbols of what's in all of us," he replied. "Our qualities. Compulsions. Our inner conflicts."

"I've heard that before," I said. "The Mahabharata is really about the war within us, and so on. It still doesn't make sense."

He looked me straight in the eye. "Not to you, perhaps," he said. "But do you expect me to accept what makes sense to you? Don't you think you might give me room to disagree?"

"Of course," I said. "But it makes no sense."

"I've lived a few decades longer than you," he said. "Don't you think I might have seen those demons as my own compulsions? Are you sure you yourself won't see that one day?"

"No, and no," I said.

He changed tack. "Do you want me to move to Delhi out of concern for me or to keep your own worries or your conscience under control?" he asked.

"When you put it that way," I said, "I guess it's to keep my conscience quiet."

"Regardless of the network of friends I have here," he said, "and of the fact that I've got used to this place and would have difficulty living in a flat, that it's much easier getting help here than it is in Delhi. And, that at my age, any change is painful."

"Okay," I said. "I won't ask you to shift. But I will ask you from time to time whether you've changed your mind."

"Please do," he said. He smiled. "The moment I think it's beyond me to manage here, I'll let you know."

He didn't have time to change his mind, for he died of a heart attack a year later while playing rummy with a group of teenagers. The teenagers got him to his family doctor in under half an hour but he was gone by then. I surprised myself by performing his last rites. Not because I believed in those rites, but because I thought that was what he'd like me to do. All through those few days I wondered about what he believed in, but forgot all about that when I got back to Delhi and my sixty-hour weeks...

So here I was, sleepless in my nephew's house, wondering...stunned, at the end of a half-century of working with the legal system, at the shakiness of my values, at the depth of my ignorance of them.

Waking up was different.

I woke up remembering what Father said about compulsions, and up came a few questions. First, if I accepted what Father said about compulsions, and gave up the idea that I was making decisions and choosing a course of action, then I was giving up responsibility for what I did. At least, that was what I'd been taught all my life. Second, were my feelings also compulsions, or a result of compulsions? I wish I'd thought of these when he'd been alive...then I understood that your understanding of the same things changes as you grow, as you see more.

I was failing to get answers to these questions when Janaki roused me from my stupor. "Are you ill, old man?" she asked.

"Just thinking," I replied.

"Does thinking make you ill?" she asked. "Or lazy?"

She was baiting me. No need to get upset. I smiled. "If you want me to do something, just say so." It struck me then that there was no need to get upset about anything at all. Being upset was simply a waste of time and energy. Besides, you tend to make the wrong decisions when you were upset.

"Nothing," she said grumpily, turning away.

I felt a twinge of compunction for her. She would have been bemused by my lack of reaction to her baiting. Then it struck me that I was helpless to do anything about it. If I were helpless against my compulsions, what could I do about someone else's? And was my compunction itself a compulsion?

It went deeper still. Why did I want to do anything at all? What stopped me from spending the rest of my life just sitting idle? I didn't need to work, or look after anything other than my personal hygiene. Guilt? Habit? Were these compulsions? The questions kept flooding in, one after the other, but no answers.

And then, on that quiet morning with the sun beginning to show through the little gaps between the curtains, came the big question, the one I'd been hiding from: if my compulsions were making me do things, and I wasn't my compulsions, then who was I?

It seemed obvious. I was the person behind the eyes and the ears and the mouth and the nose, inside the skin, through which I knew and felt the world.

Oh, really?

I sat up, shocked.

"What else can I be?" came the question in my mind. "What else is there?"

I'd experienced nothing else. Did that mean there wasn't anything else? Was it that I couldn't experience anything else, or that there *was* nothing else? Just for a moment I wished I had no memory, nothing that would tie me down to my history. Then I remembered Jasmine's misery at losing her memory and came back to reality.

But the question lingered: what was real?

Was this what the scriptures mean when they said the world is illusion? But there was nothing else!

Or was there?

I knew no way to answer the question. It didn't have a logical or reasonable answer. Perhaps those who got the answer, or thought they got the answer, were insane.

I didn't want to know the answer for I feared it brought insanity.

Benares, the holiest city for Hindus, was also home to monks and saints and mystics, fake and real. If any of them were real, I always wondered, did they know something I didn't? If they did, I didn't want to know it!

And then came panic, and a strong sense of claustrophobia, neither of which I'd felt before, though they'd been described many times to me by many people; at the base of the panic was the realization that I was trapped in this body, with no way out! I felt my heart beating wildly, and my mouth went dry. The urge to charge out of bed, or to scream, was almost irresistible. I forced myself to lie still for a while, breathing as slowly and evenly as I could, until the panic turned into regular fear. I had no idea how long it had lasted, but it had felt like hours.

Then came the urge to speak to someone about it, to seek reassurance in talking about it and "sharing" it, as they say these days, but as I continued to lie still, that urge too passed.

The clock on the wall said it was only a quarter-past-six: there was no great rush to get out of bed, and I decided to stay in for a little while longer. I was unused to thinking about these matters, my mind more tuned to the law and its limitations, but I somehow felt their weight much more than ever before.

What, for instance, were Jasmine's compulsions? If she and her compulsions were separate, should she be punished for her actions?

Should any criminal be? I remembered my father telling me that the world was an illusion. The way it seemed to me now, it was more of a distraction from questions of essence...

It struck me that I'd evaded these matters all along because there were no easy or apparent answers. Easier to do what you know can be done rather than beat your head on the wall of unanswerable questions.

The thought came out of the blue. Jasmine obeyed her compulsions, I obeyed mine, and everyone else obeyed theirs. The idea of responsibility was another compulsion, just like guilt. That left my value judgements meaningless. All the things I'd been beating myself up about, or crowing about...all that was unnecessary.

Jasmine would have to face whatever came her way, and so would Ashok. As would Janaki, and myself. It was as if a great weight had fallen off my shoulders. I slept.

Chapter Twenty-two

Jasmine

The memories come flooding back. It's as if a logjam has been cleared. I remember, decades ago, my thirst for blood, a thirst that I shrink from now. But there's no denying it.

The memories that have already returned become much more detailed. There are names now, and faces that I can put together. There are rivalries and friendships, moments of defeat and victory, of joy and utter bereavement. And now, in some measure, memories of love and tenderness that make me weep.

I remember him well. I remember his smiling eyes, his long eyelashes, his gentle hands, his scarred legs where he had burnt himself getting a colleague out of a burning hut...I remember the poetry he quoted, in a voice that rose and fell, from a poet called Pablo Neruda, who wove magic into love and revolution both in a song from the heart, that in which we could drown.

I remember our closeness, and our baby, conceived

on a night in the rains, never born, a life interrupted by a midwife at the command of some soulless Mao-worshipper.

I remember his farewells, brief moments of quiet before he went off to do something violent. "Treat this like the last," he said before each one. "Don't expect me back." And just the third time he said that, he never came back, lost in a CRPF ambush near Sambalpur. I remember the photograph of his broken body in one of the newspapers. Others had brought word of his death, of course, but I had hoped that he survived; that hope died with the newspaper photo.

I remember his inner conflicts. He told me more than once in the quiet of the night that he wanted to give up, but couldn't because that would mean turning on those who helped him when he needed it most. Far easier, he said, was to play the part and hope to die. There was no other release.

I remember the farmhouse and the wealthy old landlord very clearly now, and even more the feelings that coursed through me then. I remember the joy of dipping my palm and fingers in the pool of blood on the floor that came from the wound in his neck, and thumping the whitewashed wall with that hand. I was telling them—the enemy, an enemy that I understood so vaguely but was certain existed—that I was here to take blood, that I would be back for more.

I remember my rage at Sister Katherine, at her holding back the truth of my parentage from me, and how quickly it passed at the sight of the guilt in her eyes. She thought she hadn't done me justice, but what else could she have done?

I remember the rage at my father. I thought of his as the personification of the Bakasura that Jejo Bapa told us about. What he did to my mother, I thought, was proof. Would he have been any different if he hadn't been a policeman? I didn't know and I didn't care. He was what he was, and he deserved a painful death.

I remember the scorn on his face when he said I could well be telling the truth about him being my father, that I wouldn't get a penny out of him on that count. I remember the disbelief in his eyes when I told him I didn't want any money. I remember my own surprise and shock as the knife came up in his hand, the sharpness of the first cut on my forearm, and his overbalancing and falling on his own knife. I remember the shock at his strength when he reared up at me despite the knife in his chest. And I remember cursing my own foolishness as I bent to put a towel on his wound to stop the bleeding.

I remember when I decided to turn myself in. I remember how we forced villagers, the very ones we claimed to defend, into choosing between their own survival and that of people they cared for, such as the runaway. I remember realizing that we could be as bad as the government.

I remember what I had decided to tell the police when giving myself up. I was going to admit to doing whatever I had done. Then, without telling them anything about my group, I was going to accept whatever punishment they gave me. I knew, though, that it would be something like life imprisonment, which meant fourteen years in jail if I behaved myself...I never wanted to give my people away.

I did think about who my people were.

I remember old Jejo Baba, long gone now. Would I give him up, Jejo Baba of the stories and the warmth and the hunger and the iron in the soul? You could say he encouraged the bloodthirst...no, he didn't. He just gave it a direction. A direction that I found out much later didn't make sense.

Are there others in the group who are changing, who have lost their bloodthirst, and are turning away? Others who stay only for fear of the consequences of trying to leave and getting caught?

I am horrified at what I have done. The burden of guilt is unbearable. There is no way to make amends, only to do a penance, and that is only to ease my own guilt, not to reduce the suffering I have caused. For a moment, only a moment, I consider how comforting it would be to die now...as I lie soaked in misery. However, one other thought emerges: is there something I can do to prevent more loss?

The answer is clear—I must give up my former

comrades. Again, I am torn. They are the only family I knew for some decades. I might have disliked individuals in the group, the greedy, the manipulative, the hypocritical. But the majority of members of the group are my family. I've lived with them, worked with them, shared danger with them, been saved by them. How can I turn on them now?

Will I be turning on them? What if I name the few senior people I know? They cannot be trusted; they will certainly name the others, my friends. And the consequences will be death or prison.

Would I give up Jejo Bapa now if he were alive? These are the people who offered support when I had no one else. How can I betray them now?

The questions go on into the night. By morning, there's only one hint of an answer. Perhaps I can give myself up, but not my friends. My friends are the foot soldiers, like myself, working for a better world. The leaders are the parasites. I cannot give up the parasites without also destroying the lives of the foot soldiers, or, at least, disrupting them to an extent that might harm most of them. I do not know what to do.

An even more difficult question relates to the Patnaiks, all three of them.

I am supposed to meet the old couple, the lawyers, at eleven. Their patience has been formidable, their kindness profound.

I am not worth it. My past has too much blood in it to deserve their kindness.

They have tried to make the best of everything I did. The old people took the trouble to travel to Malkangiri at their own expense to find out what I did before I met my father. The old lady fell ill too because of the travel.

I cannot face them, to tell them that I will not share what I know with the khakis, but I have to. I am afraid...I am afraid that their kindness will overcome my resolution. So I should not meet them.

This is so very difficult.

Chapter Twenty-three

Govind Patnaik

There's a surprise waiting for us at the prison. There's a message from the Jail Superintendent asking us to see him. Janaki and I go up to his office and find the NIA investigating officer, Ramesh Arora, with him. "What's the matter?" I ask.

"Jasmine has made a statement," replied Arora. "I find it disturbing."

"What has she said?" I asked.

"She says she's willing to confess to most of the killings that we've accused her of," he replied, "but remembers nothing more."

"Is the confession valid?" I asked.

"She made it in my presence," replied Arora, "and the Superintendent's, in this room. She says she's willing to sign it again in the presence of a magistrate."

That would make it valid. In any case, I didn't think Jasmine would give in to any ordinary coercion. She must have done it voluntarily. It would be difficult for her to deny that statement, or go back on it. I was wondering what to do when Janaki nudged me. "We need to discuss this," she said when I turned to look at her.

"Of course," I said. Then, to the Superintendent and Arora: "Janaki and I will discuss this and get back to you."

"Please do," said Arora. "If she takes this course, she won't give us what we need to prevent whatever her former friends plan to do."

They found us a room in which to talk alone, one of the interrogation rooms, seedy and equipped with a desk and a few chairs. "She's got her memory back," Janaki said as soon as we were alone. "She's realized that she's done many of the things they're saying she did."

"So what?" I asked.

"She thinks she's guilty," Janaki replied. "Put yourself in her position. She knows what she's done, she doesn't want to let her old friends down. She doesn't want to let her new friends down either."

"What do you mean?" I asked.

"She doesn't want to let us down," came the answer. "You, me, Ashok. She can't face us."

It struck me then that she was right. That was the only explanation I could think of that held water.

Poor Ashok. "What do we do about this?" I asked. "I can only think of one way."

"Yes," she said. "We ask Ashok," she said. "We might have to work through him if necessary. It's for his sake anyway. But it's better all-around if you and Ashok can persuade her."

"You and Ashok might be better at it," I said.

"Perhaps," she replied. "But perhaps all three of us..."

When we went back to the Superintendent's office, Arora opened up a little more. "Tell her," he said, "that if she has any former colleagues willing to surrender, we'll consider giving them an amnesty."

"How do we do get the message across without endangering her?" I asked. "She is my client, and I have to ask you that question. What if the news gets to the wrong people and they try to finish her off?"

He nodded. "I understand. We have our own channels in both directions. Let me see what we can do."

"Whatever you do," I said heavily, "you must make sure that her life is not endangered."

"Right," he said. "We'll take care of that. We need the information she has, you know, so it's as much in our interest to keep her alive as it is in hers." He smiled.

"I'm going to talk to my nephew about it," I said. "I'll be back tomorrow, and we'll see how we can persuade her to tell us without endangering people she considers friends and family."

At his flat that evening, after a quiet dinner, when Janaki went off to the guest room, Ashok listened in silence when I told him that Jasmine had confessed to many of the charges against her, refused to name her ex-colleagues, and said that she would plead guilty to any crimes she could remember having committed. "We have to hope that her friends will accept the amnesty," he said.

"Yes," I replied.

He sighed. "People have this inertia. They stick to what's not good for them because they don't know what's going to happen to them if they break free. There's this fear of the unknown. Her colleagues will hesitate before they give up, if at all they do."

"What are you saying?" I asked.

"Some of them won't accept the amnesty," he said. "The chances are that they'll go for it only if they can discuss it in some detail in safety. That they most probably can't. Certainly not in large groups. So don't expect many surrenders."

"I thought that might happen," I said. "Now what?"

"Now we try to get through to her," he said. "We must. Otherwise she's going to spend at least fourteen years in prison, and be branded a bloodthirsty murderess, which I think she's not. Besides, if her old pals find a way to finish her off while she's in prison, they might just do that."

He seemed caught up in his own thoughts, and I didn't blame him, but I had to ask, "How do we get through to her?"

"Only one way," he said, looking me straight in the eye. "I talk to her. And that might not work."

"What do we do then?" I asked.

He shrugged in what I thought was a fatalistic manner. "Accept it."

"I'm surprised to hear you of all people saying that," I said. "There's a difference between acceptance and resignation."

"I know," he said. "But I don't have a choice. I've told you several times that she's bound by her conscience, that she tries to be true to it, and that she's strong." He looked away for a moment. "We were all deluded, hoping that something good would come of this..." He looked me straight in the eye. "Perhaps me, most of all. I apologize for dragging you into this."

The depth of loss showed in his voice. "What will you do?" I asked.

"Try," he said. "I'll try to persuade her that the people she cares for will get a good deal if they give themselves up. I don't know if she'll believe it."

"Why shouldn't she believe it?" I asked.

"She doesn't trust the government," he said.

"Why not?" I asked.

"Look at her history, Uncle," he said. "She's been cheated by everyone with any authority. Her mother and grandparents suffered most of all, of course, but her too. Look at why she ran away from the orphanage. How much would you trust the authorities if you had that in your background? And you know what? You have some form of corruption in almost everything the government touches. You and I might not have to pay the way others do, you because you're a lawyer and me because I'm a doctor, but have you any idea what the man on the street goes through? I'm not sure I trust the government myself..."

The bitterness in his voice took me aback, though I couldn't really argue with what he said. If people like us had no way to get rid of the corruption that pervades the government, what would a poor villager with no connections do? "You're the only one who might get her to change her mind," I said. "Do what you think is right."

"I would if I knew what that was," he said heavily.

"What do you plan?" I asked.

"She refused to see me alone," he replied. "So I've arranged for a medical examination for her at the Institute. We'll scan her head to see how her skull and brain are recovering from her injury. The day after tomorrow, around four in the afternoon, after the outpatient departments all close for the day. We'll put her through some tests before the NIA record her confession and shift her back to the prison."

"But won't that risk her life?" I asked.

"The NIA care about that only to the extent that she's willing to give up her colleagues and their plans," he replied. "That she's not willing to do, so...besides, shifting her back to prison might signal that she's not willing to talk, so it could get her former colleagues off her back."

A possibility strikes me when he describes this arrangement. "Do you think we—Janaki and I—could meet her at the hospital?" I asked.

"I suppose so," he said. "It depends on the security arrangements, and, as far as I know, you're still her lawyer. Let me talk to the police."

"Let me know," I told him. Then, a question I'd been trying to avoid, "Do you think she's perhaps lost her sanity, with all the memories coming back?"

"I doubt it," he said, "but that's one of the things I want to check before she confesses before a senior police officer. If there's any chance of stopping that confession on the grounds that she is unwell, I will."

"What if she's well?" I asked.

"I won't compromise there," he replied flatly.

"All right," I said. Neither of us felt like a conversation after that so I went off to the guest room where Janaki waited.

"What did you discuss?" she asked.

"Jasmine's confession," I said, and gave her some of the details, of the medical tests and so on.

"There's no happy ending unless she gives the NIA names and dates," she said. "No matter what."

"Yes," I replied.

She glared at me. "I wish..." she began.

"What?" I asked.

"I wish we hadn't got into this," she said.

"I've wished that several times," I said, "but never after we discovered that Jasmine really wanted to turn herself in."

"What were you hoping for?" she asked.

My mind cleared as I discovered what was in my heart. "Some acknowledgment of the circumstances that made her what she was," I said. "Not just for her, but for all victims. So people keep asking questions of themselves about what's right and what's not. That's all."

Epilogue

Janaki Patnaik

At times he was the worst of men, at others the best. At times he was a five-year-old, and at others a cantankerous ninety-five. And then sometimes he was a hero, and at others a shrinking coward. No one else I have ever known was as full of contrasts as he. I hated him at times, and loved him at others. One thing I sensed in him always was a kind of decency: for the rest, he was a mystery.

I still don't know what he really was. What I do know is that living without him is darkness without end.

I never got used to using his given name. My mother never once referred to my father by his name, saying that it was disrespectful in our tradition. I inherited the tradition, too, but now I think it is time to break it.

Three months have passed since Govind—there, I've used his name—died, and I still wake up with a hollow where he used to be. It used to be unbearable at first, so I used to wake up and stay in bed with my eyes shut tight because I couldn't face the world, and perhaps hoped that he would one day come back to wake me up from the nightmare.

But now the time has come to finish the story that Jasmine began in the solitude of her hospital room, a story that he supplemented with his notes. I tell her story because it deserves to be told, far more than mine or even his.

Jasmine was scheduled to go through a series of tests, X-rays and scans and blood and urine tests, at the All India Institute of Medical Sciences, Bhubaneshwar, at 4 pm that afternoon. The purpose of these tests was to ensure that she was in good health when the NIA handed her over to the state police. The only people who were supposed to know that she would be undergoing these tests were Ashok and us and the NIA officer in charge of their investigation; even the radiologist at the hospital only knew that a female patient who was an undertrial would be undergoing those tests, and was given a reference number instead of a name to file her by.

Govind woke up that morning in good spirits. By the time I finished my prayers and started on the tea, he was ready and waiting at the dining table. "We're going to arrive at some kind of decision today," he said. "It'll be good to put all this waiting and uncertainty behind us."

"Aren't you nervous?" I asked.

"No," he said. "I have a feeling it's going to work out well."

I was cross at him, perhaps envious of his sense of wellbeing. "We'll see," I said shortly.

He smiled at me. "Don't worry so much," he said, picking up his teacup. "Enjoy the morning."

My irritation subsided, but not the premonition that matters weren't going to work out. Still, I sat beside him, smiled back, and did my best to enjoy the morning.

His good feeling lasted. After lunch, taking a little rest before leaving for the Institute, he said it was time to take a break. "No matter what," he said, "we'll take a week off and go away to somewhere quiet, with good food and good air, and relax."

"I'll hold you to it," I said. I'd heard this many times before, but it had happened only once.

"Of course," he said, the lightness persisting. "This is my only case now. It's been difficult, but it'll be over soon." He looked at his watch. "Time to go."

Jasmine was brought to the Casualty entrance of the Institute in a police SUV with darkened windows, so no one would be able to identify her from the outside. Her guard consisted of two policewomen in uniform and two armed policemen in plainclothes. She herself was in neutral clothing, with her hair cut short, so it was difficult to make out at first glance whether she was a man or a woman.

Ashok was inside, with a group of doctors. At my insistence, Govind and I waited by the Casualty entrance on the off chance that she would see that we were still with her as she went from the vehicle to the doctors waiting in Casualty. I was told later that there were also three armed plainclothes policemen apparently loitering in the area looking for suspicious activity or people; one of them had checked our ID tags and checked with someone on a radio and been told that we were to be allowed to wait there.

The police learnt some of what followed from the CCTV camera footage covering the emergency entrance. Less than a minute before Jasmine was due to arrive, a man emerged from the parking lot reserved for doctors working in the Institute. He had on a white smock that's the uniform of doctors here, and was striding purposefully in the general direction of the Casualty entrance as he passed the parking lot exit. He wore what seemed to be an ID tag on a blue lanyard around his neck, and held a stethoscope—also part of doctors' uniforms here—coiled in his hand.

A policeman intercepted him some twenty metres from the Casualty entrance, but as he was asking for ID, the "doctor's" cellphone rang. He took it out of his pocket, indicating to the policeman with a smile that he'd answer the call first, and spoke into it, withdrawing into the shade of a window ledge nearby, well within the policeman's range of attention, fumbling in his trousers pocket, apparently for a document to show the policeman.

The vehicle carrying Jasmine drew up at the Casualty

entrance while the man in the smock was speaking into his cellphone some feet away from the plainclothesman who had stopped him. A policewoman in uniform stepped out of it, reached inside, and, holding Jasmine's left hand, helped her out. Behind Jasmine came another uniformed policewoman, holding Jasmine's other hand.

Govind and I began to walk towards her car even before it stopped moving; I think I was impatient. Behind us was a plainclothesman. We were within feet of the rear door when it opened and the first policewoman came out and began to lead Jasmine out.

A second identical vehicle drew up behind it, and from it emerged an armed policeman from the front passenger side and two more armed policemen from the two rear doors. At this time, the policeman who had intercepted the "doctor" was looking at the cars and the people emerging from them rather than the man he had stopped.

The "doctor", who was holding the cellphone in his left hand, drew a pistol from somewhere inside his clothing with his right hand and took a quick aimed shot at Jasmine. It passed by her and hit the body of the car, and he had just enough time for another shot at Jasmine.

Meanwhile, Govind, hearing first the shot and figuring out where it came from, moved to cover her. The fake doctor's second and last shot hit him in the chest, and he crumpled onto the concrete. I hardly heard the fusillade that brought down the shooter.

The policemen brought a trolley and immediately took him to the doctors waiting at Emergency. I held his hand while they pushed the trolley and I think I felt his hand squeeze mine but by the time the first doctor got to him he was gone. My life had turned upside down. Darkness overcame me and I don't know what happened for a few hours afterwards.

I regained some control over myself sometime later, enough to meet the children when they arrived next morning, and to go to his funeral the next afternoon, where our son wept as he lit the pyre, as did our daughter and Ashok, who had been at my side throughout. Jasmine came to the funeral too, guarded by many policemen and women, and hugged me briefly at the pyre-side. I was stiff with her in the beginning, because at the time I blamed her in part for taking him away from me, but when I saw how distraught she was, the stiffness went away.

They told me later that, after the shots were fired, the policewomen guarding Jasmine pushed her back in the car, which took off in a curve and back out of the main gate of the Institute, back to her safe house. She was unharmed, but wailing in distress after watching Govind being shot.

That night she changed her mind about not speaking to the NIA. They worked out some kind of a deal with her. They took a long time to debrief her. At her insistence, they allowed Ashok to participate in her debriefing, which I believe is a long and complex matter because they take pains over verifying much of what she told them. Ashok is in touch but he isn't permitted to tell me anything about it, and he takes these matters seriously. But he assures me that the information Jasmine has already provided is enough to ensure that she won't undergo a trial or spend time in prison. He hasn't told me any details, but I think Jasmine will disappear and another woman will surface somewhere else with another name, perhaps with Ashok for company.

She also left me her notes. I think I understand her much better now.

I am now with my daughter. They, our son and daughter, both believe that spending time with their children is the best thing I can do now, while trying to get over Govind's death. They are right, for some time, and I still find relief in spending time with the little ones, but it is time now to return to Delhi and to give the rest of my life to my work. I have been trying to set things up by email and internet conversations, and hope to return in a month or two. They don't like it, but then it's my life and I want to follow Govind's example.

We were both right on the morning of that fateful day. It all worked out for him. Jasmine changed her mind, and her story has the kind of end that he would have wanted. As for me, the doom that I felt was coming did come. And, if there is an afterlife and I meet him again, the first thing I will do is hold him to his word.

Acknowledgements

Thanks to the many people who contributed to this book: my sister, Tara, and brother-in-law, Mohanan; Suresh and Chitra, who have always been there; Sankar and Uma; MC Dinakaran; and, last but not least, Jay, my occasional neighbour and friend.